Cages on Opposite Shores

JANSET BERKOK SHAMI

A Novel

INTERLINK BOOKS
An imprint of Interlink Publishing Group, Inc.
NEW YORK

First published in 1995 by

INTERLINK BOOKS
An imprint of Interlink Publishing Group, Inc.
99 Seventh Avenue
Brooklyn, New York 11215

Copyright © Janset Berkok Shami 1995

Library of Congress Cataloging-in-Publication Data

Shami, Janset Berkok.
Cages on opposite shores / by Janset Berkok Shami.
p. cm. — (Emerging voices. New international fiction)
ISBN 1-56656-165-5 (hbk.)—ISBN 1-56656-157-4 (pbk.)
I. Title. II. Series.
PR9570.T873S48 1995   94-9347
823—dc20   CIP

Printed and bound in the United States of America
10 9 8 7 6 5 4 3 2 1

Cages on
Opposite Shores

1

Meral leaned against the bow frame of the salon's window and dialed the number of the lawyer, while two pigeons lingered on the ledge as if they too had calls to make. The white pigeon remained on the far end and darted looks to the right and left; the gray one paraded up and down displaying its steel blue necklace of feathers.

The lawyer's secretary answered the phone. "I'll make an appointment for Mr. Vedat to see you, but I am not sure if he will take your case," she said. "Normally he doesn't handle divorce cases." The sound of the flipped pages at the other end of the line reached into the silence of the room. The pigeons flew to the new café across the street, while the secretary consulted the diary; they remained perched on the edge of the slanted roof while the appointment was fixed. By the time the uncomfortable conversation ended they were two gliding specks above the gently fluctuating coastline of suburban Istanbul.

Meral turned her back to the sunlit window. Her tall, angular figure created shadows in the room. The broken sun rays spotlighted the chairs, the tables and the wall hangings. The figurine of Johann Strauss on the shelf held its violin bow gracefully ready to fill the room with the music of his waltzes. An Anatolian peasant woman pictured on an empty vase offered a basketful of wild flowers to whoever would take them. They all might have been parts of a stage decor. Meral half expected a pretty French maid to enter, wearing a shiny black uniform and a starched white apron. There would be a feather duster in her hand. The telephone would ring. The doorbell would ring. People would trickle into the story. The story would develop. The story would envelope you. The story would block out everything from your life.

She moved away from the warmth of the sun. No French maid had swished in and out of this room during Meral's childhood. Instead, an elderly woman dragged her slippered feet over its carpets. This had been Emine, Meral's nanny.

Meral's mother had read endless books in this room. But her more absorbing activities took place at the table that nearly filled the adjoining room. She sat there writing and scratching out again and again. She sat there painting tiny flowers on tiny canvases. Painting and painting over the paintings once again. Meral could see the untidy surface of that huge table through the open door. She once again felt its sharp edges pressing under her chin as when she had tiptoed to see what was being done on top of that table. She had listened eagerly to her mother's vague answers to her questions. Every time she tried to get close to this table her mother had sent her away to her nanny. She was sent away politely, but firmly.

She walked towards the big table which was comparatively tidier now than when she had first returned to her mother's house two weeks ago. She had found on top of this table paintings, verses of poetry, short stories without titles, first acts of three-act plays and even several bars of musical composition. Her mother worked so constantly that she might have been working on something even on the day Death came and took her away, two years ago.

Meral had propped the miniature paintings against the wall. A great number of turbaned men who rode black horses, who carried books with gilded covers, and a great number of willowy women who reclined on long chairs, who smelled multicolored flowers, looked at her from the edge of the table touching the wall. She had straightened out crumpled, single sheets of paper which contained verses of poetry and had secured them under a glass paperweight. She had gathered the stories which were written on long, unlined sheets of paper and had heaped them on one side of the table. They were folded in half and some of the covering sheets carried comments about the stories.

Her walk towards the table was slow and cautious. She could not hope that the few weeks she had spent here since her separation from her husband could bridge the gap of eleven years of absence through marriage.

She took the diary with the broken lock on its dangling strap. Its tattered binding was secured with a heavy rubber band. When she attempted to remove the band, it disintegrated in her hand. The pages of the diary were stuck to each other as if time had been its adviser in the tactics of defense. Meral had to penetrate its ranks from the weakest point. She pried the book open by carefully separating the two pages which clung to each other less firmly than the rest.

May 18, 1928

The new geography teacher called on me today five minutes before the bell rang. I was checking my watch every now and then throughout the lesson hoping the bell would ring before the teacher called on me.

She asked me to point out Vienna, Berlin and Frankfurt on the map of Europe. It took me a long time to point out Frankfurt. But I did it. She had a list of our class in front of her. She ran her finger down the list and tried to place my name without asking me. But she couldn't. So she said, "What's your name?"

I said, "Nar."

"Nar? What kind of name is that?"

I had to explain. "My mother gave me this name because it is a shortened form of Nartuhi—an Armenian name."

The teacher ran her finger down the list of students again.

"Nar Demiray," she said. She knew from the family name that I was not Armenian.

There is only one month left to the exams. After the exams, I'll say "goodbye" to this school, and go to the American High School in Uskudar.

3

I have to survive this one month at this school. I just have to close my ears to the whispers of my classmates and ignore their curious looks. One thing I know, none of them will come and ask me how come my mother is Armenian. Why would anyone ask? I do not have any good friends among them. None of the girls will give me the chance to explain the circumstances of my father's marriage to an Armenian woman. If any of them did ask, I would be proud to tell them that my father married my mother in order to save her. I would tell them that during the massacre my father was a judge in Marash. He married my mother, and made her convert to Islam. Perhaps the girl who asks the question would respect my father for saving a life, as I respected him.

How I wish my father were alive. How I wish he hadn't gone to a "better place," leaving his six-year-old daughter in the arms of an Armenian mother.

Why did they have to transfer the old geography teacher to another school before the year was over? Why did I tell this teacher that my name was Armenian?

Meral's trembling fingers were unable to turn the page. Her eyes were fixed on her hand. After some time, she stood up and walked to the tall gilded mirror opposite the table. She looked at herself.

She studied the defiant look of her large hazel eyes. She studied her long, narrow nose. She studied the abundance of auburn hair above her forehead. And then she lowered her eyes, and fixed her gaze on the childlike determination of her small mouth. Her tightened lips were barring the way of a thousand questions.

Throughout her growing years, nobody had spoken to her about her grandmother. It was as if she had never had a grandmother.

She closed the diary and looked at the remnants of the rubber band which were like the hardened skin on an improperly healed scar. She collected the rest of the diaries and made a neat pile of them on the table by putting the largest one at the bottom.

*

The setting sun outlined the opposite shore, and advanced the slim minarets and the curved domes of European Istanbul nearer to the

Asian shore. A ferryboat approached the wharf. Meral walked to the waiting room door. The clock on the wall as well as her wristwatch showed that the boat would dock on time. It would take her to the appointment on time.

She saw herself circle around the Ayasofia Mosque, walk along the gray walls of the Topkapi Museum and reach an office building where she had never been. She saw herself enter the office of a lawyer she had never met. She heard the echo of her voice answer questions she had not been asked.

The boat slowed down, gave a few shudders and turned parallel to the wharf. A tall sailor on the boat threw the rope, a stocky sailor on the landing stage caught it and slid its loop over the bollard.

The grumbling machines objected to this slavery, but their protests were unheeded. The boat was dragged closer and closer to the crowd standing behind the glass doors of the waiting room. The sailors rolled the flat gangways on their noisy wheels by pulling the ropes attached to iron rings at their unprotected sides. The gangways were balanced between the landing below and the exit of the boat above, and the flow of people transformed them into giant see-saws. The rhythm created by this flow grounded and lifted the opposite ends of the planks alternately. The people came out with hats and briefcases, with scarves and printed dresses, with parcels and swinging arms. They were laughing and frowning, talking and arguing.

The passageway held their merriment, their anxieties and resentments, while their footsteps carried them along in the same direction.

The floodlights of the wharf skipped over the rippling waves by the time the passageway was empty of all the people. Stripped of its golden outline, the opposite shore looked cool and far away, with rings of lights on the minarets. An unexpected fury at the lawyer's secretary reared up in Meral's heart. An appointment at 7:30 p.m.!

She was almost ready to go back home when the cabin boy approached the waiting rooms. He slid open the door of the first waiting room and walked to the second one where she stood. She was pushed out by the pressing crowd, and forced to walk towards the boat. As she stepped on to the gangway, intending to take a secure position at its center, the weight of the people ahead lifted its dock side end off the ground and caused her foot to slip off. And before she could take a backwards step, a group of newly embarking people brought down the gangway on her foot. The heavy wooden plank landed flat on her toes together with the people it carried. The people in front of her walked on, while the pain crept upwards from her toes, leaving her quite helpless. She began to scream while those behind her walked on and passed her by. She was still screaming when two people took her by the arms, and helped her to the nearest seat on the boat.

Several people who witnessed her accident watched her for a while before they walked on to find seats for themselves. One tall, shabbily dressed man spoke to his friend in a disappointed voice. "It is nothing," he said. "You should have seen what happened the other day. A man pushed clear off the plank while the boat was starting to move. He couldn't even fall in the sea. The boat plastered him flat onto the wall of the landing." "Don't throw words about," said his friend, rushing ahead in his unwavering pursuit of a good seat. "I swear," said the tall man following him. "They took him straight to the hospital."

One of the people who had helped her to the seat sat down next to Meral. He was urging her to drink a cup of tea. She was holding the teacup placed in her hands, but half the tea was in the saucer. She knew she should take care, and not spill any of it on her new suit. She knew she should smile and thank the man who brought it. She wanted to pay for the tea. The man did not let her.

"I am a doctor," he said, as he knelt down and took her shoe off. He flexed and straightened her toes one by one. "Does it hurt?" he asked. She shook her head. But when he touched her big toe, she winced.

The doctor took out a bunch of papers from his briefcase. He removed the clip which held them together. Trying to unfold its curves, several papers fell from his hands. Then he searched his pockets. He brought out a lighter, he flicked it and heated the tip of the clip on its flame. "This won't hurt," he said and he punched her toenail with it. He covered the nail with tissue paper and after several tries he managed to put her shoe back on her foot. His movements were jerky. He was desperately in need of conversation.

"You know," he said, "a similar thing happened to my brother-in-law some years ago. Under different circumstances, of course. And after that he never left the house."

Seeing the startled look on Meral's face, he added quickly, "Oh, to be sure, the accident was not the only reason. He is burdened with personal problems."

He stopped short as he caught sight of the tea-boy weaving his way through the rows of seats carrying his glasses of steaming tea. "Two teas here," he called out. "You will have another cup of tea, won't you?" he asked. "I need some myself," he added.

The long search for the right change in his pockets interrupted the doctor's previous train of thought. When he spoke, he said, "Your nail may fall out, but not before the new one grows halfway."

After this, he chatted all the way to the European shore, sustaining a forced gaiety on his large, flat face. The effort he put into his conversation flushed his cheeks and deepened the color of his salmon-pink skin.

When the boat slowed down, his talk became less energetic and he grew thoughtful and hesitant. When it was time to leave, he stood up hastily, slid his hand into his jacket's inner pocket and produced a card. "May I present my card?" he said. "Please come and have tea with us. We shall be so happy to see you in our house," he said.

"Well, thank you," said Meral without moving from her seat. Her accident had broken her resolution to see the lawyer.

He went on standing in front of her and shifting his heavy weight from one leg to the other. "Our telephone number is on the card," he said. "Please choose a convenient day. Any afternoon will do. We are at home every afternoon."

He was waiting for her to stand up. When she remained seated, he became confused. "May I help you?" he said, bending towards her.

"I think I'll go back home," said Meral. "I was going to see my lawyer. I can do that any other day."

"Well then," said the doctor as he straightened up, "we'll see you then. Monday? Tuesday? Any day. Just give me a call."

Meral stayed on the ferryboat, which returned to the Asian shore of Istanbul. The image of the doctor's round face and the wave of his short-fingered hand saying goodbye accompanied her all the way back home.

The doctor had said "Monday? Tuesday?" As she arrived home, she teased her loneliness with a scornful question. What was there between now and Monday? What was there between now and Tuesday? An appointment with her dentist, a meeting with the ladies of the Fine Arts Committee and an appointment with the lawyer. She must call the lawyer and renew the appointment.

When she arrived home, she removed the doctor's card from her handbag, and placed it on the piano.

*

Three days later, leaving her bed too early for her appointments, Meral paced the salon in her nightgown and slippers, and caught herself stealing secret glances at the doctor's card on the piano.

After some time, however, she showered, had her breakfast and started preparing herself for the day, doing everything as slowly as possible. But pulling a dress on did not take too long. And she never was one to spend too much time in front of the mirror.

Once, a friend had a sharp comment about her makeup-free face. "You know, you are creating a vain image by leaving your face untouched," she had said. "It's not enough to dress elegantly. It's not enough to have your hair nicely set and tidy. You have to use some color on your cheeks. Put some shadow around your eyes."

When Meral had laughed, she had continued. "I'm serious," she had said. "Would you like me to tell you frankly the message I receive when I look at you? 'I am beautiful without any unnecessary help. I am perfect. I look perfect!' That's the message I receive. That's the message you send me. Do you think that the kind of image you create is helpful in your relations with your female friends? I would say not! I would say *tout au contraire!*"

Remembering her friend's advice, which had astonished and amused her at the time, she put some rouge on her face. But she could not continue with the makeup as she had never learned how to apply eye-shadow and one didn't go to the dentist wearing lipstick.

The 11 a.m. appointment with the dentist was perfect. She had to meet the ladies of the Fine Arts Committee at noon. The Fine Arts Club was almost opposite the dentist's clinic. After their meeting she would walk to the gallery to inspect the arrangement of the exhibition of prints which was due to open the following day. The committee members had expressly requested her to go and give her opinions of their work.

She heard the sharp orders of the head-waiter from the café across the road as soon as she went down the marble steps of the building and walked out into the glaring sun. "Bring the tablecloths. What are you waiting for?" he said, scolding one of the waiters. The legs of the chairs made scratchy sounds on the tiled floor as the other waiters pushed them against the tables.

Meral had to accept many changes. She had to accept that when she left the house the sea would not meet her directly over the profusion of wild bushes. The open space in front of her mother's house had been tamed into a garden café. From now on, she had to peek at the sea through the piles of tables and chairs. The café intruded into her past. The narrow balconied façade of the two new blocks of apartments next to the café intruded into her past.

Meral walked on, averting her gaze from the patch of garden in front of another block of apartments. This square garden had scanty blades of grass and was bordered with tiles on each side. At the end of the road was a supermarket where the polished surfaces of the artificially ripened fruit presented themselves to the pedestrian's attention. A stone house had once held that spot with unassuming dignity. Carried by salty breezes from the sea, the generous scent of the roses in its garden had filled the neighborhood.

Meral felt relieved when she arrived at the taxi rank. A young driver ran to one of the cars lined up alongside the road. "To Galatasaray," Meral said to him before entering his car.

The driver grinned. This was a long drive.

Meral's decision to go to the European shore over the Bosphorus Bridge reminded her of her last trip on the ferryboat; and the remembrance curved a question-mark in her mind. Should she accept the invitation of the doctor or not? She paid the driver and took the elevator up to the clinic.

The dentist himself answered the doorbell. "Oh, welcome, my dear," he said as he retreated all the way to the vestibule, hanging onto the brass knob of the heavy door. "You know what," he added, as his frail reflection appeared on the full-length mirror on the opposite wall, "when you called me this morning, you reminded me of something." He continued as he slowly closed the door: "You were a little girl, ten or eleven years, you came all the way to my clinic."

Meral stole glances at the mirror as she advanced slowly, listening to the dentist. On its shiny surface his irresolute gestures looked sharp, his soft-spoken words sounded expressive.

After seating Meral at the chair he continued, while he carefully selected his instruments. "Yes, you came all the way to my clinic with a friend. A pretty little girl. You made me extract one of her canines. It was a perfectly good tooth. But you said it spoiled her looks. Your mother called me later."

Meral had heard this story from him several times. But this time it was a little different.

"My mother?" said Meral, surprised.

"Yes, and she scolded me bitterly. She said . . . well, she questioned my integrity as a professional man. She accused me of being an 'opportunist'."

"My mother?" Meral asked again. "Did my mother really call you?"

"Of course, dear," he said, bringing the drill close to her mouth. "God rest her soul, your mother was a fine lady. But she could be cutting at times. Mind you, I deserved it. But you were so convincing, my dear."

The one-sided conversation could not go on much further. Although the part of the story concerning her mother was probably a figment of the dentist's aging imagination, it had not failed to stir a certain curiosity in her mind. What if her mother really had called him?

The dental instruments moved in and out of her mouth. She thought about her mother's sudden death. It was the maid, Fatma, who had told her the news. "She is dead. She is dead," she had repeated on the phone in panic. Meral had come as fast as she could while the unbelieving voice of the maid rang in her ears. Her mother had lived and had died. Had anyone been aware of her living? Had her existence made any difference to anyone?

Meral's nanny Emine died many years before her mother. When that little woman had died, Meral's pain was so strong that she felt the world itself had come to an end. After so many years she still felt

10

the pain caused by her nanny's death whenever a silly, frivolous, unconnected word or action stirred any happy, sad, childish memories in her mind.

She did not shed many tears for her mother although her heart was filled with sadness. This sadness was kept immune from daily emotions. The feeling stood alone—as her mother had stood alone throughout her life.

The elevator which carried Meral down from the dentist's clinic opened its door to a mosaic mural on the opposite wall. A woman's pearly teeth smiled in front of a sea represented by even waves of different shades of blue. Meral wondered, as she did every time she visited her dentist, if he owned the apartment building. The mosaic looked like a cunning advertising device.

When she arrived at the Fine Arts Club, she was pleased to notice that the secretary had remembered her request. The last name on the tag the secretary pinned on her suit had been changed from her husband's to her father's family name—from Sardan to Demiray. The meeting was short and to the point. All the ladies had carried out their duties to the letter.

Meral walked to the gallery of the Credit Bank where the print exhibition was to be held. The first thing she checked was the spacing of the panels. This met her approval. Then she looked at the composition of each panel. Everything was fine. She could find nothing to criticize in the arrangements.

The pictures were mainly works by Orientalists. They were rare prints. Scenes from Turkey and the rest of the Middle East. One attracted Meral's attention particularly. It was a black and white print showing a slave girl. She was naked and was being offered for sale. Meral felt the embarrassment of the girl under her own skin. She almost heard the extravagant words of the oily salesman. Is that how her grandfather had saved her Armenian grandmother?

After her tour of the pictures, she went back to the print of the slave girl once again. She looked at the raw nakedness of the picture and tried to fasten her jacket's single button. It came off and broke into two pieces. For a while, her eyes fixed themselves on the broken pieces in her palm. Then she closed her fingers around them and went out of the gallery.

11

Her mother used to talk about a *tuhafiyeci** shop every now and then. She remembered that the shop was somewhere in this area. She even had a vague memory of seeing its façade. In her memory, the shop's window held yards of lace which crisscrossed each other like streamers frozen in mid-air; it had round and oval buttons sitting on bright colored velvet cushions like pebbles scattered over patches of sandy beaches. The linen tablecloths at the base of the show window were arranged so that, in spite of their crowded appearance, one easily appreciated the richness of the embroidery on each and every one of them.

The *tuhafiyeci* shop was the third shop on the steep road alongside Galatasaray College. As soon as Meral entered, a woman in her sixties looked up from her crochet work and removed her glasses. "Yes?" she said. "May I help you?"

Meral held out the broken pieces of the button.

"Do you have a similar button?" she asked. "Just one."

The woman stood up with some difficulty, walked to the wall unit and pulled out various drawers with peeling paint and chipped handles. She put her glasses on again, dipped her fingers into several shallow cardboard boxes and sifted through the assorted buttons. The right button did not fall into her hand. She spoke to herself in anger. She spoke in Armenian.

At last she held up a button, planted it in Meral's hand, and raised a victorious look towards her face. At the same moment her expression changed.

She came closer to her, pushing her slipping glasses into position and read Meral's name from the tag on her lapel.

"Meral Demiray," she said and kept on looking at her.

Meral took this remark as a pretext for starting an idle conversation and said nothing.

The woman murmured to herself. "It cannot be. It cannot be," she said.

"How much?" asked Meral.

The woman was still looking at her.

---

* **tuhafiyeci**: *shop selling notions*

"Is your mother's name Nar?" she asked.

"It is . . . Yes, it was," answered Meral in surprise.

"Then," the woman said. "Then," she repeated, "you must be Satinique's granddaughter."

"Satinique?" said Meral.

A sad little smile hung down her faded lips. "Naturally it was changed. After marriage she was given a Muslim name. But she was Satinique all right. Satinique is not just a name. There are legends attached to that name."

The woman was not talking to Meral. She was talking to herself and to all the surviving Armenian race.

Meral was not listening to the woman, she was listening to her own thoughts. Her grandmother had walked on the same sidewalk as Meral when coming to the *tuhafiyeci* shop. Her grandmother had talked to this *tuhafiyeci* woman. Meral's chance meeting with her grandmother in her mother's diary had been followed by another chance meeting. Was she following or being followed? Was her grandmother searching for her? What was the matter with her?

Meral put some change into the old woman's hand, and walked out.

*

Arriving home she made a note of the date of her next visit to the dentist. She reminded herself with relief that this was going to be her last visit. She also reminded herself that she had to come to a decision about calling the doctor she had met on the ferryboat.

She looked at the card on the piano, as she had several times before. She read every word written on it: Dr. Zeki Yuksel, Kasimpasa Clinic of the Ministry of Health. She read the home telephone number and address: 77850012, Villa Yazan 178, Arnavutkoy. She was surprised at her willingness to accept the doctor's invitation, in spite of her constant warnings to herself against rash decisions. Rash decisions, together with her impulsive curiosity about other people's lives, could lead her in unforeseen directions. At this stage of her life, she should avoid mistakes.

Since Meral had left her husband, since she had pushed aside eleven years of her life, she had come up with various philosophical ideas. Her favorite among them was the one about the tree. She looked at living as climbing up a tree. The branches of the tree provided the choices you make. You choose one of the main branches and you climb up. After a while you discover that it divides into several other branches. You are faced with a decision. You make your choice, and you meet new choices. While the climbing is going on, you come to realize that the tree has more than one main branch. You could have chosen a different one than the one you did. But by now it is too late. Your previous choices have carried you to a distance from the other main branches. It is too late to retrace your steps. You have left too much wasted time behind. If you break a limb, if you start all over again, it won't be the same kind of climb.

This reminded her of a story about the Anatolian folk philosopher Nasreddin Hoca. On his way from one village to another, a man sees Hoca perched on top of a tree. He is busily sawing a branch. Just as he is about to pass Hoca by, he notices that the branch he is trying to cut off is the very branch he is sitting on. "Hoca," he says, "what are you doing? You'll fall and break your leg." Paying no attention to the man, Hoca goes on with what he is doing and before long he ends up on the ground with an injured leg. He runs eagerly after the man in spite of his limp. "How did you know I was going to fall?" he asks, amazed at his prediction. "Do you also know when and how I am going to die?" Meral knew the man had given Hoca an answer; but she could not remember what it was.

Was Meral about to cut the branch she sat on too? What kind of injuries would she suffer from the fall? What sort of questions would she ask?

2

"How could a man say so much and make so little sense?" Meral thought, leaving the taxi cab. She had caught a taxi on the busy street of the lawyer's office after the unpleasant meeting was concluded, and left it at the corner of another busy street. Now, she had to find the place of the appointment following the complicated directions given by her friend Rezan, the president of the Fine Arts Committee.

Now that the sweet shop faced her, now that she saw the sign Guven Muhallebi, she stood looking at it, still thinking about the lawyer's long-winded talk. She needed to regain her concentration and collect some courage to cut through the traffic. If she chose an inappropriate moment for crossing the street, she might be hit by one of the vehicles speeding along its four lanes in both directions.

Her attempt was successful, and the cool atmosphere inside the sweet shop rewarded her. The round clock on the forehead of the green wall showed her that it was 11:30. She had arrived at the right place at the appointed time. But where was Rezan herself?

However, she did not mind waiting for her friend in this freshly painted, pleasant place. She did not mind her being late. She settled at one of the round, marble-topped tables and propped her injured foot against its cast-iron leg.

But as soon as she began to feel comfortable, the lawyer's voice started to scratch her ears. She was in his stuffy office once again and was doing her best to listen to his long, unbelievable success stories. A great number of "unfairly accused" swindlers, forgers and thieves who were lucky enough to be his clients, were acquitted promptly because of his cleverness in handling their cases. "I saved them from the claws of the law," he said, throwing out his chest. She was having difficulty in deriving any consolation from his ill-chosen words. Their meaning demonstrated nothing more than his self-confidence. He had said that he was going to save her. (From what? From the "claws of the law?") He said that he would lead her "to the green pastures of peace and independence." (Would she be there alone or would she be accompanied by a herd of swindlers, forgers and thieves?)

The expensive, pure silk suit was a clever cover for this man who seemed to be constructed of snugly-fitting electronic parts. There was no room for self-doubt between the components. A simple friction with this artificial being, such as shaking hands, might cause an electric shock for a person made of flesh and blood.

When the time had come for Meral to leave the office, she had hesitated to give him her hand.

It was time to dismiss the lawyer from her thoughts. She turned her head from side to side and looked at the evenly distributed round tables on the marble floor. She counted them as if she were working on an inventory. As she started to count the empty chairs which were pushed against them, two young women came through the door of the Muhallebici and approached the counter with leisurely movements of swinging hips. One of them spoke to the man who peered from behind the huge jars which lined the edge of the counter. "A kilo of mixed candies please," she said. "Be generous with the cinnamon and lemon drops," she added. "As you wish, *hanimefendi*,"* said the man, producing a red velvet box with golden trimmings, and starting

---

* **hanimefendi**: *respectful address for a woman; equivalent to "Lady"*

16

to shovel pieces of candies of all shapes and colors from the jars. He lifted off the polished, mirror-like brass caps of the jars, one after the other, with flourishing movements. A spicy smell filled the air, and the intoxicated reflection of the sunlight performed a momentary oriental dance among the painted flowers on the high ceiling. The soft rhythm of the dance rubbed off the assertive spikes of the lawyer's statements, it replaced his unpleasant voice with another, a gentler voice. "Monday, Tuesday; Monday, Tuesday," she heard Dr. Zeki say, as if whispering the words in her ear.

The rhythm of the repeated words gave in to the crisp tempo of Rezan's approaching steps.

"Sorry, dear," she said, pulling out a chair opposite Meral. "It's the traffic," she said, as she sat down.

Rezan was prepared to compensate her delay in arriving with a few pleasantries, but the tolerant expression on Meral's face revealed that there was no necessity for it.

Ignoring the waiter who appeared at the table as soon as she settled down, she started talking about the exhibition she was organizing.

"Two lemonades, please," said Meral to the waiting man, as Rezan poured her groomed ideas into carefully chosen words.

"It's going to be the most fantastic exhibition Istanbul art lovers have ever seen. Imagine fifty young artists' works side by side. What do you think? Tell me what do you think?"

As she expounded on the subject, her tone of voice made it clear that she would be unable to accept any kind of criticism. Even the suggestion of a minor alteration in her plans might make her burst out with undefeatable arguments.

"I think it is a very good idea," said Meral, "but I don't think I can help you."

"Oh no," said Rezan. "Oh no," she repeated. "What am I to do? Who will help me?" she said, spreading her wiry fingers in a gesture of helplessness. "What is the matter with you anyway?" she asked.

"I have left my husband," said Meral.

"Oh, I am sorry," Rezan said, in a voice which lacked sympathy. It also lacked the usual tinge of curiosity. It seemed that the news had already reached her ears.

17

"Don't be," said Meral, speaking as dispassionately as her friend. "It was bound to happen."

Rezan's chain of thought had remained intact in spite of the interruption. "I'm not asking you to do anything against your wishes, but this exhibition of mine is going to be. . . ."

Meral changed the position of her leg against the table's stand and started speaking before Rezan completed her sentence. "Does your husband have anything to do with the Municipality Hospitals? Does he know the doctor in charge of the Kasimpasa Clinic? Do you happen to know Dr. Zeki Yuksel?"

The successive questions she had posed received a calm answer. Keeping the surprise off her face, Rezan told Meral what she knew about Dr. Zeki. "I know of the Yuksel family. They were socialites, but suddenly dropped out of the scene. They used to live in Yesilkoy. I believe Dr. Zeki moved to Arnavutkoy to live with his sister and brother-in-law. Why do you ask?" she said, stopping herself from giving out further information. It was obvious that she had suddenly become suspicious of Meral's motives. She thought that Meral was trying to distract her. She was losing hope of recruiting her for the new project.

Meral drank what was left in her glass. "I had an accident on the ferryboat," she said, pointing at her bandaged toe sticking out of her sandal. "Dr. Zeki came to my aid. He has invited me to his house to have tea. I don't know if I should go."

"Why not?" Rezan said, shrugging her shoulders. "I would. He is from a respectable family. Anyway, since when are you so conventional that you need to wait for proper introductions?"

*

On Tuesday morning Meral sat by the window and sewed the new button on her suit. As soon as this was done, she was going to wear it and go out. Out to visit Dr. Zeki, his sister and his brother-in-law. She was expected in their house in an hour.

But after she sewed on the button, she put the suit back into the wardrobe. It was almost the end of May. She needed something cool. Her fingers pushed clothes on hangers to the right and left inside the half empty wardrobe. There wasn't a dress suitable for the weather. There wasn't one right for the occasion. She rested her outstretched arms on the disturbed lines of skirts and blouses, missing her old ones left in the house she had deserted. She waited for an encouraging sign from the replacements. But the newly-bought clothes remained perfectly still.

She pulled out the first dress which came to hand.

The taxi was the same one she had taken to go to the dentist. Recognizing her, the young driver's face broke into a broad smile. "Here is a regular customer," he seemed to say.

"What's the telephone number of your office?" Meral asked.

The driver's answer was prompt: "It's 8660632. And my name is Ahmet. Here is my card," he said, presenting it to her with a flourish as soon as she entered the taxi.

"Arnavutkoy," Meral said, slipping the smudged card in her bag. She leaned backwards on her seat to discourage further conversation. But there was no need for the precaution. The driver was an intelligent person. He knew when to speak and when to keep silent. Hearing the general location where his passenger wanted to be taken, he started the car before asking for the exact address. She gave him the written-out address after they left the inland roads.

When they crossed the bridge and turned to the seaside avenue, some modest boutiques and crowded juice stands started to slide by between imposing old buildings and majestic mosques. As they continued towards further districts of the Bosphorus, some Yali-mansions* appeared between the heavy traffic, dazzling Meral's eyes with the shimmering white exteriors of lace-like woodwork.

The Yali with the long lawn stretching all the way to the sea used to belong to her grandfather's family. Her mother had pointed it out to her when they passed it on their way to the only visit on which Meral had been allowed to accompany her. But Meral was too full of excitement to pay attention to the mansion and to what her mother said about it. She had learned earlier from her nanny that the lady they were going to visit had a daughter of her own age.

---

* **Yali-mansions:** *waterfront mansions built on pilings over the water; common on the Bosphorus*

19

One thing she was sure of was that her mother had not told her anything about her grandfather's and his Armenian wife's life in this Yali. She had not told her that her father had brought his young bride there after saving her from her uncertain fate. She had not told Meral that her grandmother had lived for seven years in this Yali, which was staffed by half a dozen black *halayiks**, a cook from Bolu and two gardeners. She had not told her that her father had a daughter from his previous marriage and that she was as old as his new wife. She had not told her that it was this stepdaughter who had thrown Meral's grandmother out of the Yali as soon as her father had died. She had not told her that after seven years of uneasy luxury, her grandmother was pushed out on the streets with a small child.

This small child was Meral's mother. The first pages of the diary came back to her while the taxi carried her to Arnavutkoy. Dry tears burned her eyes, as she was carried to the depths of Bosphorus.

They passed Beylerbeyi and approached Arnavutkoy. Meral watched the careful, unhurried movements of the fishermen who lined the edge of the sidewalk. They attached their baits onto their bamboo fishing rods, they swung their rods into the sea and they fussed with hooks and tangled lines. She watched these men—some young, some old, some middle-aged—go about their business uninterrupted by the noise and the motion on the avenue. She watched these men who had stretched the few yards of distance between themselves and the busy avenue into miles. For a moment she forgot the past and the present. For a moment she forgot where she was.

"Here we are," said the driver. The taxi had brought her to her destination. It had stopped in front of a villa.

The driver held up the address on the paper and compared the number written on it with the number on the brass plate over the huge black iron gate.

Meral did not leave the taxi. Her hands fumbled for several minutes in her purse, while the firmly planted huge villa towered above her like a formidable schoolmaster. What was she doing there? The message sent through the stone walls of the house was clear; she was

---

* **halayiks:** *female servants, almost slaves, who serve the same family throughout their life*

trespassing. It would be best if she returned home.

She finally paid the patient driver and walked to the gate, returning to her usual self with every step she took.

After pushing the heavy gate open, she sailed through the overgrown hedges on the sides of the graveled path, and gave the doorbell several short, firm buzzes.

The door opened before Meral had removed her finger from the bell. "Hello, hello," Dr. Zeki said, his broad smile reaching up to his small eyes. "Welcome, welcome," he added, while he made way for her.

Although the door was pushed wide open, the vestibule remained dark. A dust-covered mirror and its heavy frame faced her with a thoughtful frown from above the sideboard. The only light came from the sun rays of Dr. Zeki's smile. She advanced over these rays laid in her path and passed through a room with deeply pleated velvet drapes at its three tall windows.

They walked into a large salon with a winding staircase opposite the door. A huge fireplace dominated the room. Covered by turquoise tiles of graceful designs, the chimney climbed up to the high ceiling. Inside the fireplace were several logs of wood. The untidy structure of the logs and the accumulated ashes under them belied the approaching summer. They belied the existence of all the bright and beautiful things in life.

"Sit down. Please sit down," said Dr. Zeki, gesturing towards the couch. The couch was placed near the stairs. It faced a wide and tall window. Seasons had come and gone outside the panes of that window. The seasons had converted the balls of dust into layers of dried mud. The lace curtains which hung down across the window were too frail to conceal the condition of the panes behind them.

"Orhan will come down shortly," Dr. Zeki said, as soon as Meral sat on the couch. He balanced his heavy body precariously on the edge of the armchair next to the couch. There was an ornate coffee table between them.

"What can I get for you?" he asked, bending towards her. "We'll be having tea in a little while. But what can I get you in the meantime?"

"Nothing, thank you," said Meral. "I'll be patient, I'll wait for the tea."

Dr. Zeki did not insist. Instead he said, "How good of you to come. How good of you to honor our house."

His polite words, to which Meral had been listening absentmindedly so far, called her to shocked attention when she heard them portray a situation she had not expected. "You cannot imagine what your visit means to us. Orhan and I have not had a visitor here since I don't remember when," he said.

Although what the doctor had said made it quite obvious that he and his brother-in-law were the only people living in this villa, the awareness seemed to travel to Meral's mind through dark channels. Two men? No wives? No women? Two men! No wives! No women! Although to Dr. Zeki there seemed to be nothing extraordinary about receiving a female visitor, Meral felt extremely awkward. She tightened the reins of her self-control to breaking point to keep the surprise off her face. While easygoing subjects rolled down the sunny slopes of Dr. Zeki's smile, Meral's panicky mind tried to find an excuse for cutting her visit short. She should escape from this huge house where two men lived alone. She should escape from this house where one of the men talked incessantly and the other was not around.

"Well, this was most enjoyable," she said, standing up. "But it is getting late. I must be going."

"Oh no," said Dr. Zeki. He was almost whimpering. "You cannot go yet. We didn't have our tea yet. You haven't met Orhan yet. I'll go and wake him up. His afternoon naps are getting longer and longer."

He jumped up with an agility unexpected of his heavy body, and almost ran to the door.

Meral had to sit down again.

Time walked over the stretched silence with the careful steps of a tightrope walker. Then she heard footsteps outside. She heard a muffled argument. She heard more footsteps. Then silence.

Eventually both wings of the heavy door opened at once. Dr. Zeki walked in with a laden silver tray. On the tray were the teapot, teacups, cakes and cookies, all mixed up. As soon as he put them on the large coffee table, soft steps approached through the open door. Unaware of her actions, Meral stood up.

"I am honored to meet you, *hanimefendi*," said the approaching man. He bent down gracefully and kissed her hand.

After this was done, he looked directly at Meral. Defiance and humility were mingled in his greenish eyes. His voice came from the depths of bygone days. His presence was affirmed by his black hair, straight nose and the mobility of his lips. He wore an old-fashioned double-breasted beige suit.

He sat on a chair close to Dr. Zeki. He seemed to be in a stupor. Time kept still, waiting for him to surface.

Dr. Zeki was up, trying to serve the tea. His actions were jerky and indecisive.

"How do you like your tea?" he asked Meral.

He lifted a teacup, and put it down again. He took the teapot, its handle burned his hand. He put it down. He looked for the napkin. It was hidden under the cake dish. He lifted the cake dish to remove the napkin. He almost dropped the cake.

His brother-in-law watched his movements all the time. His face failed to express approval or disapproval. Nothing had been prepared for anyone in this house. There was no one in this house to help with such preparations. Loading the tray must have been a monumental effort for the doctor.

Meral felt that it was time she came to the rescue of the struggling man. "May I help?" she said, wrapping the small napkin neatly around the handle of the teapot.

"Please, *hanimefendi*," said Orhan, "do not trouble yourself."

Dr. Zeki said, "Actually the tray is much too crowded."

"Why don't we put some of the dishes on the table," said Meral.

"What a wonderful idea!" said Dr. Zeki.

Meral laughed as she removed the dishes of cake and cookies from the tray and put them on the table. A soft echo of laughter reached Meral's ears. It came from Orhan's direction. Then Dr. Zeki broke into laughter of relief.

"What a wonderful idea," he repeated with relish. His simplicity was the source of the miracle. He was the cause of the laughter.

Meral poured the tea and handed the first cup to Orhan. "Sugar?" she asked, extending the sugar bowl.

Dr. Zeki answered. "No sugar for Orhan," he said. "He is diabetic." He handed him a bottle of pills from the tray.

"Oh, I am sorry," said Meral. She knew nothing of diabetics.

When Orhan spoke after some time, Meral almost failed to relate what he said to her sympathetic comment.

"That is the least of my problems," he said.

"Come on, no self-pity now," said Dr. Zeki. He turned to Meral. "Orhan and I have been friends with each other since I do not remember when," he said. "Self-pity has always been Orhan's weakness. Once I found him in the basement of his house where we used to play together. He was in tears. He was seven or eight at the time. He had a poem on a piece of paper. He had written it himself. He was reading it aloud and crying at his own lines."

"I suppose writing is compulsive," Meral said. "My mother died two years ago and I found heaps of writing on her desk. At present my job is to sort them out. I remember her as a self-effacing woman. But there is so much fire in her writing."

"Speaking of writing, do you know who Orhan's father was?" asked Dr. Zeki. "He was Haldun Benenli."

She remembered the villa now. She had seen many photographs of Benenli, the well-known poet, in front of it. It was often alleged by his enthusiastic readers that the scenery from this villa had inspired most of his better known poems. His fans who eagerly awaited his forthcoming poems were inconsolable when they learned of his death following an operation in London, five or six years ago. The lamentations for his untimely departure from the literary scene echoed in numberless articles.

Haldun Benenli's photographs presented him as a flamboyant man. She looked at Orhan to search for a resemblance. His head was bowed.

"Orhan could have become a famous poet like his father. But his father insisted that he should study international law. We both studied in Germany. We shared an apartment."

Orhan was studying the prominent veins of his large hands. His hands were resting on his knees.

Dr. Zeki threw a quick look at Orhan. "We had better change the subject," he said. He waited for a while, then he continued. "OK. Let's see. What about sports. Orhan was a champion swimmer in his youth. He has many cups. He keeps them upstairs in his room. Fenerbahce Club was very sorry to see him go to Germany."

24

"Zeki," said Orhan, "you are boring *hanimefendi*. You sound like a doting mother."

Meral laughed. So did Dr. Zeki.

"I also love the sea," she said. "I used to have a boat when I was a girl. We used to swim the whole summer through. This was before I married. My husband hates all kinds of sports."

She continued after a pause. "What about you, Dr. Zeki?" she asked.

"Now there is a dull story. I used to water-ski. Not very well. Later, I sold my motor-boat," he said. "Now, all I do is go to the Kasimpasa Emergency Clinic. I examine the patients. When they have minor problems, we treat them. If we cannot help the patients, we refer them to other hospitals. You see, it is a small clinic. Not enough medicine. Not enough instruments." He was getting depressed.

This time Orhan spoke. "Who is indulging in self-pity now?" he said unexpectedly.

He continued after some time, as if he were cued by a prompter hiding somewhere underneath the dusty furniture. "Zeki was the brightest among us neighborhood kids. His father had high hopes for him. Zeki decided to become a surgeon when he was quite a little boy. Whenever we went to fancy-dress parties as teenagers, Zeki always came dressed in overalls and an operating mask. We wracked our brains to come up with interesting ideas. Zeki did not bother himself. He came to every single party dressed as a surgeon."

Dr. Zeki spread his fingers and held them up. "In Germany, I was told my fingers were too short for a surgeon," he said.

"Nonsense," said Orhan. "You make it up."

Dr. Zeki did not answer.

"You simply became lazy in Germany. Too many girls. Too much money from home."

Meral was confused. On the ferryboat she had understood from Dr. Zeki that Orhan had not been out of his house for ten years. He had hinted that Orhan shut himself up because of a tragedy in his life. How could a man like him fail to show understanding towards the weakness of others? Orhan denied self-pity to Dr. Zeki while he seemed to live wrapped up in the very same emotion.

"It is time I went home," said Meral. She stood up.

Orhan approached her with a serious face. "We are privileged to know you, *hanimefendi*. We hope we did not bore you too much. Would you come and have tea with us again?" he asked.

Meral had to change the hardened expression of her face.

"Make it soon, please." He kissed her hand.

This was the birth of a friendship.

3

Meral's husband called again. This was his fifth call since she had left him. His two visits and four calls so far had resolved nothing. Yet he was not able to accept that the worn-out thread of their married life could not hold them together any longer, that they had come to the end of their life together.

During the conversation, Fahri kept saying, "Hello. Do you hear me?" every time Meral was searching for appropriate words.

"I hear you," she answered each time.

One would think he was calling from New York or Tokyo.

"We must talk," he said. "We must solve this misunderstanding."

"To talk . . . to solve . . . since when did we talk?" she asked herself. But to her husband, she said: "Look, Fahri, we have talked all we need to. About solving our misunderstanding—there is no misunderstanding between us. I wish there was. Then perhaps we could solve it. On the contrary, it is understanding that has separated me from you. Understanding that there is nothing in this marriage for me. There is no room in this marriage for me."

She was pleased with what she said. During their previous arguments, she had been lost for words. But now, helped by the crutches of sturdy, time-proven speech, she touched the core of the matter. She was not sorry for the way she expressed herself. Was it not true that she had been pushed out of space? Was it not true that she had been denied sharing his life? Was it not true that she had been deprived of personal growth?

Fahri lived with publishing. He slept with publishing. Photography was his hobby. Hobby? He saw life only through lenses. Anything which remained outside of the borders of the lenses did not exist. Once he had taken a photograph of Meral and Bekir, his nephew. Meral's arm was around the shoulders of the boy. According to Fahri, the photo summed up the happy relationship of the two people. It was definite. It was final.

"Hello, hello," he said again. "Do you hear me?"

He had not said anything. It was Meral who had spoken last. Did he want her to go on and on?

He probably wanted her to decipher the weak stretches on the thread of their relationship and fasten a quick knot over them. Well, she couldn't. She couldn't do it by herself. It was unfair that she should be the one to stop their marriage from slipping down. They had to go their separate ways.

Her hand put the receiver down. Her movement was slow and deliberate; gentle and sad. This was her final goodbye to eleven years.

The telephone rang. She went to the kitchen to make some tea. The telephone rang. She grabbed her bag. The telephone rang again. She picked up her bathing suit and a towel. The telephone might have rung again, but Meral was already out of the house.

She went out to swim.

She walked to the taxi rank as fast as she could. That morning there were only two cars in the line. This time an old driver walked towards the car in the front and opened the door for her.

Meral entered. "To the Ada Wharf," she said.

She folded the towel lengthwise twice and rolled it over the bathing suit. The taxi was on its way. In no time, the driver pulled up near the newsstand at the wharf.

"This is as far as we can go," he said.

CAGES ON OPPOSITE SHORES

Meral paid him and walked among the crowds who waited for the ferryboat. The wharf for the boats going to the islands was always more crowded than the one for the European shore, as the increasing pollution of the Marmara Sea sent people off to more and more distant beaches. On weekends it was hard to find seats. But this was Thursday and early summer.

As the doors of the waiting room opened and she walked up to the upper deck of the ferryboat, she began to regret her sharp retorts to Fahri's pleading on the phone. She should have acted in a wiser manner. She should have used the opportunity of Fahri's call to talk to him about the divorce. Now, she would have to call him herself. She would have to tell him that she had already consulted a lawyer. She would have to prepare him for the official procedures which had been explained to her by her repulsive lawyer.

The court sessions were going to be painful for both of them. There would be many questions asked by people who had nothing to do with their lives. The whole matter could be settled more easily if Fahri did not raise objections. The lawyer had told her that if Fahri agreed, the divorce might not take more than two or three court sessions.

The boat drew a giant circle on the smooth surface of the sea, and made its way around the greenery of Moda Burnu. As the engines accelerated into fuller speed, a whistle broke from their depths. The sharp sound filled the air while the wooden boards shuddered under the passengers' feet. After the boat had reached and passed Moda Burnu, it followed a straight line towards the islands.

Meral sat on the top deck. A teasing wind pulled at the hair and scarves of the passengers. Several children ran between the legs of the seated people. They played hide and seek. This game used to be Meral's favorite when she was young. But she had not been allowed to mix with the neighborhood children. Books with colored pictures were pushed into her hand, and she was encouraged to read all the time. However, once her nanny Emine had taken her to the Moda children's playground. Meral was full of excitement on the way, but when they arrived they found out that the swings had been removed. There were only a few children playing in the sandpit, under the shade of chestnut trees. Nanny had not allowed Meral to go into the sandpit. Her nice clothes would become dirty. She took her to another playground. The Wharf Playground. As soon as Meral had seen the children crowding around the swings, she had joined them. She had swung, queued for her turn and swung again. After she repeated this several times the mothers of some children started to object. They said she was being unfair to other children. The mothers could not understand what Meral really wanted. What she wanted was to be among the children who pulled and pushed each other all the time. It was the waves she needed, not the swim.

The beach on the far side of the island was nearly empty. Meral changed in one of the cabins nearest to the entrance. She walked into the sea. As soon as the salty waves embraced her, she felt cleansed of her problems. She had one very long swim and came out. She walked to the open-air shower and queued for her turn, watching the multi-directed spurts of the shower's pipe which was about to create a lake around its base. The large slabs placed around the soaked circle of ground gradually disappeared under the abundance of running water as the swimmers took their turns at the shower. The last one before Meral was a fat lady. She remained under the shower almost five minutes rinsing the rich lather of the soap from her hair. She looked at Meral apologetically as her fingers rubbed the dark roundness of her head with quick, graceful fingers. Meral watched the soapy water running down the white polka dots of her black bathing suit.

After taking her shower, Meral walked towards the changing cabins drying herself. The open space above the cabin's short door gave her a view of the beach's café. She saw the tea boy take a tray with several tiny glasses of tea from the counter. Holding the knob where the tray's three raised arms joined together, he zigzagged around the sprawled bodies of the sunbathers on the sand. The tray swung slightly as he walked along, and the hot steam from the glasses climbed up the tray's copper arms. The sight tempted Meral to order a cup of tea for herself when she finished dressing. But she changed her mind. She might miss the next boat.

She walked to the landing and bought her ticket. The man at the ticket office had loosened the collar of his white uniform. He was singing a nostalgic Anatolian folk song to himself. "Right. Here you go, lady," he said, interrupting his song, and pushed the ticket out through the small window. He continued to sing. "The tulip says

'Look at my swan-like neck, look at my velvet-like petals. I'm the prettiest among the flowers. Surely no flower can match my beauty.'"

As she went up to the middle deck the boat started. She took a seat which gave her the moving scenery alongside the boat. She looked at the motorboats tugging at the tight ropes which held them fast to the pier. She looked at the empty tables of the seaside restaurants. Those tables which lined part of the shore were stiff, but the skirts of their covering cloths waved to the departing boat. When time would replace June with July these skirts of the covering tablecloths would be stifled between the crowding legs of the tourists filling the tables. July and August would end the tablecloths' breezy holiday.

The restaurant grew smaller. The island grew smaller. The bordering surf around the island turned the scenery into a postcard picture. A formal postcard picture taken by an unimaginative photographer. A picture resembling the photographs taken by her husband Fahri. A restaurant with tiny tables. A landing with a doll's house building. An insignificant island—a spot on the sea.

When the boat was about to arrive at Kadikoy, Meral had a glimpse of the mid-sea tower of Leander—the ivory tower of her husband.

Soon after she had met Fahri in mid-summer, he had joined their friendly group of swimmers. At the end of the summer, while her relation to him was at a standstill, she and her friends had found themselves in the middle of a stormy sea. On that day, while they fought with the waves, Fahri had busily photographed them from Leander's Tower. After the storm, he had come to her and said, "How would you like to see yourself in the same storm again?" His words, to which Meral had attached more meaning than they carried, had been accompanied by a mysterious smile at the corners of his mouth. The smile had molded and re-molded the sparse flesh on his dry face and kept Meral looking at him spellbound. The indignation she had felt towards him for remaining at the Tower during his friends' moment of danger was forgotten.

The ivory tower he created out of his work and his hobby was responsible for the failure of their marriage. In Meral's mind, this man's ivory tower was fixed in the shape of Leander's Tower, which stood at the gateway of the Bosphorus, halfway between the shores of European and Asian Istanbul.

31

JANSET BERKOK SHAMI

*

As the taxi approached the door of her mother's house, she saw Fahri leaning on the railings of the marble steps. He was smiling at her in the afternoon sun. He had grown a mustache since she had seen him last. She took out her key and opened the door.

"Come in," she said.

He quickly seated himself on the couch, and Meral chose the upright chair opposite him.

"Yes?" she said.

"I am sorry," he said.

"We are both sorry," she said. "But let us think about the future now. Not the past. Now that I have left you, what are you going to do about it?"

"I'll beg you to come back."

"That will not help," Meral said. Her voice was firm. "Please try to understand, I'll not come back. Now, my question is, are you going to make the divorce easy or difficult?"

"Divorce?" The bomb which exploded in his question had been planted long ago.

Meral spoke after some time.

"Yes, divorce," she said. "Would you like a cup of coffee?"

"Divorce?" he repeated. "We never talked about divorce before. What is going on? I hear you have found yourself new friends on the European shore. I hear you are neglecting your beloved committees."

Meral stiffened and remained silent for a while. Then she said, "What you hear does not concern me, Fahri."

She had been able to speak calmly. "Would you like a cup of coffee?" she said again.

The calmness of her question made him jump out of his seat. "Coffee?" he shouted. "Is this time for coffee?"

He walked out of the room. He walked out of the house.

*

After her husband left, Meral remained standing, trying to think about the conversation they had had. But instead she found herself think-

32

ing of her coming dental appointment. It was going to be the last one. Then her thoughts switched to the old Armenian woman at the *tuhafiyeci* shop. Finally the interrupting distractions allowed her thoughts to turn back to the divorce. She made a mental note that she should contact the lawyer again. First the minor accident on the ferryboat had prevented her from keeping the appointment with him. And when she had made a new appointment and gone to see him, she had come out of his office without a firm decision in her mind. He had talked about the interesting cases he had handled. Among them there were some divorce cases too. But there were no similarities between these complicated cases and her straightforward desire to be let free. After the lawyer had gone on and on, he had suddenly asked her, "Do you really want a divorce? Do you really want to break up your marriage?" After that first visit she had let the days slip by. But now she was firm in her decision that this marriage which hung onto her life like an unnecessary, unattractive accessory should be severed. She should contact him as soon as her final dental appointment was over.

The last time she had gone to the dentist he had been in a talkative mood. He had surprised her with the new slant he had given to the old story of Meral's friend Lamia. He had claimed that Meral's mother had called and scolded him when she had learned that he had pulled Lamia's tooth. This was hardly believable. Her mother had not even scolded Meral for taking her friend to the dentist. Meral's old nanny was the one who had scolded her. "Who did you think you were?" she had said. "Her mother? Her father? Her brother? Who?" Meral had thought that the tooth spoiled Lamia's pretty face. That was all.

Meral's mother neither had the courage nor the energy for such scenes. As far as Meral knew, her mother would make any sacrifice not to create a scene.

The dentist's new version of the story caused a possibility to surface in Meral's mind. This possibility threatened to drown her old image of her mother. Meral remembered an unfinished episode, experiencing once again her frustration of years ago.

Once, only that once, her mother had wanted to take a step forward. Whatever the incident was, it must have been important for her. Meral, herself, could not remember it now.

"Look here," her mother had begun. She talked with emphasis. Her voice carried a meaning which Meral hoped to understand soon. "I'll not hit you. I'll never hit you. Mothers should not hit their children. Nobody should hit children. They are human beings. They have their pride. I'll only tell you that what you did was wrong."

Meral had never experienced an outburst from her mother before. She wanted her to go on. "What? What have I done wrong?" she asked. Her voice was eager.

Perhaps it was the eagerness in Meral's voice which warned her mother off.

"Wrong?" she said. She seemed to be contemplating the word.

She walked to the other side of the room. She sat on her usual chair. She folded her hands in her lap. She remained in this position and said nothing more.

Meral ran out. She shed bitter tears. She cried for her behavior. She cried for the denial of punishment.

Meral received all her punishments from her nanny. All her praises were sung by her nanny. All her problems were solved by her nanny.

Meral's mother did not wish to be understood by her daughter. Facts were hidden from her. Only after her death, only after Meral was a fully grown woman, did she have the chance of knowing her mother and her grandmother. Had her mother protected Meral from the truth then? Or was this a belated punishment for the wrongs she had done in the past?

Now, through her mother's notes, Meral was allowed to discover that her mother spoke the Armenian language. Now she was allowed to learn that her mother's mother was Armenian. At the age of thirty-eight Meral's identity was taken away from her. Her religion was taken away from her. All the presumed facts of her family were taken away from her. The very ground she stood on was slipping from under her feet.

Would Meral's life with her husband have been different if she had had the chance of knowing her mother better? Would she have married him if she had known her mother better? Why had she stayed with Fahri so long? Had it been the presence of Bekir which had delayed the breakup of the marriage?

Bekir had come into her life during the second year of her marriage, while she still hoped to have a child. Fahri had mentioned that he had a nephew back home in his village. He said he was about thirteen or fourteen, quite an intelligent boy, but completely uneducated. He did not even know how to read and write. Meral was shocked to hear her husband mention the ignorance of his nephew in such a matter-of-fact tone.

"Do you mean that the poor boy was allowed to grow deaf and blind? Wasn't there anyone to help him?" she asked.

To her, the situation was a horror story. A crime.

In the following days Meral brought the subject of Bekir into several conversations with her husband. And then she openly suggested bringing him to Istanbul and helping him obtain an education. To her husband, this was a serious undertaking. "You wouldn't be able to handle the social complications," he said. "You know nothing of our village and our villagers."

Her answer to his objection was a strong one. "What complications are you expecting?" she asked. "He will not be coming from Mars. He will be coming from the heart of our country. Like you did."

This venture might be a serious undertaking for Fahri, but for Meral it would be a joy. She remembered the day when he finally accepted her suggestion. It was an overcast November day, but the invisible sun was warming Meral's whole being from inside.

A letter was sent to the boy's parents in the village to invite him. Meral started to work on a program of education for him before he arrived. She was a constant visitor to the local library, searching for more and more books on adult education.

He arrived within a week. He was a chubby boy with a broad face and a straight cut mouth. His chin was square and prominent. Although he was only thirteen, it appeared that his physical growth was already stunted.

Meral organized everything for him, including his daily bath. She was full of life all of a sudden. They started his studies, wasting no time.

Within a year, his five years of primary education were completed. He almost drank the knowledge. He had been so thirsty for so long that no amount of learning seemed to quench his thirst. Meral searched for more and more books. She gave him knowledge which went beyond the requirements of the primary school examination.

During that year she obtained many introduction letters from the high-ranking civil servant husbands of several ladies with whom she worked in different societies. These letters were addressed to the heads of the relevant departments at the Ministry of Education. She presented the letters as each office sent her to another. She presented the letters and they made her write half a dozen petitions. Some people she talked to were sympathetic, some were not. Some were so dissatisfied with their own jobs that they did not care what happened to this young man. One official answered Meral's probes into the matter with an angry question. "Do you want us to break all the rules just because your husband has an uneducated nephew?" he asked. Meral argued. "Please try to look at this from a broader angle," she said. "We are talking here about a clever boy who should be given the chance to improve himself. You and I were given this chance." Meral talked to half a dozen such men. Talking to them, she was sometimes understanding, sometimes impatient. And sometimes she showed her impatience in quite harsh ways. But in the end she won. He was accepted to sit for a special examination. If he succeeded he would be able to continue with his secondary school education. He sat for the examination and he passed.

Everything seemed so easy. It seemed that Bekir and Meral were getting along so well. He filled her whole life. She was a different woman. Even her husband seemed to notice the difference. Bekir never objected to whatever she asked him to do. Alongside his formal education, she taught him social manners. She was particularly concerned with his table manners.

Bekir once was upset because being left-handed he could not use the knife if he held it in his right hand. "We'll go round your problem," said Meral. "How? How?" asked Bekir, erasing the temporary lines anxiety had written on his young face. "You'll cut your meat holding it with your right hand, but you'll peel your fruits with your left hand," she said.

Meral managed to enroll him in the Military Secondary School. He was a boarder, coming home only on the weekends. He remained stocky, but he looked taller in his school uniform.

He studied for three years in high school obediently. But it was obvious that he had no inclination for a military career. This time Meral started visiting the military offices, nagging the people, pulling strings, and eventually got him out of the army without paying the compensation due for the three years of his education.

After that, she made him study accounting. This seemed to suit him. From the beginning he was good at mathematics. He completed the required course in a year.

He was eighteen then, and ready to take on his responsibilities in society. Meral was thirty-five. She had been married for eight years and was still childless. A confrontation with Bekir brought home her frail relationship with her husband.

It was a darkening afternoon in December. Bekir turned his key in the door to come in. Meral was at the door, dressed and ready to go out. She had on a silver fox jacket and a fully pleated skirt. She had a shoulder bag which matched her shoes. They faced each other across the dimness of the vestibule. Bekir said, "Hello," scrutinizing her from top to toe, and walked inside.

When Meral arrived back home at dinner time, Fahri was still at the publishing house. Bekir was sitting on the couch with a book in his hand. He looked up, and turned his eyes back to the book without saying anything. This was unusual. He had been taught to stand up when Meral or his uncle walked in. Through these formalities she had wanted to make him a better man.

It was not hard to notice that there was something wrong. She sat down in the armchair next to the couch, without removing her jacket, and put her handbag on the coffee table. Bekir turned his gaze towards the handbag. He studied it, sliding his eyes to the very end of its dangling handle. "Nice bag," he said. He lowered his eyes to her shoes. "Nice shoes," he said. Then he returned his eyes to his book. "You are wearing a nice animal skin," he said.

"It is called a fur," Meral said.

"Whatever," he answered.

"Yes?" said Meral tempting him.

"Yes?" he said, pretending to be naive. "Do you want more compliments, Auntie?"

Bekir had been asked to call Meral "Auntie" as soon as he had come from his village. But he avoided addressing her as "Auntie." When he wanted to talk to her he simply waited till she looked his way.

Finally, he made his point. "My sister back home doesn't have a sweater to wear," he said. "You have everything," he added. A sweeping movement of his hand turned her clothes, the house and the furniture into "everything." Meral would not have minded what he said, if he had not added the following statement. "You have all the questions. You have all the answers."

The comment was more than sarcastic. It was bitter. But what was he really trying to say? The sweater problem of his sister could be remedied easily——but the problem of Meral having all the answers?

At that moment a thought which must have been hiding among the folds of her everyday life came out into the open. She was not happy with her marriage. Her mother's death which followed this incident with Bekir within a year disclosed Meral's dissatisfaction. It was as if the shadow of her mother's presence had been a lid over the faults of her marriage, as if her mother's existence had something to do with Meral's remaining married to Fahri.

Bekir found a small apartment for himself somewhere near Fatih. He said he wanted to live there as that area was close to the university. He said he wanted to complete his education. But his formal education had a gap of three years. He could never be accepted by any university without first closing this gap. Only Meral could help him in this matter. With her energy. With her knowledge of the weak points of the laws governing the educational system. But he refused her offer of help.

4

Although Meral's talk with her husband was more abrupt than she would have liked it to be, she was pleased to have informed him about her decision to seek a divorce. This made her feel better than she had felt for a while.

In the early morning light, everything in her mother's two sitting rooms looked benign and docile, candid and mundane. On her way to the kitchen for a cup of tea, she glimpsed the row of pictures she had arranged on the table in the next room, and she smiled at the naive chivalry of the turbaned men and the guileless beauty of the willowy women. When this train of pictures standing against the wall led her eyes to the pile of folded stories by the end of the table, she felt confident that reading one of them could not change her good mood.

The telephone rang just as Meral unfolded one of them and read the title: Cinderella and Her Best Friend.

"Meral *hanimefendi*," said Dr. Zeki's voice on the telephone. "Why do you neglect us? We were hoping to see you again. It's been nearly two weeks."

Meral did not know what to say. The opening notes of "Polonaise-Fantasie" that came over the telephone, and the title of the story she still held in her hand, tugged at her attention at the same time.

"Will you come tomorrow? Please do! Orhan will be so pleased to see you. You cannot imagine your effect on him. Will you come?"

"Tomorrow?" said Meral.

"Yes, tomorrow. At five. Settled then," he said. "Goodbye," he said. He put down the phone before giving her a chance to say another word.

She looked at the unfolded papers in her hand and started reading the story.

"Mommy I forgot my hankie!"

My mother handed me the handkerchief and disappeared.

The teacher came over to me with a honey-sweet smile and took me to a group of children who were chattering in the corner.

"This is 'A,' our little friend," she said.

The children's little feet in shiny black shoes circled me and the look in their cunning eyes examined me thoroughly. They were to decide my exact position among them. Kamuran, the girl with golden locks of hair, took my hand into hers and studied it carefully.

"Your fingers look like our Armenian gardener's fingers. They look like Monsieur Aram's fingers," she said, and giggled.

It was then that my tears started to run.

I cried for the early morning hours I woke up to see my mother bent over her sewing in her room. I cried for her unintelligible mutterings in a strange language, and her intermittent sighs. I wanted to shout. I wanted to say, "Stop it. Throw away the thimble and the needle. Throw away the cloth and all the thread. We don't need the money. I don't need to go to school. I don't need to study."

On the carefully folded and ironed hankie my mother gave me were pictures of children sitting in a rowboat. They looked so happy. The children around me were happy too. Kamuran's curls hung so securely next to her pink cheeks.

The teacher said, "Who made 'A' cry?"

The children pointed at Kamuran who stood near me, guiltily.

40

CAGES ON OPPOSITE SHORES

"Please call my mother back," I begged the teacher, "I need another hankie. This one is all wet."

The bell rang, calling me to a class filled with children I did not know. I was six and this was already the second school to which I had been.

*

It was playtime. "Now, who is going to be the rabbit and who is going to be the wolf?" asked the teacher cheerfully.

An invisible wind churned the air and the children became a huge wave. I was part of the wave. I was carried by it and floated away from my desk. My hankie was left on my chair.

Kamuran whispered to me. "In the next play I am going to be Cinderella," she said. "Would you like to be the Fairy Godmother?" I nodded my head quickly, scarcely believing my ears. We were the best of friends, till my mother decided to change my school again.

I met Kamuran several times when I was about to start university. Then I stopped seeing her. Later, I learned that her diplomat father had been posted to Paris and he had taken his family with him.

*

"Kamuran," I shouted through the snowflakes, seeing the same blonde locks of years ago. My call sounded like the sob of a six-year-old girl.

She turned sharply, and our eyes met. For a moment I thought, "She is not Kamuran. She is wondering why I called her by this name." But it was Kamuran.

The cable car came and left, we stayed at the stop looking at each other. Kamuran was able to talk first. "I am glad to see you. You have changed so much! I mean, we've both changed," she said.

What she said was true. Who can stay six years old? Who can stay seventeen? Nobody! The eyes touch seventeen and go by. The mouth smiles seventeen and then a hand smears it with lipstick. The hand which held the blood-red lipstick and the hand which waved with a studied negligence saying "never mind" to a friend who hurt her, are no longer parts of the people who are standing at the cable car stop years later. These people who are making conversation while snow settles on their clothes are not the same people of the past years.

Kamuran talked incessantly. "Paris was definitely a gay place," she said. "But we did not stay there for long, you know. My father was transferred to Rome and we packed and followed him. My mother was very upset about it all. You see, the packing company which handled our furniture was very careless. They broke the leg of the our genuine Louis Quinze chair. I was upset too. But then . . . I stopped worrying about it. You see, I had met an Italian count. He was so handsome, 'A.' He was out of this world. He asked me to marry him. And I accepted. Then my parents discovered that he was penniless. Really, some people . . . What did he take us for? Luckily my father was transferred to Spain and we got out of Italy just in time. Now in Spain. . . ."

Kamuran's rush recount of her recent past rang false to my suspicious ears. Everything she said sounded like a chapter from a romantic novel.

The cable car which would take me home arrived before hers did.

I embraced her. "Perhaps you would come and see me some time," I said, as I climbed up. "Call me to make sure that I am at home," I added.

She looked old and yet so young with her golden hair capped with snow. She looked old and yet so young with murky clouds passing through her blue eyes.

Although my warm embrace was that of a victor, a curious nostalgia stained my victory. I missed the old, self-assured Kamuran of my childhood. I missed the Cinderella-Snow White-Sleeping Beauty of my childhood.

As the cable car moved away, a sudden gust of wind opened her coat and exposed the shiny party dress underneath it. So she must be going to a party. But if she was, she was late. Why was she waiting for a cable car while the unoccupied phaetons passed by? Perhaps she had already been to a party and was going back home. But it was too early for that. It was not midnight yet and she had not lost a shoe. Her shoes looked rather worn out. . . .

I remembered the news I had read that morning. It was something like, "He returned from Spain accompanied by his wife and daughter. He was taken straight to court. He faces charges of. . . ." I had paid no attention to the names.

Wasn't Kamuran's father's return from Spain rather sudden? Did this news mean that she would not go to those faraway places anymore? Did this mean that she would not have the chance of meeting the prince of her dreams? It can't be! It is not fair!

Kamuran with old shoes. . . . Kamuran in court. . . .

The judge will ask her, "Why did your father rob the embassy safe?"

She will answer truthfully. "To buy me a pair of diamond shoes," she will say.

The judge will not understand. The prosecutor will not understand. None of the people in the court will understand that Kamuran needed diamond shoes as we, ordinary people, needed ordinary leather shoes.

I left the cable car at the last stop and walked home on the soft, melting snow shivering with fear. I opened the newspaper harshly.

"The daughter of the diplomat, who is the wife of a young diplomat herself and the mother of three children. . . ." continued the news.

Kamuran is not married yet. She is not old enough to be the mother of three children. Her respectable father is free of my shameful suspicion!

While a silent laughter narrowed my happy eyes, I looked at my fingers clutching at the corner of the newspaper.

"Your fingers look like our Armenian gardener's fingers!"

France, Italy, Spain.

Spain, Italy, France.

France, Italy, Spain.

Spain, Italy, France.

Stop it. Stop it.

I walked from France to Spain a hundred times, as the telephone rang. It rang while I walked from Spain to Italy. It rang again while I walked from Italy to France.

The telephone is tired. And I am tired.

I only wish that she would find her prince and leave me alone.

I only wish she would leave me alone.

*

As soon as Meral entered the villa, she realized that Dr. Zeki had translated Orhan's feelings literally. Nothing more, nothing less. Her effect on him was clearly written on his face.

He was standing at the salon door, waiting. Meral entered, followed by Dr. Zeki. Immediately he bent and kissed her hand. He had imposed strict restrictions on himself. But his delight at seeing her was betrayed by his jaunty movements. He followed her across the room and watched her seat herself. After this, he walked to the chair opposite hers. He lowered himself into it. His watchful eyes were fixed on hers.

The awkward moment was in need of words, sounds. Dr. Zeki's generosity provided them. He welcomed her volubly. He sprinkled his smile over everything. The light aroma of his trifling remarks filled the room.

After some time Orhan voiced an opinion.

"I think we have done enough talking on matters not related to any of us," he said.

Dr. Zeki picked up the statement from where Orhan left it.

"You are absolutely right," he said. "The problem is, we do not know much about each other."

"Okay, then," volunteered Meral. "Here is my resume. I was born in Istanbul. My father was a wealthy businessman. When my father married my mother, he was sixty years old. My mother was thirty-three. They lived together for five years. When I was four years old my father died. My mother died only two years ago. I studied at the German High School and then I studied Ottoman History at Istanbul University. I never learned to drive. Swimming is the only sport I enjoy."

Meral's straightforward account made Orhan think deeply.

"Wouldn't you like to go on?" asked Dr. Zeki. His voice was hesitant.

"Certainly," said Meral with the crispness of a saleswoman. "I married a young man who came from the heart of Anatolia——from one of the villages of Konya. He came to Istanbul to study. He is a graduate of Istanbul University too. After he finished his studies, he did not go back to his village. He worked in a publishing firm for several years. Later he established his own publishing house. I met him when he was about to venture into that business. I suppose I helped him a little. He was a friend of my friends. He was an amateur photographer. He used to come swimming with us, but he would spend his time taking photographs."

"He must have photographed mainly you," ventured Dr. Zeki.

"No, no," said Meral. "He took photographs of each one of us, turning his lens from one to the other. Sometimes several of us would be squeezed into the same photograph. But this would be just a co-incidence."

She was waiting for a question. But there was none. Both men were silent. So she passed the judgement herself.

"I think he was searching for an answer in his photographs. I think he is still searching for an answer. He thinks the answer will come through the lens."

Still no comment. "Well, at least, I think so," she said. She tried to smile.

"So, this is it? The happy ending?" asked Dr. Zeki.

"Far from it. On the phone you asked me why I didn't come to see you. I'll tell you why. I was busy with my lawyer. I am asking for a divorce."

"I am sorry," said Orhan.

"Now you know everything," said Meral.

Orhan amended what she had said: "One never knows everything."

"What do you mean?" asked Meral.

Orhan did not answer. His eyes followed Dr. Zeki going out of the room to prepare tea. "We do not know what he looks like," he said suddenly.

"What?" said Meral. "Who?"

"Your husband."

"Oh, well," she said, "he is rather tall . . . and dark. He has thick wavy hair. When I first met him he had a mustache. After we married I made him shave it off. It did not suit his face. You see, he doesn't really have enough space for it. But he kept on growing it and shaving it off again every now and then. That man changed something in himself the minute I felt I was getting close to him. He changed something in his looks, in his speech, in his clothes. . . ."

She tried to give her voice the same light touch it had at the beginning of the conversation. "His eyes are round. They give his face an expression of permanent surprise."

There was a silence.

"Your turn now," she said.

"You want to know what I look like?" he said, pretending to misunderstand her.

"Well, I would be interested. I am sure we all see ourselves quite differently than other people do. Don't you agree?" was Meral's good-natured response.

"I agree," said Orhan. "But who cares what I look like, anyway?" he added.

"What about your life story?" Meral asked, tinkling the school bell and calling Orhan to attention.

Orhan acknowledged the end of the recess with a sigh. "Well," he said, "not much to tell really. Zeki already told you that I am a great sportsman(!) a poet(!) what else? Oh, yes, a cook(!). I am the cook of our makeshift family of two."

Meral's silence urged him to continue.

"I married Zeki's sister," he said. "I continued my education in Germany after my marriage. I came home only for holidays. My marriage didn't work out either."

Although Meral did not give voice to any of the questions which quivered on her tongue, Orhan continued after a short silence. But this silence had carved out a major chunk from his life.

"I am forty years old. I have no children. Zeki is forty years old too. He never married. He came close to marriage once. But he never did. Both of us have been alone in this house for the last ten years. At the beginning Zeki used to invite some people. But as I did not come in to meet them, they stopped visiting after one or two times."

Dr. Zeki brought in the tea tray.

"Here we are," he said, placing it on the table in front of the couch.

Meral moved to the couch and started serving. She dropped two tablets of saccharine into Orhan's cup before she handed him his tea.

Dr. Zeki's laden tray dictated the codes of a ritual. The ritual involved just the three of them. They drank the tea. They ate the cookies. This was to be repeated.

5

The memory invaded Meral's mind just as she was about to fall asleep in her bed. She remembered entering her mother's room one evening without knocking and catching her partially undressed. She was about to put on her nightgown. Meral had noticed long strips of plaster in front of both her mother's uncovered shoulders. They ran down towards her armpits. Meral must have been quite a small girl at the time. She had thought that the pink strips of plaster were part of a grown-up body, like the puffy breasts.

Since the first entry she came across in the diaries had introduced Meral's grandmother to her, since the *tuhafiyeci* woman had confirmed the introduction by stamping a name, an Armenian name, on her, she had lost the courage to delve deeper into the diaries. She had become inclined to weave her way through the fringes of the table, through her mother's stories. She imagined that this longer path to her mother's personal life would be less thorny, easier to get through. The stories would warn her of dangers on her way, they would prepare her for unexpected shocks, before she arrived at the path's irreversible end.

But her leisurely walk did not last long. The diversion joined the main road sooner than she expected.

And what challenged her earlier thoughts, what caused the change of heart was the sudden return of the memory.

She had to take up her mother's diaries and read everything written in them. She had to! Deciding to read from the first diary, as she had before, she sat and opened its cover. The mature handwriting of the lines on the first page contrasted with the writing on the following pages of the diary. It was obvious that these lines were added several years after the diary had been completed.

"Beware of your mother!" This is what the Guardian Angels must whisper daily into the ears of each and every child. "Beware of your mother!" they must whisper from the day they are born to the day they die.

"My God. My dear, merciful God," Meral whispered to herself. She left the diary on the table and went to the salon. She turned on the table lamp first. Then she turned on all the other lights in the room. She went back to the big table and brought the diary to the salon. She sat down and opened it once again.

There was another line below the bitter warning. Obviously it had been written at a still later date. It said: *My mother died years ago. How do I feel now?* The writer had not tried to answer her question. But she had written out the date. *May 21, 1955.*

Meral's mother was forty when she wrote this. At the age of forty she was not sure if she forgave her mother or not. Meral would have been three years old then.

She turned the pages of the book.

February 12, 1948

My mother was a perfectionist. She believed in perfection with all her heart. She talked of perfection. She always produced perfection. (Correction: she almost always produced perfection. My very existence is an exception.)

Each one of her handiworks was a perfection. Her tablecloths were masterpieces. I loved the look of them. I loved the feel of them. I loved the smell of them. I watched them being made; being wrapped up and

48

being sent to the tuhafiyeci *shops to be sold. I watched them being born, growing and being sent out into the world.*

A note scribbled in the margin commented:

I was expecting my mother to make me a present of one of these tablecloths when I married. But she gave me a ring instead.

Meral went back to the beginning of the diary again:

June 7, 1928

My mother is very busy today. She is not working on her lovely tablecloths. She is making something ugly. She went and bought thick, coarse linen. This material is the kind they use for tents. She cut it up with big scissors. Her hands were hurt. She had wrapped her fingers with gauze, so that she can press hard enough on the scissors to be able to cut the material. And now she has started sewing it. Her metal thimble was pierced. She broke several needles. And when what she did was partly ready, she made me wear it over my naked flesh. It is a corset. A very hard corset. It is to hold me straight. For years my mother has been telling me to stand up straight. She slaps me every now and then to make me stand straight. She could not make me stand straight. Now, she has found a new way. This wretched corset!

*

June 9, 1928

My corset is ready after five fittings. The fifth fitting took fifty minutes. I nearly fainted while standing but she kept on adjusting the side straps and the back straps. At the end my mother was quite pleased with her work. But the corset is scratching my flesh. I told her. She didn't pay any attention to me. "You'll get used to it," she said.

*

June 10, 1928

My mother came into my room and made me put on the corset. Yester-

49

day's scratches have become red and very painful now. I told my mother that the corset hurts. She said: "It is to make you stand straight. If you stand straight, it will not hurt you."

*

July 5, 1928
Miss Lucy came back today. I thought I had got rid of her. My mother wants me to continue with the ballet lessons. I begged her to stop the lessons. But it is no use. Miss Lucy says I have no talent. My mother knows I have no talent.

*

July 8, 1928
I was beaten this morning. The new Armenian maid showed my mother the blood stains on my slip. My mother showed them to me. "The corset is cutting me to pieces. All my slips will be bloody from now on. My shoulders will stay like this," I said. First she hit me with her hands. Then she used the stick she keeps behind the door. The corset is cutting into the flesh of my armpits. The rest of my body hurts from the beating.

*

July 10, 1928
The Armenian maid (her name is Susan, I learned today) and my ballet teacher talked to each other for a long time this morning. Their talk was fast. I could not understand a word they were saying. I wondered if they were talking about me. I told my mother I could not understand what they were saying. She said, "Because you do not study your Armenian language."

*

July 11, 1928
The English neighbor has a nice white dog. I see him outside sometimes. He followed me today when I was sent to the grocer's. I patted

him. His hair felt like silk.
It was a nice, warm day today.

*

July 12, 1928
There is pus in the cuts under my arms. My mother looked at them.
She put some kind of cream on them and covered the front of my shoul-
ders with strips of colored plaster. But she made me wear the corset all
the same. The strips start from the tips of my shoulders and run all the
way down to my armpits. They are supposed to protect me from the harsh
texture of the corset.

Meral lulled herself to sleep. In her dream she hugged her mother's body for a long time. When she let her go, her mother's corset
clung to her body. It burned her flesh all over. She cried, she tried
to tear it off. But she could not get rid of it. Then Orhan appeared
out of nowhere. He removed the corset from her with ease. Averting
his eyes from her he placed a light kiss on her shoulder.
As soon as Meral woke up, she continued reading the same diary.
She had to finish it that day. She wouldn't dare to continue if she let
any time pass.

September 14, 1928
I am happy today. I am starting my new school tomorrow. New friends.
They will not know that my mother is Armenian. I am determined to
find myself a good friend among the girls I'll meet.

*

September 15, 1928
The carriage came at seven. My mother placed one of her rare kisses
on top of my head, as this is the first day of the new school. The carriage
is very pretty. Paintings cover its sides and ceiling. The paintings are of
lakes, trees and flowers. There are no people. The red-roofed houses on
the shores of the lakes are not lived in. I'll occupy one of these houses.
I'll make some curtains for its windows. I'll carry wood to warm myself

in winter. I'll fish by the lake in summer. I'll swim in the nearby river. I'll climb the trees.

*

September 16, 1928

The carriage was late this morning. The driver takes us six girls to school in the carriage. I am the fourth girl he collects. After me, he goes to Vedia's. Her mother stretched her head out from an upper window of their house and told the driver calmly (quite calmly) that if next time he doesn't come on time, he had better stop coming. She said she'll send her daughter to school in another carriage. She made my heart jump. Vedia is in my class and I like her very much. She is a clever girl. She is helping me with my English. After a few months, I'll try to write this diary in English. Then my mother will not be able to read it. I won't need to keep it under the loose wooden board in my room. When Susan takes the carpet to clean it my heart starts to beat violently. The board remains bare while she hangs it on the balcony rail and beats it with the bamboo stick. There are several loose boards in my room. The one which hides the book is not the only one. But my mother is a very cunning woman. I am also worried about the carpet. One day that old carpet with its magnificent designs will fall to pieces. What will cover the boards then?

*

September 17, 1928

I hate Mecdi, our driver. He was late again. This time he had his scolding from my mother. Well, my mother's scolding was incomparable. She was loud. She was bitter. She was as cutting as a whip. After we had gone a little further from my house, Mecdi took a bottle from the wooden box next to his seat. He drank from it. He started cursing my mother and whipping his horse. His horse is white with brown spots. Her name is Naciye. Mecdi loves her. He talks to her. He calls her Lady Naciye. But he whipped her again and again this morning to make her run fast. If I were Lady Naciye I wouldn't run. However much he whipped me, I wouldn't run. I'd show him that he could not scare me.

CAGES ON OPPOSITE SHORES

The strong expression of resistance in the last entry made Meral grip the diary so tightly that it hurt her fingers.

She released the diary, opening her fingers one by one. She put it on the table and looked at it respectfully. Not daring to move her eyes from the pile of the diaries, she picked up the next one.

Part of this diary was written in German, other parts were written in English and French. She had switched from one language to another, according to the different schools she was moved to every other year. Meral could only read the parts which were written in German and English and these parts had several entries about her grandmother's relentless efforts to marry her daughter to the English neighbor's son. When she had finally understood her daughter's lack of interest in the young man, when she had realized that she would not succeed, she had praised the young man in a way which belittled her daughter. "The boy is an Oxford graduate," she said, "and funnily enough he is willing to marry you." She reminded her daughter that her "drooping shoulders" gave her a "caved-in appearance." She reminded her of the unproportional size of her hips, which obliged her to enlarge the left side and tighten the right side of all her skirts and dresses. Then there was Meral's mother's silent answer to these hurtful comments. "There is no need for her to remind me of all that," she wrote. "I cannot forget the alleged unproportional size of my hips as long as she continues to stick pins all over them while she makes her adjustments. And 'funnily enough,' as my mother would put it, I look and look and I do not see any difference between my hips."

To bring her point to the bitter end, the mother said this to her daughter: "You do not have much chance of marrying a Turkish man, anyway, because of me."

Although Meral put down the diary in her hand and took up another one covering the more mature years of her mother's life, the struggles to get rid of the corset continued. Her mother's long-awaited liberation seemed to have been realized only after the rarely washed garment caused an infection requiring an operation. The entries immediately following the operation mentioned a stretch of scars from her shoulders to her armpits. What she wrote about herself prior to her marriage, however, made it clear that she had gained some self-confidence about her looks. She met her future husband at the

Ministry of Tourism where she worked. Several foreign businessmen were on their way to Istanbul to meet him. His secretary had just married and there was no one to help him with the preparations. After their meeting at the Ministry he called her on the phone and asked if she would be good enough to arrange some business dinners and some sightseeing tours for his visitors. He was prepared to pay her generously.

Meral's mother offered her services for this and other occasions which followed. One day, while they were discussing arrangements for another group of visitors arriving soon, he turned to her and said, "I like you. You have a good head on your shoulders. Will you marry me?" He had never married. "Good head on my shoulders? Good head? Yes. Good shoulders? No," wrote Meral's mother.

She married him. She came to live in this house where Meral was reading the diary now. She brought her mother with her. She also brought her big table.

The diary said that Meral's grandmother died from burns. She tried to light the oven when the maid was at the grocer's. She wanted to bake Armenian bread. Her woolly hair caught fire first. She was senile at the age of forty-eight. Her condition made her behave like a child. Every now and then she cried on her daughter's shoulder. "My Nartuhi, why don't you like the Armenian bread I knead with my own hands? My Nartuhi, why don't you share your bread with me?"

There were some tender entries in the diary. Meral's mother wrote: "I smelled my mother's hair and I cried."

That line made Meral go back through the earlier diary to search for "crying." There was only one other entry about crying. But it was a secret cry:

October 18, 1929
My mother made me chop onions, to help Susan. "Chop them finely! Finely!" she kept telling me, moving in and out of the kitchen. The chopping made my eyes watery. My mother would not notice if I cried. So I cried. My mother would hit me if she realized that I cried.

All Meral's mother was allowed to do was to work beyond her capacity, to be clever and to be smart looking. "If I am moody, I am given an Optalidon tablet. There are cures for everything. There are cures for every kind of behavior," she wrote.

According to Meral's grandmother, life would give nothing if it wasn't wrested out of it. But she was mistaken. In the end, life had given her daughter the love and trust of an elderly gentleman. He thought she had a good head on her shoulders. Life had also given her a child. What more could she ask for?

Meral kept on reading the diary at random.

November 30, 1929

Yesterday I saw my mother lying in bed—doing nothing. She was just looking at the ceiling. Her eyes were fixed on something close to the pink frills of the overhanging lightshade. Her eyelids fluttered frequently. Her breathing was fast and shallow. Despite her reclined position, she was charged with agitated energy. "She is ready to jump at me," I thought. I wanted to run away. At the same time, a gush of emotion pushed me towards the bed.

She heard my hesitant steps. She tried to look at me with her wide open eyes. But her look was buried inside her eyes. Even her greatest efforts could not divert her eyes towards me. Her gaze was roaming among the dead. Dead people, dead hopes. Killed father, killed mother, killed brother.

I needed to take two steps, just two steps, to reach her. I needed two steps to reach out and to put my arms around her. I could not do it.

*

December 3, 1929

Yesterday my mother was operated on. They call the operation "middle ear operation." I am at home. I wanted to see my mother's room while she was in the hospital. I went in. Her bed was made. A photo of me was stuck to the edge of the mirror of her dressing table. This photo was taken last year. My hair was combed straight down. It nearly touched my shoulders. I had a ribbon on the top of my head. It wasn't a good photo. But I looked tidy. Perhaps that is why my mother chose that photo to stick at the edge of the mirror.

There were some folded clothes on top of the chair near the dressing table. I took the green cotton blouse my mother wears often and put it to my cheek. I pressed it harder and harder. Its faint smell made me dizzy.

For a moment I saw my mother lying under the sheets of her bed. She was immobile. She was absolutely calm. I saw her dead. I ran out of the room.

*

December 5, 1929

It is three days since my mother had her ear operation. Susan is complaining that there is too much work in the house. I think she is complaining because mother could not pay her salary for three months. Why doesn't she go away? There would be one less Armenian in the house. The Armenian ballet teacher, the Armenian blind man who brings the threads and materials for the tablecloths from Mary's tuhafiyeci *shop, and now we have this Armenian maid. I told my mother several times that I would work harder, if only she would send her away. "You'll work harder? That will be the day," she answered. "You are the laziest girl I know. You didn't even finish your wooden eggs. Customers are waiting for them." My mother makes me paint flowers on wooden eggs used for darning stockings. How can one see the flowers when stockings are pulled over them? Do people really pay more money for the eggs when they have been decorated? I think my mother is just trying to fill my time. Anyway, I like to paint flowers.*

*

March 5, 1930

My mother has had an abscess on her forehead for some time. Now it has become as big as one of the wooden eggs on which I paint the flowers. We went to the doctor who always pins a carnation in his lapel. His villa is just off the main road, near the tennis courts. He looked at the abscess. "Shall I open it?" he asked. It seems that my mother already knew that it had to be done. "All right," she answered. The doctor prepared his instruments. He cut it open. I watched him. He did not have a nurse. He did not ask me to do anything. After he stitched it up, he said, "You need some injections, so that you will not have an infection."

My mother had to have the injections done every four hours. The medicine had to be kept in the refrigerator. "Do you have a refrigerator?" the doctor asked. "Of course," said my mother. But we did not have one.

CAGES ON OPPOSITE SHORES

"Do you happen to know someone in the neighborhood who gives injections? Shall I recommend you a good igneci?"* *he asked. "No need. I do know an* igneci. *He lives quite close to us," said my mother. She knew no* igneci *who lived close to us. She did not know any* igneci. *I was the one who gave her injections, whenever she needed them. She herself was the* igneci *who gave injections to the neighbors. The neighbors paid her for the injections she gave them.*

We bought the medicine from the pharmacy on our way home. My mother rang the bell of our next-door neighbor's house. She made me speak to the English woman who lived there. While I talked to the English woman, her skinny son roamed around and listened to our conversation. He smiled at my broken English. But he whistled and pretended not to hear.

My mother was telling me what to say to the English woman, bit by bit. That made it hard for me to translate.

"The doctor gave a medicine," I started. "Injection. Every four hour my mother must have. Every time we must take it from refrigerator. We have no refrigerator. Your refrigerator, if we put medicine in it, we will trouble you at night. Will you be trouble?"

The mother of this English woman, who lives with her, is a witch. She wears an invisible black net around her crinkly white hair. She roams the streets and collects newborn kittens. When she catches them, she drowns them in boiling water.

But this woman I talked to is a nice woman. She smiled at me. "No trouble at all," she said.

My mother and I went home. I inserted the needle into the rubber top of the vial, and drew the necessary amount of liquid into the syringe. I gave my mother the first injection. Then I went back to the house of the English woman and gave her the vial. At six in the evening, I went there again and took the vial again. I gave my mother another injection. I returned the vial. At ten I was at the house of the English woman again. And at two in the morning again.

---

* **igneci**: *a person trained to give injections*

57

March 6, 1930

This morning at six, I gave my mother another injection. I'll continue giving injections to her throughout the day. I am very tired. I am also very scared. My mother's bottom is looking lumpy because of the injections. Her bottom does not have much flesh anyway.

*

March 7, 1930

I did not go to school today in order to continue with the injections. At two o'clock in the afternoon, when I went to the house of the English woman to take the vial, the skinny boy appeared again. His name is Michael. At six in the evening, he was there again. He looks at me in a strange way.

*

March 8, 1930

My mother is all right now. She had forgotten to scold me during the injections. Now she doesn't miss any opportunity to scold me. Our life is back to normal.

Meral had to go and see the *tuhafiyeci* woman once again. She had to have a long talk with her about her grandmother.

6

The *tuhafiyeci* woman was bent over the crochet work in her hands as before. Her thick spectacles were hooked over her nose as they were before.

Meral felt that no time had passed since her last visit to the shop. She tightened her fist around the pieces of broken button which weren't there. She waited for the woman to see her. The old woman raised her head and spoke with no surprise in her voice. "Oh, here you are," she said. "You look so much like Satinique. Her hair was curlier . . . and a little darker. But you have the same fearless forehead.

"If you knew your grandmother's struggle for life. If you knew how hard she worked for her daughter. Her daughter—your mother— was her life. She lived for her. She transferred her from one foreign school to another so that she would learn all the important European languages. She wanted her to learn everything, so that she would not suffer as she herself had. She knew her suffering was caused by her ignorance. She knew she couldn't have been thrown out of the Yali

59

if she had known anything about law—if she had known anything about her rights. She was aware that her ten or eleven gold bracelets, given by her husband when they first married, would not last long. She sold them one by one.

"Although she lived very modestly, her little treasure was coming to an end. She lived in Sikkeli Street, you know, the Jewish Quarter. Those days it was a very poor street. The unpainted wooden houses were so old that one wondered how they remained standing. Perhaps it was because they were so tightly crammed together. The sewage water used to trickle down the cobblestone street. Half-naked children used to run from house to house carrying messages from their mothers to their friends' mothers. They borrowed rice and sugar. They borrowed loaves of bread.

"I am an old chatterbox. I am repeating to you things you already know," she said. She stopped talking suddenly and bent her head back to her crochet.

The interruption made Meral forget where she was, what she was doing there, and what she was going to say. She couldn't think of a single appropriate question. She couldn't think of a single question to encourage the woman to go on. The harder she tried to catch the questions, the farther away they ran.

The *tuhafiyeci* woman smiled at Meral's troubled face and went on. "Yes, your grandmother was an ignorant woman. But the centuries-old culture of her homeland had endowed her with a refined taste. When Satinique finally met my mother and my mother taught her the craft of embroidery, you should have seen the wonders she created with what she learned! She invented such imaginative patterns on the linen that her tablecloths became a craze among the members of the snobbish class. Her embroidered pieces covered the dining tables at the richest dinner parties."

She sighed. "So to speak, Satinique supported herself and her beloved daughter by the tip of her needle. She made the tablecloths and my mother sold them. There was always a waiting list for her work. But you could not hurry Satinique. No, no, no. You couldn't hurry her. She offered the customer her best—or nothing.

"It was when she started to lose her eyesight that she stopped embroidering. By then, she had a small amount of savings. She had

60

moved from her room in Sikkeli Street. She had rented a small decent apartment of two rooms near the Folk Music Center. And she had bought an enormous table for your mother. This table was so big that it nearly filled one of the rooms by itself. Once my mother and I visited her place. I saw your mother's table. On the way back home, I asked my mother to buy me a similar table. She refused. She said I had a desk. I still remember my argument with my mother, about Nartuhi's table.

"You know what your grandmother did with her savings? She opened a hardware store near Iskele. Can you imagine a woman opening a hardware store sixty years ago in Istanbul? She did it. And she ran it all by herself. She made lots and lots of money. It was the only hardware store on the Asian shore then.

"When your grandmother stopped making her tablecloths, my mother kept the last one for herself. My mother said that she had sold it and paid her for it. But she kept it for herself. My mother used it a few times. But it is still in good condition."

The *tuhafiyeci* woman stood up, opened a drawer, and pulled out a package. "I wrapped it up right after you left the shop last time," she said. "I knew you would return. I would like you to have it."

She walked to Meral and held out the flat package. Meral stretched out both her arms and received the package like a newborn baby.

*

The next morning Meral woke up feeling surrounded by a complete hush of silence. She woke up with an emptiness devoid of any sense of time. She recognized her being alone as "loneliness." She recognized it, and yet it seemed to her that this loneliness was not hers. Her thoughts and emotions had abandoned the accepted forms. They floated about her leisurely like strangely shaped and unusually patterned tiny seahorses.

There was a lapse of time she could not bridge. How had she come back home from the European shore? By boat? Had she really been to the *tuhafiyeci*'s? The package on the chair was the only witness to reality.

In the past, when mornings awakened her with a slight depression, she would hang onto her day's projects like lifesavers. "Who are the people I should telephone today? What are the things I'll ask them to do? What are the things I'll be doing for them?" She padded out these thoughts with details and remained in bed wrapped up with other people's lives. Then she would get up, leaving her depression in bed, and go about her daily routine energetically.

Now she would no longer be able to do this. She had quarreled with Rezan. She had resigned from her various committees and societies. While previously she had worked for these societies with all her sincerity, she now came to understand that certain committee members had worked against her. They undermined her work. They gossiped against her to Fahri. No reason was left for her to go on. She had burnt her boats.

She did not miss her old life. But something stopped her from moving into her future. She was not given a key to her future, because she did not have the key of her past.

She walked to the next room and looked at the diaries piled on her mother's table. The diary on top was the tattered one in which she had made her first important discovery about her grandmother. She lifted it carefully and reached for the bigger size volume underneath. This diary with the green leather binding was the one where she had read about her mother's marriage. She searched for earlier dates in it.

The date of the page she opened was *December 20, 1937*. The entry started with a well-known proverb.

There will be "blind buyers for the blind sellers" says the proverb. Michael's childhood crush on me has been revived since he left for Oxford. He comes back to his family in Istanbul every holiday, whether the holiday is short or long. He says that he comes back mainly to see me.

I wonder what the students and professors at Oxford make of him. His accent must sound quite strange to their ears. One cannot truthfully call him English, nor could one call him Turkish. Of course we have a name for people like Michael in our country. We call these foreigners who deprive themselves of the salt of the nation among whom they've lived for generations "sweet water foreigners," but what would the British know about this?

CAGES ON OPPOSITE SHORES

He says to me, "I have never met a girl like you." Every time he says that, I answer, "I believe you." Every time he hears my answer he laughs and looks into my eyes to see his reflection. He doesn't find it and turns his head away in disappointment. He never thinks of asking me why I agree to his comment so eagerly. Probably he thinks that I take what he says as the compliment it is meant to be.

The conditions of my life have to be duplicated in order to produce another girl like me. People similar to my parents and grandparents have to marry each other to produce a girl like me. And this is difficult. So, I suppose I'll enjoy being unique all through my life. Correction: I'll suffer from being unique all through my life.

I never explained all this to Michael. He is a college boy studying astronomy. I wonder what made him choose this subject. The clear, starry nights of Istanbul? Astronomy is a new and an old science. I think Michael did not consider this aspect of astronomy when the idea of becoming an astronomer attracted him somehow.

When years and years later he becomes a professor (although it is easier for me to imagine him walking on the moon), he may discover a certain infirmity in the movements of our earth, which revolves insistently around the sun. If he discovers the variable movements of our earth and measures the extent of its irregularity, he will stop being amused by my "unusual" ideas. He will no longer search for his reflection in my eyes. Anyway, by that time our ways will be separated. Just give it another year or two, and Michael will stop disturbing me with his unwelcome attentions.

She left the diary open on the table. She went to the kitchen and put the kettle on. She watched the kettle boil. She carried the cup of tea to the window and looked out. The café across the road was being prepared for a fresh day. The head-waiter was pointing his finger in this and that direction and the waiters were running to their pointed destinations. She could not hear their footsteps. The usually sharp voice of the head-waiter was not even a whisper this morning.

She left the empty teacup on the window sill and returned to the table. She flipped the pages, which were written in a determined hand, till she met the name Michael again. This entry was towards the end of the diary.

JANSET BERKOK SHAMI

July 30, 1941

Since Michael graduated and came back to Istanbul last month, my mother is pestering me into agreeing to go and visit Michael's mother. I am doing my best to explain to her that we cannot visit an English family without an invitation. It would be an invasion of their privacy. But who is listening to me?

*

August 3, 1941

Would my mother stop and think for a moment that her decision primarily involves me? Would she care to know that my whole being is repelled by her decision? I know that in a day or two she'll carry out her decision. Why wouldn't she? Does it matter how I feel about it as long as the visit will serve her purpose?

She hopes to marry her daughter off through this visit. According to her, when we visit our neighbor, Michael will see me and fall in love with me once again. I will see Michael and will like him better than I did before. I cannot convince her that I haven't had a drop of interest in Michael all through the years I have known him. She refuses to believe me.

Today she opened the subject which is on her mind all the time in the following delicate manner. "Michael is not bad looking. He is certainly better looking than yourself," she said.

I answered that I agreed with her.

"And he is well educated," she said, searching my face for more agreement and she received it easily. I gave it to her willingly in order to stop her from creeping inside me. I did it because if she crept inside me, she would shuffle my thoughts, rearrange them to her liking and drag a new bundle of thoughts out of me.

"Then what is the problem?" This was not a question. It was an expression of surprise at her easy victory.

When I said nothing, she gave her verdict. "You'll become an old maid," she said.

*

CAGES ON OPPOSITE SHORES

August 6, 1941

I had known all along that I would succumb to her wishes eventually.

My mother stopped my continuous objections. She stopped them as easily as she stopped the run in her only pair of silk stockings. She stopped my objections with one threatening look; she stopped the run in the stocking with a drop of nail polish. She put on her black suit and squeezed her feet, permanently swollen from long hours of sitting at her sewing, into her high-heeled shoes.

Just before she rang the bell of the next-door house, she gave me a look of appraisal. Then she started her improvements. She pulled down the side of my pleated skirt over my "wider hip" to make the length of the two sides of the skirt equal. She patted my back to check if the padded strip of cushion which has remained strapped to my waist since I became a teenager was in the right position. She made sure that the cushion filled the "hollow area" above my "sagging buttocks" properly. She wetted her index fingers on her tongue and rubbed my eyebrows energetically with the hope of changing their place from their present position "so close" to my eyes, to a higher spot on my forehead. She rubbed them so forcefully against their natural direction of growth that she might have shifted their roots underneath my skin.

When she finally removed her hands from my poor, physical existence, I gave another chance to my objections. It was no use.

At first Michael's mother was only surprised by our unexpected visit. But as my mother's conversation progressed through my translation and became bolder with the hints of marriage, she became flabbergasted. I could see what she felt clearly in her face, although all she did was give short, crisp answers to the questions asked of her. I could see that the woman had an enormous amount of self-control.

When my monotonous translations loaded with hints started to have the effect of a snake charmer's flute on Michael, when I saw his colorless lips move and stretch into a mile-long smile, I could not act the part imposed on me any longer.

My mother went on with her one-sided conversation in the same manner, but my translations stopped having anything to do with what she said. In order to give myself courage for what I was doing, I kept on reminding myself that my mother did not understand a word of English. I spoke in a sing-song voice so that my mother would not guess the meaning of my words.

JANSET BERKOK SHAMI

"Madame," I said, "I am here just to obey my mother's orders. I did not wish to come. What I say may sound strange to you as your customs are quite different from ours, but here, in the East, we have to obey our parents' wishes. Please excuse our presence in your house. Please ignore all that is said to you. I am doing only what I am told to do. This is the way it goes in the East!"

Michael's mother must have heard about the importance of obedience in our country. But in all probability this "sweet water foreigner" was not knowledgeable enough about the limits of the obedience we have to give to our parents. People like her live in a no-man's-land in Turkey, they live without having any real contact with the Turks. So, when I said, "this is the way it goes," she might have believed me. The bitter truth of the matter, which unfortunately I cannot hide from myself, is that this is not the way it goes in Ataturk's Turkey. This is the way it goes between my mother and I.

*

August 10, 1941
Michael's mother had forgotten to offer us anything during our stupid, stupid visit to her house. I heard my mother complain about this to Susan, our maid. She spoke in Turkish and spoke quite loudly. Perhaps she wanted her voice to reach my room. "You stingy Gavurs!" she said, forgetting that she herself had been a Gavur before she was converted to Islam. "Stingy Gavur," she repeated several times, referring to the nice Christian woman with this rude word.

The unnatural silence went on. Meral had to hear a voice; not just her mother's silent screams. She spoke. "I must clear away all the papers today," she said aloud. She hoped her voice would awaken her from the nightmare of silence.

The silence persisted but her definite words brought her into action. She went to her bedroom. She opened the wardrobe, removed several newly-bought shoes from their boxes and carried the empty boxes to the table. After tying the five diaries together, she started sifting through the papers. When this was done, she arranged them into the boxes, sticking labels on each one of them. Except for one

66

box which contained her mother's literary efforts, she carried everything to the bedroom and put them on the bottom shelf of the wardrobe. Then she went to the kitchen and came back to the table with a duster and a tin of polish. Going in and out of the rooms had helped her regain her usual vigorous movements. She rubbed the surface of the table. She rubbed it with all her might again and again.

Then she went to her mother's room. The framed, embroidered words of a prayer hung above the head of her bed. She released the string of the frame from the rusty nail. She was not going to concern herself with the space behind it, which would be murmuring the prayer it had supported for all those years.

She brought the frame to the big table and propped it against the wall right in the middle of the miniature paintings. The graceful fingers of the gold embroidery reached out from the background of blue satin. "Oh God, keep us under your protection," said the prayer.

Meral had been very religious when she was a little girl. She had memorized many prayers. She learned them from her nanny. When Emine finished her work, she would settle herself down on her cotton wool mattress on the floor, take the string of prayer beads and run them through her fingers to the rhythm of her constant prayers. Meral would repeat after her. Emine did not know the meanings of the Arabic prayers. Meral did not know what she repeated. But she loved everyone and everything after she repeated the prayers. She particularly loved her nanny who sat next to her and listened to her prayers without any comment.

Once Meral had asked her nanny a question about God. She had asked her question just after Emine had completed her ablutions and walked into the room wearing her wooden slippers.

"Nanny, where is Allah?"

"Allah is everywhere."

"Then we must be walking all over him," concluded Meral.

"*Tovbe estagfrullah, tovbe estagfrullah*! Allah forgive me!" said Emine. Blood rushed into her old face and filled the deep creases of her dark skin. She looked very frightening.

"Are you cross with me?" asked Meral. But Emine had removed her wooden slippers and was busy drying her washed feet with a threadbare towel. She did not answer her. She unfolded her prayer rug, spread it on the floor and started to pray.

Meral brought her own prayer rug and spread it next to Emine's. She placed her small rug exactly parallel to Emine's so that she would face Mecca as all Muslims did. She started praying too. She knew the prayers by heart, but she stole sidelong glances at Emine in order to follow her movements. She sat over her bent knees when Emine did so. She placed her forehead on the ground when Emine did so.

"May Allah accept your prayers," said Emine, when they had finished praying.

Meral took her rug, folded it and placed it next to her nanny's over the trunk. Emine's room contained her cotton-wool mattress, her wooden trunk and a Quran. The Quran was kept in a bag made of blue linen. The bag's flap was held in place by a brown button, of the kind used for men's suits. Its strap was a braided cord. When the Quran was not in use, the bag dangled from a huge nail. The nail was hammered into the highest spot on the wall. Nothing should be higher than the Quran. When Emine wanted to read the Quran, she reached it by standing on a chair.

Meral read the prayer in the frame aloud: "Oh God, keep us under your protection," and then she brought the wrapped up gift of the tablecloth and placed it on the table right in front of the framed prayer.

The prayer and the tablecloth—this combination had to mean something. She planted her elbows on the table; she supported her head with her arms; she cupped her burning face with her hands and remained sitting. She did not change her position on the chair while she cried. She cried for the thin coat of knowledge that brushed lightly over her hardened ignorance. She cried for her mother's foolish challenges.

7

The last time Meral had spoken with the lawyer on the phone, it was decided that she would go to his office one afternoon to discuss some details about the divorce procedure. He had sounded flexible about the time and the day. "Come any time between four and six," he had said.

But after being driven through the most crowded streets of European Istanbul, after arriving at the wrought iron door of the Derin Han office building, after taking the grimy elevator up to the narrow corridor, all she achieved was reading a scribbled note on the lawyer's door: "I will be back at 5 p.m."

This was no good. There was no place for Meral to wait, and she could not walk around the crowded streets for forty-five minutes. She decided to give up seeing the lawyer. She came out of the building and walked away, zigzagging among the convoy of boys carrying half a dozen shoe boxes from one shop to another. The boxes were held together with heavy strings and swung in their hands as they tried to talk to each other, raising their voices above the noise of the street. The sidewalks were filled with the goods of unlicensed street vendors. They sold wristwatches and transistor radios; they sold multi-purpose knives which would peel, slice and dice all kinds of vegetables; powders which would polish silver, brass, copper and God knows what else. Perhaps shoes and furniture. Metal parts of the wares glimmered under the sun, as the vendors praised them with eloquent speeches and watched the end of the street with anxious eyes. If a policeman's nose appeared round the corner, their possessions would be collected in bags, the legs of the supporting tables would be pulled together, and the vendors would dive into the crowds and disappear. During this panicky moment one wouldn't think of taking sides (the policeman or the vendor?) and would mainly concentrate on maintaining one's balance in order not to be knocked down.

Meral was relieved when she reached the corner and signaled to an empty taxi. The car started towards the Galata Bridge down the one-way street before the driver half-turned his head and asked, "Where to?"

Meral was not prepared for the question. She did not know how to answer. She wanted to go away from the lawyer's office. That is all she knew. Was she going back home? And to do what?

She saw herself roaming between the walls of her mother's rooms like a wounded, caged animal. "To Arnavutkoy," she said to the driver, when he repeated his question.

She rang the bell of Orhan's villa. No one answered the door. She rang it again to make sure and listened to its echo coming from inside the house. When still no one answered, she started back towards the garden gate, walking along the graveled path as fast as she could. She had to leave this house which was frightened of life. There was nothing in it for her. She had enough troubles of her own. She was not going to burden her life with other people's troubles.

When she half-opened the heavy gate, her eyes following its unwilling motion towards her, she felt the presence of someone. When she looked up, she came face to face with Dr. Zeki's sunny smile. "Oh, Meral *hanimefendi*," he said. "What a pleasure. Come in, come in."

In addition to his briefcase Dr. Zeki was carrying several plastic bags filled with vegetables and fruit, and he was having difficulty in squeezing himself through the narrow opening of the gate. Meral pulled it further in and stood back.

"I have been to my lawyer. He wasn't at his office," she said.

"Oh, what a nice man your lawyer is. I must thank him for not being in his office. Please, please come in. Don't bother to close the gate. I'll come and close it later. Orhan will be so pleased to see you."

"Are you sure?" asked Meral, closing the gate. "Then why didn't he bother to open the door for me?" She tried to keep her voice free of emotion.

"But Orhan never answers the door. Never."

Dr. Zeki remained behind her, and coaxed her towards the house, saying, "how nice," "what a pleasant surprise," at every step. When they reached the door, he deposited the plastic bags on the steps and started a search of his pockets for the key. One of the plastic bags turned over and several apples rolled out. Meral bent to collect them, as Dr. Zeki found the key in the breast pocket of his jacket. "Please, please do not bother," he said, as he tried to insert the key into the lock. "You come in, I'll collect them later." She had already put the apples back into the plastic bag.

Dr. Zeki held the door open and let her in. On the other side of the hall were a pair of eyes looking at them. Orhan was standing there and trembling.

"Look, Orhan, look who is here!" said Dr. Zeki. "I nearly missed her. She was about to go away. Can you imagine that? She came to see us—to honor us with her visit, and she was about to go away."

Orhan was still trembling. Only after they came closer to him did he seem to calm down. He held her hand, looked at her and bent deeply over her hand to kiss it. A Chopin scherzo played on somewhere behind closed doors while his humble gesture asked her forgiveness and tried to explain something without using words.

She understood and her understanding pleased her. Although she was seeing this strange man for only the third time, although he had not said anything relating to his condition, Meral felt she understood him more than she had understood her husband during their eleven years of marriage.

"Now," said Dr. Zeki, as if talking to a child, "you take Meral

71

JANSET BERKOK SHAMI

hanimefendi to the salon and make her comfortable, and I'll go and prepare our tea. We'll have tea together. Won't it be nice?"

Orhan cupped Meral's elbow with his hand and led her towards the salon. His hand was still shaking and it transferred its tremors into Meral. She wished he would let her walk alone. She had walked alone all her life.

When she reached the chair next to the couch, she sat down as Orhan released her arm unwillingly.

He sat on the other side of the couch facing her. He rubbed his hands on his knees, following their movements with his eyes. "I am sorry," he said.

"What for?" said Meral, just to help.

"For not opening the door. I meant to. I guessed it was you. But I couldn't do it."

Meral hesitated for a while before she asked another question. Somebody had to. "Why?" she asked.

"I haven't done it for such a long time."

"That is not a reason."

He said nothing. He wasn't able to talk and was looking at the door and waiting for Dr. Zeki's return.

It was only after Dr. Zeki appeared with the loaded tea tray that Orhan started shedding his anxiety.

"This Orhan," said Dr. Zeki, while they were sipping the tea, "he never was one to answer doorbells. Even when we were youngsters, he always sent me to open the door. Imagine, I'd be a visitor in his house and would open the door to other visitors."

Orhan grinned at his cup of tea.

"So," continued Dr. Zeki, "while I was in the kitchen, I had a brilliant idea. Why don't I give you a key?" Having said this, embarrassment crept up into his face and turned its pink color into crimson. He hastily placed his teacup on the coffee table and started to search his pant pockets. Objects jingled in them. Coins, pieces of string and rubber bands came out. He even produced a Coca-Cola cap from his pocket. Finally a tiny skeleton with loose joints dangled from the tip of his fingers, while he held the key attached to it in his hand.

Both Meral and Orhan started laughing. Dr. Zeki joined in heartily.

"It was the only key holder I could find," he said, extending the skeleton and the key towards her.

"Are you sure?" said Meral, looking at the face of each man before taking the key.

"Absolutely," said Orhan before Dr. Zeki had a chance to answer.

"Don't you think," Dr. Zeki said to Orhan, "don't you think we owe some explanation to our friend for your behavior?"

"Absolutely," said Orhan again, almost before Dr. Zeki had completed his sentence.

"May I?" asked Dr. Zeki.

"Go ahead," was the answer.

Nobody asked Meral if she wanted to know what they were offering to tell her. She wondered what her answer would be if they asked her.

"You see, my sister, Orhan's wife, is. . . ."

"This is not the place to start," said Orhan. His voice pleaded with Dr. Zeki to stop.

"All right," said Dr. Zeki. "Then you try."

"Not today," he said. The finality of his decision was written all over his face. Dr. Zeki retreated.

Meral offered the two men fresh cups of tea. She also filled her own cup.

"My lawyer seems to be a very unreliable man," she said. "He told me I could come any day between four and six, but he wasn't in his office this afternoon. I am considering going to another lawyer."

They talked about her divorce. They talked about her marriage. Orhan was a very good listener, but Dr. Zeki was jittery. He came in and out bringing the tray and the dishes. He made her feel that what he was doing was more important than what she was saying. He interrupted her with questions which would have been answered without asking if he had waited a little longer. But he did not pass judgement. He was totally sympathetic when Meral told them of the frustrations she had faced while trying to help her husband. Meral told them her husband had accepted her financial contribution when he was establishing his publishing business. But as soon as his work started going well, he had done everything to discourage her from having anything to do with the business. She told them that when she had tried to learn photography, he had constantly made fun of the pictures she took, till she stopped touching the camera.

*

Meral's days following her visit to the villa were spent in suppressing an uprising—an uprising by her indulgent side, which wanted to repeat the visit without a breathing space. She managed to keep these wishes under control for seven days. On the seventh day, however, she yielded and found herself on her way to the villa.

Having rushed out of the house too soon, she arrived at 4:30 p.m. Assuming that Dr. Zeki would not be at home that early, she decided to use the key she had been given. But she was mistaken. A lively conversation between the two occupants of the house met her in the vestibule. The sound of their voices carried a disarming child-like gaiety. She hastened her steps. She wanted to be part of the merriment. She called out. "Hello, hello," she said. Two smiling faces came into view in the shady room.

She announced herself gaily. "Here I am," she said. "I am sure you didn't expect me so soon."

"Oh Meral *hanimefendi*," said Dr. Zeki, jumping up with clumsy agility and going towards her. "Oh Meral *hanimefendi*. Welcome, welcome. We are always happy to see you."

Orhan followed suit with a broadening smile, as the pleasure of seeing her heightened his happy mood.

"What is going on?" Meral asked, looking from one man to the other.

Orhan kissed her hand and escorted her to her seat.

"Nothing much," said Dr. Zeki, while his eyes followed Orhan's confidently performed gallantry like a proud parent. "I was telling Orhan that the teacher next door has a peculiar walk. I don't know why but Orhan wanted to know more about it. I am afraid I expanded on that walk too much. I exaggerated. Orhan laughed. We both laughed. Poor Miss Emel, I wonder what she would say if she knew that we were sitting here and laughing at her."

"How does Miss Emel walk?" asked Meral.

"Well," said Dr. Zeki, "first she looks sideways as if someone is following her. Then she puts her hand behind her dress and straightens it. She repeats these actions again and again with clockwork regularity."

"What is so funny about it?" said Orhan, trying to look serious. But one could see the crumbs of swallowed delight on the corners of his lips.

"You mean she walks like this?" said Meral. She stood up and walked around the room imitating the walk of the woman she had never seen.

The two men laughed. She was in the team of harmless conspirators now.

When Dr. Zeki went to the kitchen to prepare tea, she continued walking around as if she was going to do more imitating. But that was not what she did.

Instead, she busied herself by straightening and flattening the cushions on the empty couch, pulling them this way and that way and hitting them repeatedly. Then suddenly she perched herself on a straight-backed chair facing Orhan's puffy one, and locked her eyes on his. The undiluted intensity of her steady look transfixed the man as she spoke. "Why don't you go and have a look at the teacher's walk yourself?"

Orhan's defense came in a frozen stare. It ousted her from the edge of the chair. It forced her to stand up and go to the window.

"I want to be your friend," she said, carrying her weakened voice away with her. She looked out. She looked at the waves of the sea admitting defeat.

Suddenly a response came to where she stood, calling her back. "I think it is time you knew more about me," Orhan was saying. "I mean about my problem," he added.

Meral did not sit opposite him as she had done earlier, but sat timidly at the end of the couch closer to Orhan's chair.

"I loved Nevin. I truly, sincerely loved her. I painted roses around the photograph she gave me. And my first love happened to be the choice of an arranged marriage. At the time I chose her, it seems that her family had already chosen me. We got engaged and I went to Germany to finish my education. I looked at the photograph with the circle of roses day after day. Then autumn came. The trees lost their leaves and the roses lost their petals.

"I wrote my intention of breaking off the engagement to Nevin in a poem and sent it to her. Then I wrote to tell my father of my decision. He replied with a harsh letter. He said that I had been a spoiled child, and now at the age of nineteen I was acting like a child again. But this time it was a person I was playing with, not a teddy-bear. As I was a member of a respectable family, I should act like one. He saw no reason for breaking off the engagement. The girl was waiting for me patiently. So why couldn't I keep my love for her? I wrote another poem to Nevin and told her that I hoped she had not taken my previous poem seriously. But my letters to her had lost their constant flow. Noticing this, our families decided to marry us sooner. I was married to Nevin when I was twenty. Nevin was only eighteen. I continued my studies in Germany and came home only for holidays. When I finished my education and was ready to return home and settle down, I found out that even the small amount of love I had felt for Nevin had evaporated. Being a member of a respectable family, I married her, but being a mean and unreliable person I let her see that I did not care for her. I showed my indifference in very cruel ways. I acted as freely as a bachelor would. I did not agree to having children. In short, I pushed her to the edge of the abyss with every sentence I spoke, with every gesture I made. I gave her the final push. . . ."

He ran his fingers through his hair, and started to do it again. But they stopped halfway and remained still. He spoke while his fingers covered his forehead. "I gave her a final push," he said, "by telling her to get rid of the baby. She was keeping her pregnancy a secret from me, till she was sure of it. I was sure of it before she was, so I told her to get rid of it.

"Next day when I came back I heard a rhythmical sound from the upper floor. When I reached her room I found it locked. I understood what was going on. Nevin was getting rid of the baby using the practices of ignorant, superstitious women. I begged her to stop. I banged on the door. I looked for the maid, the cook, the gardener, nobody was around. She had sent them away. By the time I broke down the door, she was just a heap in the corner. Then hospitals—she had done it, she had got rid of the baby. Then hospitals—she had got rid of me. Then hospitals—she had got rid of all the miserable, cruel world. She was put in a nursing home.

"Some months later, one morning when I was on my way to visit her, a motorcycle ran over my toes. Isn't that ridiculous? But this is what happened. I had to stay at home for a few days. Then I suddenly felt I needed to get away from people. I had to stop having contact with people I did not care for. I got rid of the gardener, the cook and the maid, one by one. I stopped going out. I stopped visiting Nevin. I am sure she is happier this way. She was always suspicious of the candies I took her . . . She thought I wanted to poison her."

His last words were almost spoken in a whisper.

After a short silence Meral also spoke in a whisper. "I want to be your friend," she said, repeating what she had said before.

The open window let in the last rays of the setting sun, and caught by the pincers of light, the sound of her voice was turned in different directions and inspected.

After some more silence Meral suddenly found herself telling Orhan the story of Bekir, her husband's nephew. When her story was nearing its end, she expected Orhan to be indignant at Bekir's ungratefulness. But he was not. What was more disappointing was that when she closed her story by telling him that she had not seen him since that time, for almost four years, he came out with a disturbing idea. "Have you ever wondered what happened to that young man after you left him? You have written on his life all you wanted to write. Then you crumpled him and threw him into a waste-basket like an unfinished story. That isn't fair."

"He is the one who left us," Meral said, defending herself. "But he will come back. I know he will."

She stood up, hoping that her upright position would rid her of Orhan's unfair comments. She hoped that his comments would skid off her like raindrops from an umbrella taken indoors and kept open to dry. The next thing she did was to walk away, as if doing this distanced her from the pools his words left on the floor.

When her faltering steps started to advance on the linoleum floor of the kitchen, the tea tray on the counter with its cups and saucers caught her attention in spite of the gathered tears in her eyes. She approached it while Dr. Zeki was busy arranging cookies on a plate. She tried to pick up the tray and carry it to the sitting room. But he raised his usual objection. "It's too heavy for you," he said. He allowed her to carry only the cookie plate, and waited for her to leave the kitchen before he curved his short fingers around the handle of the tray. She walked out with her light burden, and he followed her with the loaded tea tray.

Why did he obstruct her actions? Why did people fail to realize that by indiscriminately sparing her of burdens, they were turning her life into a burden—a burden of uselessness? How could Orhan accuse her of being unfair? How did he know what was fair? She had done everything for Bekir. She had done everything in her power for him. Had Bekir been fair to her?

8

onfusing thoughts and feelings which came to her and left her as they pleased caused the hours of the days to pass at a confusing tempo. She had been to the European side, but she had not been able to see her lawyer. No real action had been taken towards her divorce. When she had visited the villa, she was given a key, a symbol of friendship and trust; but when she had told Orhan the story of Bekir, when she had assumed that the ungratefulness of the boy she took care of for so many years would horrify him, instead of receiving understanding, she had been accused of being heartless.

These futile episodes and the accumulated frustrations finally started to affect her sleep. She slept fitfully. She slept and woke up; she slept and woke up again. She started having many dreams.

One of the dreams she had was of Bekir. He looked angry. He spoke, gesticulating fiercely and banging his fist on a table or desk. But the sounds he made did not reach her ear. What did he say? Why couldn't she hear his voice?

The other dream was of Orhan. In that dream she was swimming with him in a calm summer sea. He was young and gay; and she wore her two-piece swimsuit with the flowery pattern. After a while Meral noticed that Orhan was no longer at her side. She turned back and saw that she had left him behind. "Are you tired?" she asked. Hearing this Orhan started swimming towards the shore.

The dream ended there, leaving her with a sense of loss. When she woke up she remembered the swimsuit she wore in the dream. It was the swimsuit of long ago. This swimsuit and the unsatisfactory end of the dream reinforced her guilty feeling towards her old friend Argun.

"Why do I speak? Why do I ask questions?" she said accusing herself. "Even in dreams, I am able to upset people."

The swimsuit of the dream was the one she had worn on that stormy summer day of her youth. She and her friends had taken her boat out of the boat-house against the caretaker's advice. The man had told them that the hole in the bottom of the boat needed repair, that they were too many for the boat, that if they wanted it to stay afloat they would have to bail water all the time, and that a storm was approaching.

They were sheltered from the bombardment of the caretaker's speech by their carefree laughter.

Fahri was among them that day. But before the storm broke out, he had swum to Leander's Tower with his waterproof camera on his back to take some photographs of them from the tower's yard.

The storm was fiercer than they expected, and Meral was fiercer than the storm. First she punished Argun bitterly for his inconsistent behavior towards her. He had showered her with his attentions all summer through and then he had suddenly cooled without any apparent reason. She had her chance of being rude to him when he tried to exchange his can for the heavy bucket with which Meral was bailing water. She ridiculed him mercilessly. "You may be a Hercules, my dear Argun," she said, looking directly at his bony, hairless chest, "but I am not so helpless myself." Then she directed her insults towards the others. When Suna panicked and Jale whimpered, she said, "What are you doing here? You should be sitting on your mothers' laps with ribbons in your hair."

They kept bailing water while their fears rocked the very foundations of their existence and brought out all their ailing and defeated emotions to the surface. They talked in loud voices, but they hardly heard each other. The awareness of danger had drawn horrid lines on their faces. Each and every one of them looked unattractive.

The boat sank. Fahri photographed them from his secure spot while they swam to shore with great difficulty.

He had returned from Leander's Tower in a motorboat, and he was ready to listen to the excited talk of his friends.

Meral learned much later that before this stormy outing there had been a visit to her mother by Argun and his mother. She heard about this visit three months after her marriage to Fahri.

Being mixed-up about her feelings towards Argun, Meral had created a detailed scenario of what had happened on that visit. The one actor and the two actresses taking part had many curtain calls during her married years. Each time they appeared on the stage of her mind, they dragged Meral's feelings of guilt and regret with them. The last dream of hers had turned the two-piece swimsuit into an emblem. An emblem of guilt, regret and frustration.

The scenario went like this: Argun walks into her mother's salon wearing a formal suit. He looks insecure without his casual clothes. He is accompanied by his mother. (Meral knew that his father was dead and she had never met his mother.) The mother's arms are lined with golden bracelets and she is fat. She sits opposite Meral's mother, and for a while they chat. (Naturally most of the chattering is done by the visitor herself.) When the fat lady thinks the time is ripe, she asks for Meral's hand in marriage for her son in the traditional way, with the traditional flowery words. His head bowed, Argun, "the young engineer with the bright future," listens to everything without a word.

The visual part of Meral's scenario ends here, but the sounds continue. Her mother's voice rings out clearly. The voice says, "I leave important decisions about life entirely up to Meral."

Meral had never seen Argun's mother. Meral had never seen Argun wearing a suit. But the scene of the marriage proposal had happened. And yet her mother had neglected to mention this to her until Meral was already married.

The advancing hours of the morning changed her reaction to the dreams of the night before. As the salty heat of July seeped through the open window of her bedroom, Meral inclined towards canceling her guilt, and started accusing Orhan. Why couldn't he give a civilized answer to a civilized question? "Are you tired?" "Yes, I'm tired." "Are you tired?" "No, I'm not tired." Why had he left her all alone in the middle of the sea? Why had he encouraged Bekir to burst into silent anger, in the other dream?

The dream about swimming with Orhan upset her most. That dream put Fahri and Orhan into the same boat. A safe boat. A boat with no room in it for her. She was in a boat too. The boat was sinking and Argun was about to disappear. Where was Argun? Where was he now? What was he doing?

Lying in bed awake in the bright sunlight and dwelling on the dreams for so long intensified Meral's resentment towards Orhan. The wounds he had inflicted on her by undermining her selfless efforts in raising Bekir started to ooze once again.

Finally she left her bed with a fully formed decision. She was not going to see Orhan and Dr. Zeki again. She was not going to visit them ever again. She wondered what to do with the key.

She removed it from her bag and tossed it on the piano, but because of her careless aim the skeleton pulled the key down to the floor.

As she bent down to pick it up, her hand slapped the key on the telephone table and pressed on it as if she wanted to crush the skeleton's bakelite bones. When she finally removed her hand from it, her eyes remained on the table and her look alternated between the shaky legs of the keyholder and the solemn and steady telephone. The two objects claimed her attention equally as guides until her thoughts started slipping towards Vedat *bey**, her lawyer.

Why was she having so much difficulty in talking to him? Why was she almost pleased when her last appointment with him did not work out? Either she should get over her dislike for him, or she should go and find herself a new lawyer.

She picked up the receiver and dialed his number with nervous fingers. For a change, the secretary was in the office. Meral started talking immediately. "This is Meral Demiray. I would like to speak

---

* bey: *Mister*

to Vedat *bey*," she said, when the secretary sing-songed her "Hello, may I help you?"

The lawyer's rushed and unequally spaced words started falling on the receiver immediately. They hit Meral's ears like torrents of rain coming from different directions.

"Meral *hanimefendi*, I'm so glad that you called. I'm so sorry that I missed you the other day. An important client needed me urgently and I. . . ."

"It's all right. Don't worry about it. I just wondered if there's anything you want me to do."

"You don't do anything, my dear lady. You leave everything to me."

"Well then, tell me . . . what is our next step?"

"Well, actually, before we take any steps there are things to be done. In this connection, by the way, I took the liberty, I mean, I went and saw your husband."

"My husband? Fahri?" Her astonishment nearly choked her.

"Yes, I arranged, I mean, we arranged to meet at his publishing house. By the way, it's quite an establishment, I must say. The up-to-date machinery . . . the uniforms of the technicians. . . ."

"May I ask what was the purpose. . . ."

"My ways may seem unorthodox to you. But if one is in this profession as long as I have been. . . ."

"May I ask what was the. . . ."

"One must find different approaches to different problems. In my profession. . . ."

As Meral could not find a way of completing her question, which was intended to reproach him for what he had done, she changed it into a different one. "What was the result?" she asked.

Her shorter question was successful in cutting through the torrent of words.

It changed the lawyer's voice, and helped the information to flow steadily. "Well, first of all let me tell you that Mr. Fahri strikes me as a very reasonable, a very well-adjusted man. And he respects you immensely. You know what he said? You know how he summed up your relationship? He said that he is a simple Anatolian man. He said that his years of education in Istanbul could not change him sufficiently. He is convinced that this is what causes problems between you and him. He thinks that you cannot accept him as he is. You find faults in everything he says and does. But he assured me that he is ready to try again. I'll repeat to you his exact words."

The distant sound of flipped pages sounded like the diminished stirrings of leaves on trees following a storm.

"This is what he said exactly. 'Nothing is up to her European standards. I tried to be what she wanted me to be. I honestly, sincerely tried. Allah knows that I tried. And I'll keep on trying if she lets me.'"

The lawyer, simulating Fahri's emotional tone of voice while relating what her husband had said, paused. This was the first recess he had allowed himself since the beginning of the telephone conversation, and it was obvious that its purpose was to provide accommodation for Meral's reaction.

It was obvious that not a crumb of doubt had lodged itself in his narrow mind to prepare him for a reaction that might not be to his liking. Although her irritation towards him had not subsided, Meral had lost her previous urge to render a blow to the lawyer by surprising him with an unexpected reaction. So she simply repeated her first question. "What is our next step?" she asked.

The silence on his side continued for some time. It must have been clear to him by then that he had been unable to impress her.

"Well," he said, "we must meet again. I have to go to Ankara tomorrow. I'll be back by Monday. Latest Tuesday. I'll call you when I return. But before we meet, I suggest you and your husband. . . ."

"Hope to hear from you on Tuesday then. Goodbye," said Meral quickly. She brought down the receiver with such a bang that the key and its funny keyholder were flung once again to the floor.

An Anatolian man! A European woman! A key attached to a mobile skeleton! Nothing made sense! Nothing!

She started sifting through her mother's records, even though she had not yet had any breakfast. She played all she found by Saint-Saens. She played his *Symphonic Variations* and *Danse Macabre* over and over again. The sporadic energy of Saint-Saens' music moved her. It expressed her moods which swung between raw anger and deep melancholy.

CAGES ON OPPOSITE SHORES

As the music went on, she approached her mother's table several times, fixing her eyes on the shoe box which now contained her mother's literary efforts.

The brightness of the red and blue lines drawing the British flag on the cover promised to lead her into the tracks of her life still to come.

She pulled the box towards her and lifted its lid. She sat down and started reading an untitled story. This was a longer story than the one she had read before, and although it was written in the form of a diary, there were no dates on the entries. It was about a Turkish girl and a German boy. The boy, Johann, is the son of a German travel agent, and the agency has a branch in Istanbul. Johann is one of the employees responsible for running the office. The girl is an employee at the Ministry of Tourism. The travel agency is cooperating with the Ministry in bringing tourists from abroad.

Johann is called back to the main office of his father's travel agency soon after a love affair flourishes between the two young people, and the unnamed heroine follows Johann to Frankfurt.

Tomorrow—29th of February—is my twenty-fourth birthday. I was born on March 1, but I celebrate my birthdays on February 29 when February is 29 days long. I think this is how it should be.

*

I am celebrating my birthday on the plane to Frankfurt. I am going to see Johann in a few hours. He does not know I am going. I did not know I was going. But here I am ... on my way.

*

I arrived at the travel agency on Munchener Strasse carrying my small suitcase, but Johann was not at the office. I was told by the elderly gentleman there that he was not coming in that day. He wrote down Johann's address and telephone number on a piece of paper and handed it to me with a smile.

The hotel is not so good. It is not too bad either, except that when I walk to the dresser next to my bed, I have to bend my head in order not to knock it on the ceiling. The room they gave me is on the top floor of the building and the slanting roof dips just where the bed is placed. Anyway I should not complain. I cannot afford a better hotel with the salary they pay me at the Ministry of Tourism. My mother did not agree to contribute "even one lira" to this trip. She did not understand the necessity of it. Well, naturally she doesn't. She does not know how much I love Johann. She does not know of the existence of Johann. I am happy to admit that there are many things my mother does not know about my life.

*

I did not call Johann at his house. Instead I called the agency, and left the telephone number of the hotel. Yesterday afternoon Johann appeared. Although he did not seem to be very happy to see me, he offered to show me around. It looks as though he doesn't go to the office that regularly. The elderly gentleman, Mr. Schmidt, whom I met when I first arrived here, seems to be running the agency single-handedly. Then, why did Johann have to leave Istanbul?

*

We went to the zoo. Of all the places in Frankfurt, Johann chose to show me the zoo. He talked about his mother while we looked at the colorful birds and tall giraffes. Why, why did I have to meet and love a boy who also happened to be an only child, like myself?

*

We had tickets for a symphony orchestra performance. Johann did not show up. "He could not make it," said his mother. I could not really understand why. So his mother and I were at the concert by ourselves. I tried to enjoy the performance but the presence of Johann's mother next to me played havoc with the music. One sideways look from her haughty profile diminished the magnitude of the cadence. One sigh from her pursed lips disconnected the two themes of the symphony by shattering its exquisitely worked-out bridges into commonplace chit-chat.

*

We were at the opera last night. Johann carried the tickets and when he was shown the way, he settled himself into the farthest seat. His mother followed him quickly, and sat by him. I took the seat next to his mother. They were performing Madame Butterfly. *The opera was in German. The aria "Leb Wohl, Mein Bluten Reich" seemed to have touched Johann. Although he was partly hidden from my view by his mother's eminent bosom, I saw him wipe his eyes several times on a well-ironed, nicely-folded handkerchief. Suddenly laughter arose in me. I stopped myself by using great self-control. If I had been in a private place, this suppressed laughter might have turned into uncontrollable sobs. How lucky for me that it happened in the opera house.*

*

I am leaving Frankfurt in an hour. I said my goodbyes to Johann and to his mother yesterday. I also told Johann that there was no need for him to come to the airport. He consented cheerfully. I remember a rude proverb: "Every cock crows in his own rubbish heap." What I mean here is that the Johann I knew in Istanbul and the Johann I met in Frankfurt are two different men. I pine for the first. I laugh at the second.

This is the end of my love story.

*

I passed by the musical instruments shop. I passed by the crowded restaurant where I had once had lunch. I passed by the housewives who walked in and out of the kitchen utensils shop. I passed between the iron-pine railings of the wooden safety walks placed in front of a damaged building. I stopped and looked at that building for some time. I tried to measure the extent of the damage the building had received from the recent war with my tearful, amateurish eyes.

The train ride to the airport did not take a long time. The plane left Frankfurt on time and arrived in Istanbul on time.

Johann had not come to see me off. My mother did not come to meet me. She couldn't have anyway, as I returned days earlier than I had planned.

*

Yesterday I received a detailed letter from Johann. In spite of its length, it was devoid of any kind of emotion. It had the tone of a business letter. It had that "We regret to inform you . . ." kind of style. He started it by summarizing our relationship and from there went on to say that his mother had strongly objected to our marriage. She had convinced her husband of the unsuitability of this marriage. "There is a wild, untamed quality about her. She would make our dear Johann suffer," she had said to his father.

Wild? Untamed? Me? Perhaps. Maybe. Probably. I like myself as I am. What about you, Johann? Do you like yourself?

Meral's heart sang out. She reached out and congratulated her mother by pressing the pages of the story to her heart. She felt her mother's death with a new unfamiliar twinge of sadness.

She stood up and went to the bureau. As she had found it almost impossible to get through to her lawyer by talking, she had decided to write to him. She somehow had to make him understand that she had totally lost interest in her marriage and anything to do with it. His news about visiting Fahri no longer disturbed her as much as it had at first. She had also managed to dismiss the picture of herself that Fahri's remarks had painted, as an unsuccessful attempt at surrealism. "That man would say anything to present himself favorably," she thought.

In her letter, she made two points. The first was that she was not interested in hearing her husband's opinions about herself. The second was that all she wanted the lawyer to do was to go on with the divorce proceedings as best he could. The only thing she asked for was to be spared the court hearings until they became absolutely necessary.

When she had finished writing it, she went to the salon and read it slowly sitting in her mother's winged chair.

She could not help noticing the similarity between her style and her mother's. The cuts in her mother's flesh burned in the lines of the letter.

Laying the letter on the coffee table, she tried to reach the source of the similarity. She had never had a disappointing love affair. She had never been rejected by a loved one (except perhaps by her mother). On the contrary, she herself was rejecting her husband who claimed that he loved her. He claimed that he tried to be what she wanted him to be.

The memory of her visit to her mother during the last months of her first year of marriage to Fahri, which had been haunting her lately, returned, finding her in her mother's salon. It found her sitting in her mother's winged chair.

She had abandoned her elbows and wrists to the armrests and hung down her hands just the way her mother had done that day. She suddenly imagined herself to be her mother.

Before going to see her, Meral had called her mother on the phone. She had asked if she would be at home that afternoon. She had to do it. Her mother did not like surprises. She had to be prepared for receiving a visitor, even if the visitor was her daughter. Fatma, her maid, was the only person who could move in and out of the house without causing disturbance to the aging woman.

Just before entering the room as her old self, and finding her new self as the mother on the chair, her eyes checked the details of the scene. The drapes were halfway over the window, blocking the bright sunshine. The door to the adjoining room was open. Everything was as it was when the conversation concerning her marriage had taken place between her and her mother.

Immediately upon enquiring after her mother's health, Meral had shocked the aging woman by a frank admission of her disappointment in her marriage. "I'm not happy. I don't think that Fahri and I are suited to each other. I don't think that our marriage is going to last," she had said.

Having made the opening, she expected her mother to ask some questions. She expected the chance to expand on her statement. But the older woman had cut her short.

"You chose your partner yourself," was all her mother said.

The swift response landed in her unattended court with the twangy sound of a ping-pong ball. It left Meral gaping at her mother for some time.

However the game had to go on. It was Meral's turn to serve. Having always supposed that her mother did not approve of her marriage because of Fahri being an Anatolian, she tried to provoke her into giving away a hidden feeling. She said, "Would you rather have seen me marry an Istanbulian, a *comme il faut* Muhallebici *bey*? Did you have something else in mind for me?"

"Why would I have anybody in mind? Were you so desperate for marriage?"

"I might have been. I was already twenty-seven. I suppose I wanted to get married. I wanted to have children. Anyway marriage was the only thing left open to me. My education didn't qualify me for a worthwhile position."

"Who stopped you from studying further? Who asked you to give up your research project at the Ottoman Archives?"

Reflecting on the heartbreaking conversation, Meral admitted to herself that she had continued in that staccato style not only because her mother had already set the rules, but also because it was easier to accept her rules than to exhibit her emotions. She had hoped that, whatever they said to each other, whichever way the conversation went, she would feel some relief by unloading part of the weight her heart had been carrying for a long time.

Towards the end of the game, Meral tried to slacken its breathless speed. "Mother," she said, "you know as well as I do that I did not give it up because I wanted to. You'll remember that those were dangerous years. The country was on the verge of being torn apart. And the building in which I had to work was in a dangerous spot. It was in the firing line of the anarchists, leftists, rightists, fascists and what-nots. But all these have nothing to do with my present situation. Let's leave the past. Let's concentrate on the present. Aren't you going to ask me any questions about my marriage?"

"I assumed that you would talk about it eventually."

Meral imagined hearing a tremble of emotion in her mother's voice as she said that.

"I want to," she said. "I want to," she repeated, bowing her head.

She thought she heard a "yes?" A "Yes" trailed by a hesitant question mark.

"What did you say?"

"Nothing."

Another silence. An ear-bursting, mind-boggling, shattering silence.

"Did you hear about the. . . ."

Meral was hopeful again. "About what?" she said.

"Oh, it's nothing really. Something I read in the paper."

"What was it?"

"It may not interest you."

"What do you care? Say it. Say it. Say it."

The volume of Meral's insistent voice had reached an unacceptable level and its desperate tone irritated her reserved mother.

"Get a hold of yourself. No need to become hysterical," she said.

This was the end of the conversation. Immediately after expressing her disapproval, her mother picked up a book from the table next to her chair, removed the marker from its pages and had held its gold-lettered, black cover in front of her face.

Now sitting in her mother's room, sitting in the same chair her mother had sat in years ago, Meral smiled bitterly at the memory.

When the aging woman had pulled the black book to her like a heavy veil in front of her face, Meral left her chair and fetched her mother's spectacles from the big table in the next room. Her mother could not read a word of the book without wearing them.

Meral remembered scrutinizing every line of that week's newspapers when she returned home. She remembered trying to find the news item her mother had referred to, with a desperate eagerness. The only likely one, the only one on the theme of marriage, was about a bride from India.

The newspaper had said that the young bride was pestered by her in-laws about the insufficiency of her dowry. She was constantly despised for her family's poverty. Whenever she visited her mother, the young bride complained about her new family's humiliating treatment and her source of unhappiness. But all the older woman did for her daughter was to advise her to be patient. The advice did not help, and the solution the younger woman found for herself was tragic:

the bride had ended her few months of marriage by ending her life. She was found hanging at the end of a rope. According to the reporter, the mother was inconsolable.

If this was the piece of news her mother was referring to, how did she relate it to Meral's condition? Fahri's mother and father had died long before Meral had married him, and the half-dozen children they had left behind, excluding Fahri, lived in different parts of Anatolia with their wives and children. So, none of the members of her husband's family were around to despise her. On the other hand, none of his relatives had bothered to thank her for taking in hand the education of Bekir.

No, there was no similarity between her and the young Indian bride who had decided to end her miserable life. The idea of ending her life had never occurred to Meral.

If that was the piece of news her mother was referring to, did it mean that she was actually worried about her? Did it mean that she expected her to do something foolish? If so, why didn't she lift a finger to help her?

Not having known enough about her mother at the time, not having read her diaries and her stories, Meral had been in darkness regarding her mother's philosophy of life. She didn't even know if the reserved woman considered herself a happy or an unhappy person.

And now? Could she evaluate her mother's reaction to her dissatisfaction with marriage? No, she still could not. Perhaps she should let the memory rest a while. Who knows, when the old conversation returned to her once again, she might apply to it the layer of her new acquired knowledge and then start toiling at it with an objective attitude. After successive rubs on its surface meanings, a genie might come out of the memory and ask, "What is your wish, my lady?" When this happened, if it happened, all she would ask from the genie would be: "Give me my past, so that I can have my future."

The last reliving of this memory reminded Meral of Fatma, her mother's faithful maid. She had not seen her since she had provided her with a lump sum compensation for all the years she had looked after her aging mother. The last contact she had had with her was a tearful one on the maid's side, who insisted that the sum she was offered was too large; and an exasperated one on Meral's side, who almost forced her to accept it. She explained to Fatma over and over again that what she offered to her came from the monthly dividends on her father's investments. These dividends used to go to her mother's account. And now they were diverted to her. She tried to convince her that the bonus was not from her, but from her mother.

Fatma accepted the sum in the end, but what Meral had said about its being from her mother made her cry even more.

Meral stood up, folding the letter she had written to the lawyer. She took it to the bureau and slipped it into an envelope.

9

The memory of her mother's abrupt manner towards her was erased from Meral's mind the next morning, but the love story between the Turkish girl and the German boy remained. It ebbed and flowed in there, propelling her steps towards the table, and tempting her hand to reach out to the box which contained the stories.

Although she knew full well that eventually she would have to read everything her mother had written, she hesitated. She acted like a child who is conditioned to beware of a dangerous object.

But in the end she dismissed her unreasonable fear and lifted the lid of the box containing the stories. The folded bunch which fell into her hands first was a fairly large one, and the story it contained was entitled "Zachariah Feast." A scribbled note right under the title branded the story as being gloomy and incomplete. "*Depressing. Needs more work*," it said.

The unflattering verdict did not stop her from unfolding the papers and reading its opening with interest.

The story started with a conversation between two women. All through the story the heroine was referred to with the initial A., while the woman she was talking to was given a full name, Leyla.

"I have never heard anything so strange," said A., after she had listened to all that Leyla said about the Zachariah feast she had recently attended.

"Have you never been to a Zachariah feast?" Leyla asked with surprise.

"No, I haven't. I wish I could attend one."

"Actually another one is coming up in three days' time."

A. was excited. "Where? Do you think you could have me . . . I mean, could it be possible for me. . . ."

She had to simplify her request. She started all over again. She talked more slowly. "Could you ask the hostess to invite me too, if this is not too much to ask?"

"Why, of course not. I'll go and see Remziye today and tell her all about you."

"What are all these things you'll tell her about me?" A. asked, taken aback. "I am only asking to be invited to a Zachariah feast, as one of the guests. Does she have to know so much about me?"

"My God," Leyla said, "you are over-sensitive. All I meant was I'd tell her that you are my neighbor, you are the wife of Mr. B. and you have a daughter of four. Things like that."

"I see," said A., thinking for a minute. "But if you tell her all these things about me, she'll jump to conclusions. She'll assume that I want to attend the feast because I want to have a son. She'll assume that I have a problem. You yourself said that the Zachariah feast was held mainly for women who wanted children. I do not want more children. At times I even wonder why. . . ." She stopped.

There was a change in her voice. "It appeals to me, this Zachariah feast, because I want a different kind of contact with my religion. We 'children of Ataturk,' we have lost something, and we don't even know what we have lost."

"What are you talking about?" said Leyla almost angrily. "Ataturk did not forbid you to practice your religion. He simply gave you the freedom to practice it or not."

"I know, I know," said A. hurriedly. She did not want to upset her

95

patriotic neighbor. "What I mean is that. . . ." She smiled. "I really don't know what I mean. I think my main purpose is to meet some new people."

"That can be arranged," said Leyla, getting up smartly. She pressed her hands gracefully over her hips and pushed her silky dress down into position. She kissed A. on both cheeks before she left.

*

The invitation for the Zachariah feast was for between noon and afternoon prayers. That meant she could go to Remziye hanim's* *house any time between one and three. She resented that the time of the invitation was not properly fixed. She also resented Leyla, who had not given her any idea about when she would be there herself.*

She sat at the mirror of the dressing table and put the finishing touches to her hair while she tried to decide when to leave the house.

Her husband came in and stood in the middle of the room.

These days her husband was everywhere and interfered with everything. If he saw her go to the kitchen for a cup of tea, he followed her and asked her why she did not let the maid bring her the tea. If she complained about the color of a book binding, he volunteered to call Huseyin bey, the bookbinder, to have the binding changed according to her taste. Lately their simple, straightforward communication had turned into subdued fights because they talked in polite but nagging voices. She wondered about other marriages where conversations might start like theirs and then might get out of hand. What did these people do? They probably ended up saying things to each other which had nothing to do with the given subject. Well, this would not happen to A. Never. If she and her husband started to talk about one theme, they would end with the same theme.

A. felt her lips curve into an unfamiliar shape. It was rare that she satirized herself and her life. But there were times that she did, and this was one of them.

Her husband started to talk to her from the middle of the room, as if there was a border line between them.

"Why?" he said, looking at her image in the mirror. "Why this sudden

---

* hanim: *Miss*

interest in the ridiculous aspect of religion?"

He stopped and started again. "You know I am not religious. But this is not the point."

The point he was about to make was the theme of this uncomfortable conversation. And it had to be placed right in the center of all they said. They should never lose sight of it.

"The point is," he said, "if you wish to resume your interest in religion, by all means do so. Remain interested. Read the Quran. Read the worthwhile books on the subject of religion. I can get you dozens of them. Do you want me to?"

"Thank you, no," said A. She was not ready to go on, even though this conversation would not last more than a few minutes at the most. Her husband would walk out of the room and fiddle with the paintings hanging on the walls of the corridor. He would adjust the positions of the frames, holding them from two sides and moving them to the right and to the left one by one. If A. had not already told him that she was going to use the phaeton, if Recep, the driver, had not already been waiting for her in front of the gate, he might have decided to take a ride along the Bosphorus and return refreshed. She had learned from Recep that whenever he took these rides, he talked about his past and expected answers from the simple man to his sudden, shocking questions. His favorite question was, "Do you think my life has been worthwhile?" Didn't a man of his cultural level realize that these simple people live day by day and never question whether lives are worthwhile or not? Didn't he know that these people do not have the luxury to even think about their own lives, let alone other people's lives? He should know that they simply lived their lives. And that was all. They also did not have the luxury of spending ten minutes flattening the folds of broad silk neckties like the one he wore and pondering where to place the pearl necktie-pin before they took a leisurely drive by the sea.

She stopped fiddling with her hair. She pinned her small black hat on and lowered the short dotted net in front of her eyes.

The thoughts which raced in her mind caused her hands to shake but she assured herself that her husband was not near enough to notice.

"I like your new hat," her husband said.

This was another habit he had newly acquired. He had to comment on everything she wore.

"Thank you," she said, standing up. "I should go," she said.

*

What she was afraid of happened. None of the invited guests had arrived. Not even Leyla was there. The minute the hostess set eyes on A., she knew who she was. "You must be A. hanim. *How nice of you to come," she said, extending her slender hand. Rings flashed on her fingers as she folded A.'s hand in both of hers. The warm squeeze increased the cold shivers A. had felt since the morning. She knew all along that she was placing herself in a trap. She knew it, but she wanted to go and meet these devout women all the same. What was she expecting of this Zachariah feast? "What do you expect of life?" was the way her husband would put it if he heard the hesitation in her mind.*

Leyla arrived after a few minutes. A. greeted her but kept her eyes averted till the rest of the people trickled in. She wanted to escape Leyla's scrutiny until she acclimatized herself to the atmosphere of this group of people who were so different from what she knew.

Her husband's business associates, who used to come by in twos and threes when he was still running his own business, did not talk like them, did not move like them, did not look like them. For one thing they were all men, and they did not bring their wives. A. did not question their reasons, as she already knew what they were. She was not fully accepted in their society. The men had to comply with the invitations in order not to hurt their business interests. Anything these men put forward, whether it was a box of sweets from Hacibekir or a thought, was weighed and measured and carefully wrapped. Beautiful words, noble sentiments, impeccable logic. Of course there must have been more underneath than met the eye. But it was easier for A. to accept everything at face value. She welcomed the guests. She gave precise instructions to the maid for the distribution of tables and chairs; she gave precise instructions to the cook for the menu. She filled out the bordered seating arrangement cards with the curvy letters of her accomplished hand. They had dozens of them, as well as headed invitation cards, in the pigeon-holes of her husband's eighteenth-century English writing desk. He kept its key on top of it, near the extra ink stand.

But these people who accepted the invitation to the Zachariah feast were a different breed. They were people who were ready and willing to accept the rules which had very little connection to their religion.

They revolved around a mysterious light which seemed to emanate from their own yearnings and desires.

Leyla came over and found a place for the two of them among the ladies who had already settled themselves on the large Persian rug. In the center of the rug there was an embroidered tablecloth covered with dishes. A. did her best to leave enough space between her and the lady at her side in order not to jab her with her bent knees. She leaned on her hand and looked at Leyla. But because of her awkward, sideways sitting position, it was easier for her to remain facing the other lady who had dressed herself appropriately for the occasion. She crossed her legs underneath her wide skirt comfortably.

There were twelve ladies around the tablecloth altogether. In the middle of this cloth a candle was planted in a silver tray. Its light flickered on the surfaces of the dishes surrounding it. In these deep, small dishes of porcelain, which filled the cloth to its very edges, were all kinds of fruits, raw vegetables and mixed nuts. The lined up dishes complemented each other's contents. Next to the confident sliced carrots were introverted prunes with their shrunken skins. Next to the serenity of fresh slices of orange where argumentative nuts, standing out in different shapes and sizes. Next to the pale, fragile chopped apples were robust cherries bursting with color.

A.'s eyes slid from one dish to the other while the hostess started her opening prayer. Turkish and Arabic were mixed up in her words and the Turkish parts of the prayer were as unintelligible as the Arabic parts. Caught in the storm of these two impenetrable languages, the listeners clung to the soothing sounds.

A. counted the dishes one by one to find out for herself if there really were forty-one kinds, as tradition required. One, two, three, four, five...

The hostess said, "Kaf, Ha, Ya, Ain, Sad."
A. continued, six, seven, eight, nine, ten.
The hostess said:
"The mention of thy Lord's mercy
"unto his servant Zachariah;
"when he called upon his Lord
"secretly,

99

"saying, 'O my Lord, behold,
"the bones within me are feeble
"and my head is all aflame with
"hoariness.
"And in calling on Thee, my Lord,
"I have never been hitherto
"unprosperous.
"And now I fear my kinsfolk
"after I am gone; and my wife
"is barren. So give me, from Thee,
"a kinsman
"who shall be my inheritor
"and the inheritor of the House
"of Jacob; and make him, my Lord,
"well-pleasing.'"

A. had reached twenty and her eyes were caught by the raisins on the edge of the tablecloth opposite her. They were small. They had been plucked out of their wholesome bunches, in summertime; they had been randomly spread out to dry. They were at this table now and they did not know where they had come from. She plucked her eyes from them and went on. Twenty-one, twenty-two, twenty-three. . . .

The hostess said:

"'O Zachariah, We give thee
"good tidings of a boy, whose name
"is John.
"No namesake have We given him
"aforetime.'"

When A. reached thirty, she realized that she had stopped counting. "John, John," she said first. "Johann, Johann," she continued silently each time the hostess said "Yahya"—each time the hostess read the name of the son of Zachariah from the Quran.

A.'s old boyfriend Johann was given to her by a whimsical arrangement of God, and he was taken away from her by his mother's prejudice. She stopped herself from thinking of Johann. She was not here to draw parallels. She counted the dishes and ended up with the forty-first dish. Cucumbers.

After some Turkish prayers, the hostess returned to the Quran. She *started reading the verse of "Ta ha" now. As her reading was about to come to its end, the lady next to A. started to search through her handbag. She took out a candle. She lit it from the candle in the tray and placed it next to it. Some other ladies produced candles too, and murmured their own prayers before they also lit them.*

The room became brighter and everyone helped themselves to the contents of the dishes on the table and chewed thoughtfully.

There was complete silence in the room. It was the silence which brought upon A. the effect of the Zachariah feast. One part of her wanted to stay sitting and looking at the candlelight, while the other part wanted to get up and perform a fantastic dance of significant movements. She did not know the way the significant movements would unfold themselves. She did not foresee the significance of the movements. She felt that if only she could get up and do this dance, her life, others' lives, everyone's lives would be as clear as everything must be clear to the sun when it dominates a cloudless sky. "Tovbe estagfrullah, *Allah forgive me," she said, correcting herself. "It would be as clear as it is to God. The only God!"*

Hadn't she just heard from the "Ta ha" verse that:

"'The hour is coming; I would conceal it
"that every soul may be recompensed
"for its labors. Let none bar thee
"from it, that believes not in it
"but follows after his own caprice,
"or thou wilt perish.'"

Hadn't she heard her hostess read:

"Say: 'Everyone is waiting; so wait,
"and assuredly you shall know
"who are the travelers on the even path,
"and who is guided.'"

Or had she misunderstood their meanings, which were crammed into two imperfectly recited languages?

The ladies who had lit candles put them out after a few minutes and put them back in their handbags. It would be the turn of the lady whose wish came true to prepare a new Zachariah feast and invite the people who were present at this feast. Then the candle she had brought to this feast would be lit in her house and would be placed in the middle of the white tablecloth.

JANSET BERKOK SHAMI

A. adjusted her hat but kept its veil up, as she knew Leyla would want to kiss her cheeks before she left. The hostess might do the same. The only other person who wore a hat was an elderly lady. She had blue eyes and totally white hair. She looked like a foreigner. The rest had scarves on their heads. One quite young woman wore a small colorful scarf. She had pulled it down and tied it under her chin with a tight knot. The two sides of the scarf's ends had neatly divided themselves on her neck like a man's bow tie. She let out small, sharp, meaningless laughter as she said "goodbye." The hostess had to explain: "She is not very well," she said. "I mean physically."

This laughter could not come from a very healthy mind. But A. was not going to judge. Suppose she broke into similar laughter herself. . . . ?

*

The butler opened the door and answered her enquiry about her husband promptly. "Sir is up in his room," he said. "He is not feeling well."

A. climbed the stairs thoughtfully. This was another one of her husband's newly acquired habits. He would make himself sick every time she went out.

She entered her bedroom first. She removed her hat. She was too lazy to put it in its box; she hung it on the stand.

It was after she changed her clothes that she walked to her husband's room.

There was no reply to her knock.

She walked in and found him sprawled over his bed. He was fully dressed. She was amazed at his behavior. This was something he never did. He never lay on covers and disarranged an orderly bed.

She allowed the shock to advance to her consciousness at a slow pace. She saw his glassy eyes. She saw the Quran clasped in his hand. She opened the marked page to find an answer to his quest. The gilded leather marker was on "Meryem's verse."

There was a note at the end of the story. It said:

According to short story writing techniques, I should prepare the reader for the ending of my sad, depressing story. But I do not agree. I do not

102

agree at all. Did life prepare me for what happened? Did I know my husband would die all of a sudden and leave me alone? He was the only person who cared for me. He gave me everything; and he asked for nothing in return. He did not criticize my faults; he found something good in every quality I possessed and everything I did. I do not know where I would be today, if he had not married me. I do not know what will happen to me from now on. I suppose I'll keep on writing. Writing to the end of my life.

The faded ink on the pages had become alive. She heard her mother's voice; she felt the touch of her grandmother's woolly hair in her hand. These two women were with her. They were in her. She was pregnant with them, and the delivery time was near.

10

Meral could no longer sustain her self-inflicted imprisonment. She rushed out of the house at about 9 a.m. with the intention of renting a rowboat. She would choose a light, easily manageable boat and row it far away from the shore.

But when she reached the café and turned the corner, she realized that she lacked the energy. Days and days of staying at home doing nothing except reading and thinking had left no real desire in her for any kind of physical activity.

She did not continue down to the boat-house. She remained fixed where she was, and kept on looking down at the beach. One side of the partitioned beach was "for women only." Beautiful women were lying on wooden platforms exposing their bodies to the maximum. The young men, who swam on the other side, watched them across the border with wistful eyes. They ignored the women who had not bothered to segregate themselves and had come to the "mixed" side of the beach. On this side a woman held onto her son's rubber ring. She was trying to teach him to swim. Another woman had pulled down the bathing suit of her little girl and was briskly rubbing her body with a towel. The little girl shivered. She had stayed too long in the September sea. Some older men sat on the broader section of the platforms, near the beach café, and played cards. Frank Sinatra's crooning voice poured out of powerful speakers with unprecedented energy. It dominated the beach and the surrounding chestnut trees.

Close to Meral, the corn-seller stood bending over his cart. He watched the same scene. But whenever he saw people come from the beach, with bags, towels and wet hair, he turned to them. He called out: "Corn, corn, milky corn!" He opened the lid of the pot and stirred the boiling corn. The steaming pot sent out an irresistible aroma to the approaching people.

She turned her back on the lives that exposed themselves on the beach. The driver of the car parked behind the corn-seller saw her move away. He called out. "Taxi, taxi!" The letter she had written to her lawyer was still in her bag. She opened it and looked inside to make sure before she jumped into the car.

"Where to?"

"Sirkeci."

Speaking with the lawyer face to face would be a more courageous act than mailing the letter. But if she did not find him at his office, she would slip it under the door.

This time he was there and he was boiling with news. He started by giving the most important of all: her husband was not willing to give her a divorce.

"But," said the lawyer-magician, "I have certain tricks up my sleeve. This case will be over in a jiffy."

He took Meral's attempts to interrupt him as a sign of panic, and raised his hand majestically. He continued. "Our first strategy will be to frustrate his reasons for putting difficulties in your way."

He kept his fleshy hand steadily in front of Meral's face like a slightly mobile statue of bravery. "The second step of our strategy will be to encourage him to talk about his publishing business."

It was during his third step that Meral managed to speak. She told him that she wanted the case to take its usual course. She did not want him to neglect it, but she also did not want him to use the "tricks up his sleeve."

When she stopped, he continued from where he had left off as if he had not heard her, as if he were deaf. Since she had signed the papers which allowed him to represent her, he had become overly enthusiastic about the case.

During his "fifth point," which sounded like a repetition of the previous ones, a sudden rage rose in Meral. She left the office while he was still talking. She left the office during his explanations of his fifth and last magical point.

As she took the elevator down, she imagined him going on with his explanations despite her absence. She felt a sudden relief when she managed to stop a taxi immediately after stepping out of the dusty iron gate of the oppressive building. But her relief did not last long. It gave way to a feeling of defeat when the unavoidable question came: "Where to?"

The bold look on the round poxed face of the driver which the car's mirror reflected seemed to disparage and ridicule her. The rough-edged voice seemed to ask more than a simple question. He seemed to be asking her her life's direction. "You have been to the lawyer. You had an inconclusive meeting with him. Where to now? Back to the cell?"

The moon-faced man repeated his question, "I say, where to, lady?"

"Arnavutkoy," she said, although she had no intention of going to the villa. She said it simply because an answer was expected of her.

"'Arnavutkoy we go,'" said the moon-faced driver, softening his voice and stretching out his words to a singing tone. Her destination reminded him of a song about Arnavutkoy, which had lately become the most popular in the Arabesque style.

But all his unwelcome performance had done for Meral was to give her time to think.

"I made a mistake," she said as soon as the taxi turned to take the asphalt running alongside the European shore of the Bosphorus. "I don't want to be taken that far. Would you please stop at the first Yali you see after you pass the Bogazkoy Wharf."

"As you wish, lady," said the driver, his voice losing its previous cheerfulness. They had nearly reached Bogazkoy and the meter of his car had not rolled its figures around enough to bring in what he considered a worthwhile fare. And what is more he might not find a new passenger to bring back to the center of the town. He might have to return empty. Using taxis most of the time as she did, Meral felt she could read the drivers' minds regarding their financial concerns. She gave the moon-faced man a good tip when she left his taxi in front of the Yali which used to belong to her grandfather.

As she rang the bell, she prepared herself to be shown into a spacious marble hall by a well-groomed butler. There would be double-winged doors at the opposite sides of the hall and these doors would be embedded with engraved crystal panes. There would be a stairway at the end of this hall flanked by sturdy banisters at its sides. It would be curving gracefully upstairs.

But the door of the Yali was opened by a scruffy little man in a gray suit, not a butler in a European-style outfit with a few oriental trimmings; and Meral's eyes were immediately thrown into a tight, airless cell. All she saw was an extremely narrow corridor faced with numberless small doors. And the far end of the corridor had no stairway. In fact, it had no opening at all.

The man, who did not look worthy of answering the door of a Yali, had no knowledge of how to address her either. "Yes, miss?" he said, as if he were talking to a teenager.

Being addressed as a teenager, Meral felt like one. "May I see the lady?" she said.

"Which lady, miss?" said the man. "There is no lady here. There is Nurhan *hanim* in the typists' room, if she is the one you want."

"Typists' room?"

"It's the third room on your right."

"Is this an office?"

"What did you think it was, miss? Didn't you read the sign before you came in?"

Meral felt the color creep up her face in patches. She could not blame the simple man for being impatient. She herself was to be blamed. So far, she had not been able to put a direct, decisive question to him.

"No family lives here?" she managed in the end.

"Why didn't you say that? Why didn't you say that you were looking for Ekrem *beyfendi*'s* house? It's in the back. It's the other half of the Yali on the seaside."

Keeping a hand on the open door, he took a step outside and started giving her directions. "You follow the hedges, and knock on the first door at the end. That would be the kitchen door. Or, you pass it, and turn to the right. If you do that, you'll end up at the glassed porch. Do whichever you prefer, miss. In either case somebody will answer the door for you. That's the place you'll find Ekrem *beyfendi*'s wife, if she is not out."

The door of the porch was opened by the lady herself. Expecting to see someone she knew, she looked at Meral with the beginnings of a smile. But failing to recognize her, she remained studying her face carefully without saying a word.

Meral was in familiar territory now. She knew what to say. "My name is Meral Demiray," she said. "I'm sorry to bother you like this, but there was no way of calling you beforehand as I did not know your name."

The lady waited patiently.

"This Yali used to belong to my grandfather. I wanted to see the building. That's all," she said.

"Come in," said the lady, sliding the glass door wider. "How interesting. What was your grandfather's name?"

"He was Fikret *pasha*.† I don't think you'll know him. He died ages ago. He died when my mother was four years old."

"Fikret *pasha*. Fikret *pasha*," repeated the woman, exerting her memory to remember at least one person carrying the same name. "I know Cemal Taskentli, who is the son of the late Fikret *beyfendi*, the internist. Had your grandfather a profession besides the title?"

"He was a judge. He had no sons. He had just my mother, and another daughter from a previous marriage. Actually...."

"Sit down, I'd like to hear all about it," said the lady, showing Meral to the couch facing the part of the garden carpeted by a carefully trimmed lawn. This lawn stretched to the sea without interruption and sloped towards the shore as if it were pulled down by the

---

* beyfendi: *respectful address for man; equivalent to "Sir"*
† pasha: *a military general; also honorary title given for exceptional service*

heavy fringes of the magnolia trees at its end.

"What happened to the other part of the Yali?"

"My husband transferred his office in there a year ago. I'm glad that he did it. This way he is relieved from driving to and fro. It's not easy to drive in the middle of the ever-increasing traffic, you know. Specially at his age. Anyway, the place was too big for us. You see our children are grown up and gone away. The space we are left with is more than enough for the two of us. We still have a salon and a TV room downstairs, and three bedrooms upstairs. And of course I have this porch."

"It has a marvelous view."

"View, yes. But sometimes our view is blocked, or let's say, distorted."

"What do you mean?"

"Some afternoons swimmers come and settle in our garden. When we tell them that this is private property, they become indignant. The other day one young man said, 'So what? What right do you have to kick us out? Haven't you heard of democracy?' And about a month ago a couple decided to make love on our lawn. Right in front of my eyes!"

"Times are changing too fast."

"Yes, they are. You may cope with it, you are young, but for me it is very difficult. It's hard to accept people's disrespectful treatment at the age of fifty."

"Are you really fifty years old?"

"Yes, I am."

"I thought you were about my age."

"You are *très gentille*, my dear. There is a generation between us."

"I'm thirty-eight. I didn't think that you were a day over forty."

"Would you like a cup of coffee?"

"Yes I would, if it's no trouble."

The hostess found a bell hidden in the folds of her seat. A uniformed maid arrived promptly, and the coffee was ordered after the questions about the quantity of sugar to be added were settled.

Now that Meral had been able to please her hostess with her compliment about her age, now that the coffees were on their way, she felt she could start asking some questions.

109

"May I ask when you purchased this Yali?"

"Oh, this Yali has been in our possession for twenty-eight, twenty-nine years. But I heard from my husband that when property prices were going up in the fifties and sixties this Yali changed hands five or six times."

"Would your husband remember any of the earlier owners? You see, actually I'm trying to find my old aunt. I have no idea if she was married or not. If she was, she may have had children. And her children might have children too."

"I'm afraid my husband is the last person who can help. You see, he is the kind of man who 'does not remember what he has eaten yesterday,' as the expression goes. His memory is all right. The problem is that he is too involved in his work. His mind is completely occupied with . . . let me be frank . . . with making money."

"We all care about money."

The coffee cups were empty, and Meral had nothing to show for the ten minutes she had spent with the self-confident lady who confessed her age so comfortably. But although her age was more advanced than Meral had guessed, she could not help her in finding a woman who would be over ninety. That was, of course, if her aunt happened to be alive.

What an incurable optimist she had become of late! And the reduced Yali! There was nothing special about it in its present state.

Meral should have asked to be taken to the Yali soon after her mother had pointed it out to her. She should have nagged her mother into taking her there. She should have nagged her mother for many things as a child. But Meral had never learned how to use that talent for personal gains. She would nag for others, but not for herself. As a child, she often marveled at other children who asked for something over and over again, never losing hope, never feeling afraid of being scolded, or of being defeated in their battle. "A child grows up by falling and by picking himself up," says the proverb. Meral did not remember ever falling down. She walked on holding her nanny's hand. Her demands from the elderly woman were reasonable; and in most cases, her nanny complied with them quite willingly.

Did this mean that she was a coward? Did this mean that it was the fear of defeat which had taught her to attack problems in her special way?

Whatever the cause was, by the time she had learned to tailor her powers to suit her needs, she was already married. By the time she had started using them, the tear between her mother and herself had become too large for mending.

If she summed up her past years, could she honestly say that she had claimed her full share of the life bestowed her? And if her answer to this question was negative, if she concluded that she had reached this stage of her life as an unprofessed defeatist, would she search for a remedy to her condition? Would she try to compensate her loss of time by making the best of the life still in front of her? In what way would she be benefiting from life's offerings in the future?

11

Time had worked constantly at repairing damages done to the newly established friendship. The elapse of two weeks had been sufficient to soothe Meral. She was inclined to forgive and forget Orhan's comments about her treatment of Bekir. So, in spite of her past resolution never to visit Orhan and Dr. Zeki, on a hot August afternoon she found herself at the villa's door. While her trembling hand fitted the key into the lock, the skeleton keyholder lauded her tolerance towards her friends and provided further excuses for Orhan by rolling its head feverishly and dangling his feet helplessly. She smiled at the skeleton with a feeling akin to love.

She found Orhan sitting at the window and waiting for her that early afternoon. Had he been doing this every single day since her last visit? Had he been skipping his afternoon naps?

How did he spend the long summer days anyway? What did he do except cook, sleep and listen to his beloved Chopin? She had not even seen a television set in that house! This missing item in the otherwise well-stocked house kindled a feeling of irritation in her, as if not having a television, not watching the silly shows, constituted a serious crime.

He received her with his usual respect and, holding her elbow, he led her to the armchair with the floral needlework. She let herself be seated in the chair of his choice sheepishly. She allowed him to adjust the silk cushions on the back of the chair feeling conscious of his presence. There was something disturbing in his physical nearness. There was something disturbing in the pleasing warmth she felt. She had to be cautious of the feelings that were encroaching on her steadily. These feelings should be stopped. She had to find a way of stopping them.

Words were the only weapon with which she could protect herself. She called them to attention as soon as she sat down.

The sound of her voice filled the room. "Would you like to continue from where you left off last time?" she asked without any warning.

The untimely question received no answer. It simply bruised the mellow atmosphere that had prevailed in the room before she came.

"So, you got rid of your maid, your cook and your gardener and you stopped going out."

Still no answer.

"I suppose you hide in your house so as not to hurt people."

What was she doing? What was she saying?

"On the contrary," came the long-considered answer. "I hide so as not to be hurt. I hide because people ask too much of me. You ask too much of me."

Although her untimely probing should have prepared her for a retaliation, it had not. She had thought she was safe. She had not expected to be flung towards the swarming depths of herself. She hung onto the edge of the cliff hoping that further talking would save her. She did it heroically. She did it with a quarreling voice. "I ask too much of you? What did I ask of you? To go and see the teacher walk? To come out of your cage? Is that what you are blaming me for? Why, I thought. . . ."

"You ask too much of me," he repeated, "and yet you don't think much of me."

"You are playing with words to confuse me," said Meral, trying to laugh. "What about you, then. Do you think much of me?"

"Yes, I do," he said, and continued as if she had demanded an explanation. He spoke so forcefully that the right meaning emerged from what he said in spite of the unusual arrangement of his words. "I think very highly of you. And I think of you all the time."

Meral was trapped in the labyrinth of words—his and hers. What did she want to learn? What did she want to ask? "What is the main point in your regard for me?" she said blindly.

"Your energy," he said without hesitation.

Meral was pleased to hear this. Being pleased, she should have said, "Thank you," and left it at that. But Meral did not behave sensibly. "You see," she started, "energy . . . fight . . . courage . . . these elements. . . ."

Orhan did not allow her to complete the sentence. The unconnected words had already tired him. "You ask too much of me," he repeated once again, sinking into depression.

Dr. Zeki came into the house, shutting the door behind him quietly. He almost tiptoed into the room. Meral smiled at him as he came over and kissed her hand.

He walked to the side of the room where Orhan was sitting in his chair drowned in misery. Dr. Zeki glanced at his brother-in-law and turned on the table lamp near him. Dr. Zeki hoped to have his presence recognized. But it was to no avail. He was ignored.

So he left the room and started sending clattering sounds to it from the kitchen.

Meral wanted to join him in there. She wanted to offer help to the man who must have been tired from the day's work at the clinic. But she did not. She could not leave the other man who was sitting hunched over in his chair, saying nothing. Besides, she knew that her offer to help in the kitchen would be rejected. Her offer of help was always rejected. She was as useless in this villa as she had been in her mother's house before she married Fahri.

*

There was a call from Dr. Zeki the very next morning. "Hello, how are you, Meral *hanimefendi*?" he asked. But he continued before she answered him. "I know that you must be feeling hurt. Orhan told me everything. I know he's been rude to you. But my dear, you must keep in mind that he is not well yet. He is recovering, thanks to you. He is recovering fast. But we cannot expect miracles."

When Meral arrived at the villa two days after this call, Dr. Zeki answered the door promptly.

"Oh, I am so glad that you came," he said. "I meant to call you again but I didn't dare. Orhan is in bad shape. And I'm the one who caused it. He told me that you were trying to learn more and more about his problem. He said that he was not ready to talk about it. I told him that your intentions were pure. I said that you were doing exactly what any good friend would do. He became furious. He behaves like a spoiled child these days. What's wrong with my telling him that your intentions are pure? Tell me what's wrong with it?"

"Nothing's wrong," she said distractedly. Her attention was divided between Dr. Zeki's words and the changes in the salon. There was a table in the room which had not been there before, its surface covered with wooden spoons, several pots and different sizes of strainers. It looked as if Dr. Zeki was transferring the entire contents of the kitchen onto that table. In addition to the kitchen utensils, Meral saw a tray full of stale food. As she took it and carried it to the kitchen, Dr. Zeki followed her with his whimpering voice.

"These days there's something wrong with whatever I do, with whatever I say. I no longer know what to say and what not to say. I don't mind his bad temper. I'm used to it. But I hate it when he shuts himself in his room."

When Meral placed the tray on the kitchen counter and was about to scrape one of the dishes into the garbage can, he blocked her way, saying, "Leave all these now. Let's go upstairs. He has shut himself up again."

He took her hand in his trembling one and led her upstairs, talking nonstop on the way.

"He hasn't come out since yesterday morning. This is his way of punishing himself. This is his way of accepting that he is in the wrong. But his injections. He has to have his insulin. He cannot do without his injections. I doubt if he bothered with them. I doubt if he cares if he lives or dies. I don't know. I don't know."

When they arrived, he stopped in front of the door for a while as if to collect courage. Then he called out to the man inside. "Open the door," he said. "Open, I have to see you," he said, trying to catch his breath.

There was no answer. "Open, Orhan, or I'll break down the door," he said, raising his voice slightly.

"He cannot stand unnecessary destruction," he whispered to Meral. Then he repeated his threat, "Open the door, or I'll break it down."

"Go away," said a weak, tired voice.

"You leave me no choice. I'll have to break it down," he said. The tremor in his voice and the repetitiveness of his threat were building up some credibility. He was about to convince himself that he was eventually going to do as he said.

"Talk to him," he said to Meral, as if giving Orhan a last chance. But Meral could not comply. She was transfixed. She watched and listened like a stranger. Was Dr. Zeki really capable of breaking down the door? In this house, the occasional orders and mild threats were usually issued by the one who was on the other side of the door.

She finally realized that she could not stand there weighing the situation. All she needed to do was exert a little effort to shake off her transitory passive mood.

She had to do something. She should not allow the situation to drive this amiable man into using physical force. She had not been invited up there to be a spectator.

"Orhan, you have no right to torture Zeki," she said, pouring her indignation into her voice. The realization of her presence sank into the silence of the closed room, and prompted the man inside to open the door a crack.

She pushed it open and remained inside the doorway. Her insistent look carried the broken man slowly back to his chair. But when he sat down, she rushed into the room as if a sudden wind had thrust her there. "Where is your syringe? Where are the ampules?" she said.

He waved his arm towards the bathroom with a tired movement. The door was open.

She found the disposable syringes near the sink. The ampules were on the upper shelf of the medicine cabinet.

Dr. Zeki was already next to Orhan and his short plump fingers were holding his friend's bared leg.

"Where do I give it?" she asked, coming back.

Dr. Zeki pointed out the spot and she plunged the needle in. She emptied the contents of the syringe and all of her heightened determination into his body. If this injection could not save him, nothing could.

She left the room without saying another word. When she noticed that the silent doctor had followed her to the hall, she turned and said, "Goodbye."

"A cup of tea? Please have a cup of tea," he said, begging into her eyes.

She shook her head and walked out.

But Dr. Zeki was not ready to let her out of his sight. "I'll see you home," he said, when their silent walk over the graveled path of the garden came to an end.

"You don't need to do that," said Meral.

But he had already stopped one of the taxis passing on the seaside avenue and held the door open for her.

"You don't need to do that," she repeated, feeling that she had lost her earlier strength. She could not stop him.

The taxi ran along the seashore carrying their silence. The silence they preserved was so solid and so complete that even the talkative driver's philosophy on drivers and driving could not slice it.

"They say our roads are too narrow. They say we drivers would not suffer if we had better roads. No, sir, it is not the roads. It is us. If we cared for each other's safety we would have no problem with the traffic. But each taxi blocks the way of the other. We human beings, we are the enemies of each other."

When they met a line of traffic at the bridge, the driver had another opportunity to express his views. He said, "If you are not in a hurry, you can enjoy the scenery. Personally I am not one of those drivers who gets irritated by a slight traffic jam."

This was practice talk for tourists. He was ready to give good impressions of Turkish drivers in particular and the Turks in general. He must have read the posters stuck here and there expressing in simple and straightforward words that tourists were valuable for the economy of the country. Meral guessed that this philosophical driver must speak a little English as well.

When they arrived at Meral's house, Dr. Zeki came out of the car and kissed her hand. But he kept the taxi waiting at the door. Meral spoke before she went in. "I had never given an injection before to-day," she said. "My mother was good at that. Perhaps I inherited the talent."

"You inherited a lot of things, my dear," he said, "and everything you inherited is wonderful. Thank you and God bless you."

She smiled at him.

12

Meral received several phone calls from Dr. Zeki in the following two days. His lengthy talks had a double purpose. He used them to invite her to the villa and to bring her up to date with the progress of Orhan's recovery. But Meral's mood had changed of late. She felt that her constant presence in the villa was not serving any purpose other than being decorative. The best thing for her to do would be to untangle herself from her involvement with Orhan, and to find another activity which would divert her attention from the slow but steady progress of her divorce.

She had already started toying with the idea of calling her friend Rezan and asking about the preparations for her exhibition.

Meral did not need to do anything about finding an activity. The call she received on the morning of the third day was not from Dr. Zeki. Her ear, which had adjusted itself to the gentle tone of the man's voice, the voice which inquired if she was busy, if he could talk to her for a moment, if he was disturbing her by his call, suddenly received a loud, decisive "hello" which sounded more like a verdict than an opening for a conversation.

Rezan's husky voice cascaded through the receiver and filled the room before Meral could reply. The persevering woman, determined to procure Meral's help for her pet project, had found a valid reason for calling her. Rezan never did anything without having, or at least inventing, a reason. And she always came to the point at once.

"I thought of something, Meral," she began. "I happen to know a good lawyer. If you are serious about the divorce, he can be of enormous help to you. His name is. . . ."

But Meral interrupted her. She did not give her the chance to tell the lawyer's name. "I decided to help you with your project," she said. "Are you at the Center? When would you like me to come?" she asked.

Rezan was delighted. "Why, thank you," she said, shaking the telephone wires with the surprise in her voice. "What made you change your mind?" she asked, but quickly added, "No, no, I don't need to know." After a moment of silence in which Meral saw her smiling to herself, the answer to Meral's question came: "I'm at home now. I'll be at the Center at about eleven."

"See you there. I have to go now," Meral said quickly. "There's somebody at the door."

The blatant lie she told was the only excuse she could think of to cut the telephone conversation short. She had to cut it short, because if she did not, Rezan would not be able to contain herself until she dug up the causes of Meral's change of mind. She would ask questions. She would want explanations. She might even channel her questioning towards Meral's enquiry about Dr. Zeki and his brother-in-law. It would be foolish to presume that she would have forgotten the conversation they had had about the two men while sipping their lemonade at the Muhallebici less than two months ago.

After she hung up, Meral kept her hand on the receiver and thought for a moment. If only she could have seen Rezan's face when she told her that she had decided to help with the exhibition, she would have had first-hand knowledge of how a cat looks after swallowing a mouse.

She dressed carefully and spent some time in front of the mirror choosing an orange-colored lipstick to go with her walnut brown dress.

120

She broke the seals of several new perfume bottles and tried them on her wrist. She seemed to be perpetually trying to find a perfume which would suit her. Every single perfume gave out one and the same aroma when they were sprayed on her: the smell of the vitamin C tablet which her mother took daily to supplement her diet.

Why would the tablets that her mother used to consume give their odor to her? Had she used them when she was pregnant with her?

She wiped off the lipstick, she wiped the perfumes from her wrist. She repeated the shower she had taken before coming to the mirror.

When she returned, she put on the baby blue dress which she had bought right after leaving Fahri.

"How are you, my darling," exclaimed Rezan, as soon as her eyes caught sight of Meral from the far end of the gallery. She rushed at her, leaving the two men who stood by her and stopping in his tracks a third one on his way towards her.

Rezan was accompanied by her ten-year-old daughter, Semra, whose lively dance-like steps had outpaced her mother's on the final lap of the race. Standing in front, and obstructing her mother from giving Meral a hug, Semra looked up, and said, "Hello Auntie!" As she spoke these two words her laughing, honey-colored eyes charred a minute spot somewhere inside Meral's chest.

That burning feeling had occurred before. It had happened on Semra's fifth birthday. It had happened when her childish voice had sent Meral a warning: "Look out Auntie, I am coming!"

Meral had arrived on that day at Rezan's house carrying a shiny red tricycle for the birthday girl. As soon as it was unwrapped Semra had jumped on it, grabbed its bars with her dimpled hands and tinkled its bell several times with an immense expression of joy and triumph. Then she had spoken, looking into Meral's eyes: "Look out Auntie, I am coming!" Instantly a spark had jumped from the little girl's honey-colored eyes into Meral's. The spark had turned into a drop of fiery fluid and had dripped to the same minute spot it touched now. It had burned the same spot it burned now.

"Go and call the waiter. Ask for a cold drink for your auntie," said Rezan to her daughter, clearing the way for herself. "I'm so glad that you decided to help," she said to Meral. "We need you so desperately! You can contribute so much!" she continued, taking her

121

arm and dragging her to the two men to whom she had been speaking earlier.

"This is the lady I was talking about. Allow me to introduce Meral. . . ."

"Meral?" said one of the men immediately.

"Argun?" said Meral.

For a moment they remained looking at one another, not knowing what to do next. Then Rezan said, "Do you two know each other?" And the man who had been waiting to be introduced volunteered an answer. "Obviously they do," he said.

Everybody giggled good-naturedly, giving Meral time to find something to say. "What are you doing here?" she asked.

The question was perfect as far as Rezan was concerned. It provided her with a chance to answer it herself. "What is he doing here?" she started, with a voice loaded with feigned surprise. "Why, he is our star artist. We are so grateful that he has consented to exhibit his work at the Art Center's most ambitious exhibition of the season."

The sudden rise in Rezan's voice as she said "season" lent so much importance to the word that Meral was confused about its meaning. Had she meant "season" or "decade"?

"Coming from you, Rezan *hanimefendi*, this is a great compliment," said Argun, clicking his heels and bowing sharply, as if he had been jabbed in the stomach.

Remembering in time that Argun was not known for his clowning, Meral stopped herself from giggling. His acknowledging gesture must have been an earnest one.

"Come and see his work," said Rezan, taking Meral's hand and leading her to the opposite wall where several canvases leaned on each other.

"Don't, please don't," said Argun. "Please," he said again, almost blocking her way. "Meral and I have so much to talk about. We haven't seen each other for such a long time. It's been. . . ."

"Eleven years," completed Meral.

"Eleven years?" shrieked Rezan, clasping her hands with a great show of excitement and grinding her numerous rings against each other.

122

"Yes, eleven years. So, would you mind very much if we left you for a while? Could you postpone Meral's duties until this afternoon? Would you make this sacrifice for me—for your obedient future protégé? I give you my solemn oath that I'll return her to you safe and sound."

As Rezan laughed at Argun's pleading, Meral tried to get used to the new Argun who seemed to have become a regular nightingale.

"Let's go," he said to Meral, as Rezan turned to the other man waiting patiently to be noticed.

"Where are we going?" asked Meral.

"First to my car. It is parked at the bottom of the hill."

"Oh," said Meral, worrying about her high heels. She would hate to stumble in front of the confident Argun.

"Once I settle you safely in the car, we are going to Yesilyurt's Cinar."

"Isn't that too far?" said Meral, raising a mild objection. Although the idea of a drive to Yesilyurt appealed to her, although her question had left the decision to him, she resented not being consulted.

"It is hardly far enough to secure our privacy. We can't risk lunching in one of the nearby restaurants. Your overbearing friend might come and snatch you from me."

"You don't seem to approve of Rezan. She is a very nice person, actually. When you know her better, you'll. . . ."

"I'm not interested in knowing her better."

Meral could not defend her friend any further, as her attention was directed to steadying her steps by choosing the least uneven cobblestones to walk upon. She almost let out a sigh of relief when Argun pointed out a red sports car just ahead of them.

As soon as they were on their way, Meral commented, "You have changed a lot."

"Are you talking about this?" Argun answered, hitting his stout stomach under the prominent buckle of his belt. "Have I gained weight?"

"No, you haven't gained much weight. You have gained self-confidence. Lots and lots of it."

"It comes with time. Time brings age, and age brings dubious gifts. One of these gifts is self-confidence."

"Some people are not given any gifts."

"Oh, they are. They simply might not know what to do with them. Lucky are the ones who receive them without the instruction slips. Lucky are the ones who don't know how to use them. Life must be more enjoyable when it's less predictable."

In spite of his nostalgic remarks about youth and inexperience, it was obvious that he was very pleased with himself. It was obvious that, given a second chance, he would do everything he could to develop into what he was now.

When they arrived at the fashionable seaside restaurant, none of the waiters bothered to show them to a table as they were busy tending to a large tourist group. Meral and Argun walked down the steps leading to the lower terrace, and settled themselves at an empty table facing the sea. Eventually one of the waiters grudgingly tore himself away from the group and came over to take their orders for an aperitif.

"A lemonade," said Meral.

"A lemonade? You still don't drink? Are you still one of those 'Green Moon' people who deny joy to themselves and to others? Am I permitted to have a beer?"

"You have my permission," said Meral, hoping to prevent him from counting her likes and dislikes in front of the waiter who was there only to take their orders.

They sipped their drinks while Argun's self-indulgent conversation turned Meral's chronic regret over his proposal of marriage into finely ground sand. A mild breeze from the sea carried her lightened feelings away grain by grain.

"So this is the bright future the woman with the golden bracelets predicted," she thought, sighing with relief.

What does a mother mean when she speaks about her child's future? How does she justify her predictions, if time proves her wrong? How does a mother who names her baby daughter Filiz, Sapling, feel when her daughter acquires an unyielding stature? How does a mother who names her son Demir, Iron, feel if he grows up to be a sickly young man?

It was time to contribute something to the conversation. "What made you take up art? Aren't you practicing your profession?" Meral managed to say, although she was busy supervising the progress of the spring-cleaning which was taking place in her mind. Now that her feelings of regret were swept away she had to readjust what remained of Argun and his memory.

"Oh, I am practicing my profession. And how! I have my Istanbul office permanently staffed with five draftsmen, two secretaries and a project manager. And about my overseas activities...."

"Overseas activities as well?"

"I'm afraid so!"

"Well, then, where do you find time for your art work?"

"I do have some free time, in spite of running the show. Or if you like, running several shows. I took up art nearly three years ago. One of my paintings is about the storm."

"What storm?"

"The storm you were involved in."

"Oh."

"Any more questions?"

"No more questions."

"But I have something to say about the subject. I would like you to know that I never blamed you for behaving the way you did on that day. I didn't mind your slighting remarks about me. Who wouldn't have acted the same? I had wounded your pride."

"My pride?"

"Yes. Why are you surprised? Didn't you expect me to propose to you personally after my mother and I visited your mother? Didn't you expect me to act after I learned that your mother left the decision of marriage to you? But I didn't. Don't get me wrong. I was attracted to you. You were so lively. So carefree. But visiting your mother was not my idea. It wasn't my idea that my mother should do the proposing on my behalf. We argued about it. I told my mother that I wasn't ready for marriage."

Meral noticed a change in Argun's manner of speaking. She noticed that his forced frankness was having a crippling effect on his speech. She even deciphered a slight stammering which reminded her of the old Argun. Meral listened with full attention and when she understood what he was trying to say, she threw her head back and laughed.

125

Mystified by her reaction, Argun fell into silence. Meral let him stay there and interpret her laughter however he wished. She did not mind. She was not going to give him the benefit of hearing her side of the story. Her only regret regarding her resolution was that it robbed her of the opportunity to thank him for freeing her mother from the weight of guilt Meral had heaped on her.

But in spite of her resolution, she could not let that episode of her past go to its last resting place without checking up on some details. This was like making sure that the fire was completely out. This was like poking gently into ashes before one went to bed. "Now it's my turn to speak about the past," she said.

"Go ahead."

"First tell me, is your mother still living?"

Somehow Argun showed no surprise at Meral's sudden interest in his mother. "Yes, she is," he replied.

"Does she have a rather full figure?"

He laughed merrily. "Let me call a spade a spade. My mother is fat," he said.

"Does she sing your praises at every opportunity, like most mothers do?"

"She does. She always did. And it's getting worse."

"Well, she has more reason to do it now," Meral said. And, "thank you," she added, folding the invisible questionnaire and slipping it into her mind.

All she had to do now was to keep the muscles of her face under control, as she felt a smile coming on. There would be no harm in allowing the corners of her lips to be pulled a little upwards, if that would be all. But she was afraid that the smile might turn into laughter. She did not want to laugh at Argun's mother. She loved her big bosom. She liked her golden bracelets. She was grateful to her for confirming the scenario that had occupied her mind for so long.

"One more thing," she said. "Why did you paint the storm?"

He looked at the calm stretch of the sea beyond the iron railings of the terrace. "I love storms. Life is too easy," he said.

"Are you married?"

"Me? Married?" He laughed even more merrily this time.

Some people from the tourist group at the upper terrace might have been watching them. If they were, they must be thinking that they were having the time of their life. In a way they were. At least Meral was. Since she had left her husband, she had not felt as care-free as she felt during this lunch. When their coffees were brought and she took a sip of hers, she felt that she had not tasted such a good cup of coffee for a long time.

On the way back, Argun parked the car on the same slope, and walked Meral to the door of the gallery.

"We'll see each other again, won't we?" he asked.

"I suppose so," answered Meral. "I have already involved myself with the arrangements of the exhibition, haven't I?"

"What I mean is that. . . ."

"And I am looking forward to seeing your paintings."

"What I mean is that. . . ."

"I have to go in, I'm already late."

*

Rezan had just completed a goodbye ceremony. The departing lady left the hall in one compartment of the revolving door still carrying a smile on her stringy lips, and Meral returned to it in another. When she was clear of the door, Rezan allowed her to see the sour expression on her face and then turned away.

Meral caught up with her before the clicking heels carried her too deep into the hall. "Hello," she said, walking alongside her. "I am here."

"I had given up on you," Rezan said, stepping ahead again.

She talked to the two porters who had carried in a panel and did not know where to place it. "Put it in there," she said, pointing to the end of the hall.

"Bring in all the others. Line them up against the walls."

"Sorry," said Meral.

At last Rezan erased her artificial expression and gave her friend a smile. "I suppose better late then never," she said.

"Tell me, what do you want me to do?" Meral said with a childish eagerness. She even came out with a proposal of her own. "How about giving me an outside job? An active job? Something to do out of the exhibition hall. Publicity. Collecting advertisements for the program. Something like that."

A stirring around the lips released Rezan's last reserve of annoyance and spoke out her ultimate forgiveness of Meral. But she had to tease her a little before she gave her approval of the suggestion.

"Coward. You are trying to escape," she said.

"I am not. I'll do my share. I'll put in more time and energy than you expect me to."

"I mean you are trying to escape from your old friend Argun."

Meral could escape from Argun, but her motives could not escape Rezan's observations. Nothing could escape Rezan's observation. "In a way," she confessed.

"You were so happy to see him. What went wrong?"

"Some misinterpreted past came in between us."

"Mysterious as always, aren't you?"

"Me? Mysterious? I'm as clear as daylight."

"You know nothing of yourself. By the way, would you like to meet the lawyer I mentioned?"

"I already have a lawyer."

"Oh, in that case forget about it."

Having completed her friendly suggestions, Rezan came back to the subject closest to her heart. "OK," she said. "Be in charge of the publicity. I'm sure you'll do a marvelous job. I expect you to bring the dead out of their graves. You'll do the whole campaign, won't you? You are the right person for that. And when the public sees the paintings, their eyes will pop out of their sockets."

"Campaign? Popping eyes? You scare me."

"Come on, my dear, you are not easily scared. Besides, you are the one who asked for the job, aren't you?"

She had asked for the job. "One usually gets what one asks for," Meral thought, as she left the hall.

13

D r. Zeki's calls continued. During each call, unaware of repeating himself, he gave the same information about Orhan: he had come out of his room, and was giving himself the injections. "But," he added, "he goes around in a daze. He doesn't talk much." Even these additional comments were repetitious.

Although Meral dismissed the commentary as a bait for her sympathy, she could not prevent herself from swimming towards it. She took the first stroke by admitting that her entry into the subject of his past had been too abrupt. Her second stroke was her acceptance of the blame for the harsh response she had received. The third stroke which brought her closest to him was her recognition of his helplessness. The stubborn man needed help. Her help.

And in order to attend to his need, she had to show some courage. She had to mail the letter she had written to Rezan on the very evening of her visit to the Center and which was still in her bag. She stepped out of the house quoting to herself Ataturk's famous speech. She knew this speech, which warned the Turks about the dangers they

129

might face following the Independence War, from beginning to end. Like the rest of her classmates she had memorized it when she was twelve. The sentence which always uplifted her was "The courage you need exists in your veins." She murmured it like a prayer, until her steps took her to the post office. She sent the letter by registered mail. In this letter, she profusely apologized to her friend for breaking her promises of help. She apologized, but did not give any explanations.

On her return home, she sat motionless at her mother's desk trying to get over the after-effects of mailing the letter. Had she been courageous or had she been cowardly? Why was the line between those two qualities so thin? Hadn't she endangered her friendship with Rezan while trying to hinder Argun's contact with her?

She bent forward to survey the surface of the table more closely. She looked at the solitary box pushed to the back. She looked at the line of miniatures with the framed prayer in the midst. Finally her look fell upon the parcel—the parcel with the tablecloth.

Why had she not asked a single question of the *tuhafiyeci* woman about her mother and her grandmother on the day she was given the tablecloth? She should have encouraged her to continue when she had interrupted herself, saying, "I am an old chatterbox, I'm repeating to you things you already know." She should have been frank with her and confessed that she knew nothing. Nothing at all. Why had she simply accepted what she had been told, and not asked for more?

She should visit her again. She should visit her right away. The card given to her by the young, polite driver was still in her bag. All she had to do was to dial the taxi office and ask for Ahmet. All she had to do was to add something sober over her acid yellow silk dress.

*

"Galatasaray," said Ahmet seeing his passenger deep in thought. "We are already at Galatasaray."

"Turn to the right at the next corner," said Meral, "and stop at the third shop on your left."

The driver did what he was told, but looked confused seeing that the window of the third shop was barred with broad, wooden boards. A chain was inserted through the loops of the iron screen underneath the boards, and a huge lock was attached to it.

"Wait," said Meral, her heart sinking.

She left the taxi and entered the next-door shop. "Why is the *tuhafiyeci* closed?" she asked the stocky salesman who walked towards her between the broad shelves fitted against the shop's walls.

Having no customers at the moment for the variety of glassware his shop displayed, he was willing to answer any question.

"The owner died," he said.

"When?"

"The poor old woman passed away a week ago."

"Why the bars?"

"I'm not sure. Madame Iskouhi's daughter came from Australia and made some arrangements. I think the shop will be auctioned."

"Where is she now?"

"Who?"

"Madame Iskouhi's daughter."

"Back in Australia."

"So soon," said Meral almost angrily. She had found someone to blame for the frustration she felt over the *tuhafiyeci* woman's death. She had let an opportunity to learn more about her grandmother slip through her fingers.

"Well, as you know, she has a husband and two children in Australia. She had to return."

"I don't know. I don't know Madame Iskouhi's daughter."

"Oh, I'm sorry," said the man. "It didn't occur to me that you could be a customer. I thought you were a friend of the family."

"Thank you," said Meral. Her timing changed the meaning of the words which meant to express her appreciation for the man's graciousness in answering her questions. It made them sound as if she were thanking him for assuming her to be a friend of the family.

The driver had moved his car further down the street, as the traffic policeman had not allowed him to linger at the busy spot near the corner. Meral walked by the windows along the sidewalk without glancing at their displays. There was more to be studied in the win-

131

dows of her mind. She saw the *tuhafiyeci* woman as a child. She heard her ask her mother to buy her a big table like Nartuhi's. Then she saw herself looking at the table which extended at great length, like the Great Wall of China, separating her from her mother. She saw Fatma aggravating her dislike of the table through her protectiveness towards the items spread over its surface. She heard her pleading warning, "Please don't touch anything. Please don't change anything on it."

Suddenly she realized her reason for not getting in contact with Fatma, except for that one time after her mother's death. She was jealous of her! She begrudged the close relationship between her mother and the maid. Fatma had been closer to Meral's mother during the last years of her life than Meral had ever been.

Since her return to her mother's house, Meral did not resent Fatma's past efforts at keeping her away from the table as much as she had as a teenager.

She repeated the silent questions she had asked herself once or twice before, as she approached the car. Where was Fatma now? What was she doing?

It was true that Meral had no way of knowing what Fatma was doing. But the answer to her question about her whereabouts was in her handbag. Fatma's address was registered and had remained registered in her constantly updated address book. And this small book went wherever Meral went, like Mary's little lamb.

She took out the book when she entered the taxi, and looked at the address.

"Can you take me to Kazkoy?" she said to the surprised driver.

"Certainly," was the answer in an admirably controlled voice. The driver was intent upon hiding the interest he felt in his passenger's wish to be taken to such a poor, downtrodden neighborhood.

Leaving Karakoy at its Sirkeci end, the driver took the seaside avenue leading to the airport. After some time, he rolled up his window against the nasty breath produced by the intermittent coughs of the tanning factory's tall pipes. He lowered it again when the car left the factory behind and started moving alongside an open-air tourist restaurant which was bordered by a shaky, wooden fence. He took a deep breath to cleanse his lungs of the factory smoke; then took another to fill them with the aroma coming from the meat barbecued on the restaurant's open fires. He had to be satisfied with inhaling the air circling this restaurant, as the heavy traffic he struggled through did not allow him to have the pleasure of watching the activity of the waiters around the *mangals** while driving. While his car passed by the fence of the restaurant, he hardly had a chance to steal a glance at the agile movements of the cook's hands beading a skewer with cubes of lamb meat, sliced tomatoes and squares of green pepper. He completely missed out on seeing him line the already beaded skewers at their appointed places on the constantly fanned fires.

Having been coaxed into wakefulness from her reverie by the sliding scenery, Meral noticed that the driver had started indulging his car into performing some acrobatics. He let it change lanes between trucks, buses and cars which moved at different speeds. Just as she was about to interfere, to tell him to slow down, he turned sharply to the right, and reduced the car's speed dramatically. He picked up the written out address which lay next to his seat and studied it while alternating his look between the piece of paper and the road in front of him.

"We can't be too far," he said, before he dived into an opening on the right-hand side of the avenue. As if to contradict Meral's evaluation that the street they had entered could not be more than an inch or two wider than the width of the car, he made it turn a corner and led it into an even narrower street. Now they were moving alongside a river of tin-roofed huts. The driver was paying the utmost attention to the sharp curves on the bridge-like cobblestone road which lay above the level of the huts. He had to do this in order to avoid the danger of slipping off the edge of the narrow road and sinking into the river. After a few minutes of this cautious driving, he stopped in front of a one-eyed hut flanked on each side by huts with two windows. These three dwellings, as well as the rest of the neighboring huts, seemed to be holding each other in a permanent hug for their personal protection. And now they all seemed to watch the car suspiciously and to be wondering what to do.

"This must be the house," the driver said, pointing at the narrow-faced one.

----

* **mangal:** *brass or copper heater using coal*

Not seeing a number either on the door of the hut he had pointed out, or on the doors of the other huts, Meral had her doubts about the driver's conclusion.

"Wait a little," she said, leaving the car. "Let me make sure."

She walked down two steps from the edge of the road. Just as she reached the door, which hung loosely on its frame, just as she was about to use its knocker, the door moved noisily inwards on its rusty hinges, and the face of a woman in her late forties appeared at the gap.

"I'm looking for Fatma. Fatma Elata. Does she live here?" asked Meral, talking fast. She was afraid that the woman would relax her hold on the door, and that its hinges would revert it to its original lopsided position.

"Ahhh, Fatmaaa," said the woman, stretching her sad voice and moving her head from side to side. This visual-vocal demonstration of hers was a shortcut to expressing sad feelings. The two words she spoke and the gesture she performed were clear signs that the question had touched an unhealed wound.

"Come in, come in," she added, pulling the door further in and showing almost the whole interior of the one-room hut.

Meral climbed up to the road to pay the driver. When she rushed back, she saw that the woman had exchanged her white headscarf for a pink one. The scarf which now framed her cheeks was decorated with loosely-attached, hand-crocheted triangles. These triangles hanging down along the woman's face like colorful Chinese lanterns did nothing to relieve the mournful expression imprinted on it. If anything they made her sad eyes look even sadder.

"Please have a cup of coffee with me," she said. Her speech was slightly impaired due to the restrictions she imposed on her lips. In order to hide her gums with the two missing teeth at the side, she allowed a minimum of space to appear between her lips as she talked. The woman's pathetic adherence to her personal appearance led Meral to conclude that this worn-out, shapeless person in front of her had been a beauty when she was younger and healthier.

She seated Meral on a lumpy mattress on top of a rickety divan constructed out of fruit boxes, and immediately started searching for coffee cups from an overcrowded cupboard hung on the wall opposite the divan. This highly placed cupboard, which had the size and proportions of a medicine cabinet, consisted of two small doors on the outside and two narrow shelves inside. The doors of this only piece of furniture in the room besides the divan, were covered with wire netting, and the shelves were skirted with frills of cut-out papers.

The woman left the room carrying the cups through a curtained opening which she left partly open. "We used to live in this house together, Fatma and I. Now that she is gone, I'm all alone in this world," she said, as she left.

"Where is she?"

There was no answer to Meral's question. The woman turned from one wall of the small alcove to the other, giving her full attention to gathering the things needed to make the coffee. First she found a jar which contained very little coffee in it, so she pushed it aside. She took a small, unused package from the shelf, opened it and stuck a spoon through its opening. The long-handled coffeepot was already on the one-burner stove. She measured the water into it by using one of the coffee cups she had brought with her, and held out a lit match to the stove. Immediately after doing this, she started scraping sugar from the bottom of an almost empty jar. She emptied the container by scraping one, two, three, four spoonfuls of sugar from it and added all that she collected to the water on the fire, without asking her guest if she wanted her coffee plain, average or sweet. If she had asked, she would have saved some sugar. Meral took her coffee plain. She also liked it light. However, the woman was not as extravagant with the coffee as she was with the sugar. She handled the newly opened package gingerly, and she added in just the usual amount of powder into the pot.

The filled cups came in through the curtain on a grass-green tin tray with large pictures of roses on its borders, and Meral repeated her question. "Where is she?" she said again.

"I hope you like your coffee sweet. I put in one and a half spoonfuls of sugar in it," the woman said, being modest about the real amount of sugar she had added.

"Yes, I like it sweet," answered Meral, wondering about the woman's false evidence. "Where is Fatma?" she asked once again, trying

JANSET BERKOK SHAMI

to prevent her mind from delving into this insignificant detail.

"Fatma," said the woman, approaching the divan timidly.

She continued, after attaching only part of her fleshy buttocks to the divan in order not to disturb her visitor by her proximity. "She lost her lady, you know," she said.

"I know," said Meral. "Her lady was my mother."

"I guessed it," said the woman. "She told me about you. She described you exactly as you are. She told me that you were beautiful. And *Mashallah*,"* she added, pulling the lobe of her ear, producing a sucking sound with her pursed lips, and knocking on the edge of the fruit-box divan with a hooked finger.

"*Mashallah*," she repeated, "she was right. Let Allah prevent the Devil from hearing what I say. Let the Devil's ears be stuffed with lead, she was right."

Having finally completed her frilly compliment to Meral's looks, she added another, a more substantial one. "She also told me that you were very generous to her."

"Fatma worked for my mother and kept her company at the same time. She deserved more than I could do for her."

"Keeping company with your mother was her pleasure. She used to talk to me about her. She told me what a fine lady she was."

Although it was Meral's wish to learn more about her mother that had led her to this unfamiliar area, she was not willing to receive it from someone who had not even met her. Second-hand information coming through the veteran maid's store of memory might have been been acceptable. But third-hand information—information offered by a stranger?

"Where is Fatma? Where is she?" she said, allowing impatience to creep into her voice.

"Fatma is somewhere in Anatolia. Allah only knows exactly where. First she went to Bolu. She sent me a letter from there. But now I don't know where she is. I haven't had any news of her since that letter. This one and only letter arrived in my hand more than a year ago."

---

* **Mashallah:** *an Arabic word for "what God wills"; in common usage, means "God protect him," praising the person while calling for her or him to be protected from the evil eye*

136

She started moving her head from side to side once again. "She should have stayed with me. I would have looked after her even if she spent all her money, even if she was left without a penny. I am younger than her. I'm still in demand for daily cleaning. I could have made enough money for both of us. I could have provided for her. I loved her and she loved me. We always got along fine. We never hurt each other in any way. I'm left with no one in this world since the anarshits shot my uncle in the coffee-house. That was many years ago. That was before, God lengthen their lives, the army people saved us from their mercy. The anarshits were looking for an enemy hiding in the coffee-house, so they came in and machine-gunned all the customers sitting around. Now the Demorc-acy is back, they say. I don't know. I think it would have been better if the Army stayed on."

"Why did she go to Anatolia?"

"She put it in her mind to find her brother. She used to speak of a brother. An elder brother. When her lady died, she started talking more and more about him. Whenever I had time to sit and chat with her, she opened the same subject. Finally she went to Anatolia to search for him."

She stood up and went to the cupboard from where the coffee cups had come. She slid her hand underneath the decorative skirts of the cut-out papers, and moved it to the right and to the left as she spoke.

"Her brother had disappeared long ago. He had not returned to his village after his military service. Some said he died, but Fatma never believed them."

Having come across what it was searching for, her hand stopped, and the woman stopped talking. But as she took out a thin envelope, she spoke again, "Here it is. Here is her letter," she said, waving it.

"Will you please read it aloud?" she added in a pleading voice as she handed it to Meral. "I haven't had this letter read to me for some time. The other day, I begged a neighbor's daughter to read it. But she laughed at me. 'It's an old letter, what do you want with it?' she said."

Meral agreed with the neighbor's daughter. The letter was old. It was old in date—as the woman herself had said; and it was old in

137

appearance—as its worn-out exterior professed. When the letter had been first received, the envelope was torn open carelessly, and the letter inside was roughly handled. Each folding and unfolding by different hands had added new creases on its paper, which came from a lined copy book. The untidy scribbling of the letter had been started with a blunt pencil, but was continued with a sharpened one. The pencil was sharpened only after its lead had become too short to make any kind of marks on the paper. It read:

Dear Safinaz,

First of all I send my sincere greetings to you. I also send my greetings to our dear neighbors Gulizar and Pervin. And also to Pervin's lovely daughter Pakize. If you ask about me, I am well. I am a little tired from the search for my brother. And I am sorry to say that I have not found him yet. A very respectable man here, the one who is writing this letter for me, told me that my brother was in Bolu until three years ago, but now went to Kayseri. He says that Kayseri is a very big place. Much bigger than Bolu, he says. He also tells me that he did not work in Bolu as a cook, as I had heard, but as a nightwatchman. He even showed me a cap he wore with his uniform. He said that my brother gave it to him before he left. This cap is with me now, and every night when I go to bed it gets wet with my tears.

But I am confident that I'll find my brother. I'll separate the clouds which envelope me, and I'll see the sun. I'll separate the clouds like I used to separate my lady's bedroom curtains. "Look, the sun is shining," I'll tell myself, like I used to tell my lady.

But until that day comes, please pray for me, my dear friend. I, for my part, am praying for you constantly.

I kiss both your beautiful eyes. I also kiss your hands, even though you are younger than me. I must kiss your hands, for they have done so much for me. Let Allah keep them and you healthy.

Your friend who
loves you so much
Fatma

"How nicely you read," said the woman, drying the gathered tears in her eyes, first with the back of one roughened hand and then with the other.

Meral folded the letter into the envelope and returned it to the woman. She followed her slow movements as she got up. She heard her sigh as she took the letter to its safe place. The letter was worth saving. This piece of writing, which managed to rub and polish the dry wood of its hard, traditional frame with the sincerity of its sentiments, was worth saving. This letter, which had kept its measured emotions intact during its transfer from Fatma's lips to the blunt pencil of "the most respectable man," was worth keeping. It had done something for Meral too. It had given her a view of her mother's mornings. Fatma had drawn her mother's curtains aside. Fatma had shown her mother the sun. But what about the rainy days?

Meral had to be content with this letter. She had to be.

"God bless you. God bless you, lady," murmured the woman as she perched herself once again at the edge of the divan, balancing her upturned hands on her tightened knees and exposing the deep cracks on her fleshy palms.

Meral gathered her bag lying next to her, opened it quickly, and squeezed a few notes into her hostess's hand. She stood up and prepared to leave before the woman started expressing surprise and uttering the traditionally expected sounds of objection. She walked out, stumbling over the first uneven cobblestone which came in her way. She somehow managed to straighten herself up, although she had come close to falling face down. She knew that the woman was watching her walk away. So Meral turned and waved at the round face smiling at her from the middle of the pink scarf's aimlessly moving triangles.

14

Although Meral admitted to herself that her entry into the subject of Orhan's past had been abrupt and, having admitted this, no longer blamed him for the way he responded to her, although she had freed herself from Rezan by writing her a letter and excusing herself from helping her with the exhibition, something prevented her from going to the villa.

She no longer seemed to possess the energy to overcome the large or small obstacles which came her way, although she kept reminding herself that she was not the only person on earth who faced difficulties. Her state of mind was not helped by the three silent days which had passed since Dr. Zeki's previously insistent telephone calls.

But one morning while clouds chased one another in the late August sky, Dr. Zeki's awaited call lifted her up from her mother's chair where she had been sitting for several hours, doing nothing.

"Meral *hanimefendi*," said the trembling voice, "if you were in front of me, I would go on my knees and beg you to come and visit us. Please, please come."

"Zeki," answered Meral. "I want to. Believe me, I want to. But I'm not myself these days. I don't think I have much to offer."

"What's the matter?"

"I don't know. I don't know."

"Well, in that case there is one more reason for you to come. Why should it always be you lifting up our spirits? Why shouldn't we try to do something for you? How about coming right away? I'm at the clinic now. But Orhan is waiting for you. If you knew how eagerly he waits for you. How he waits for you day after day. How unhappy we feel when the day ends without you."

Meral would have smiled if she was not so depressed. She would have found his tactful switch from "he" to "we" towards the end of his speech interesting. But now what he said made her identify with the old woman who is remembered by her son living abroad.

The son makes a call to one of the flower shops in the foreign city where he lives. He orders a bouquet of flowers for his old mom. The bouquet of flowers is instantly at the old woman's doorstep. It makes her ecstatically happy. "My son loves me. He sent me flowers from the end of the world," she exclaims.

The simple woman does not know that this bouquet was made of flowers grown in one of the nurseries of her own country. She does not know that it was put together by hands which knew nothing of her son. The feeling was transferred from ear to ear, the flowers were passed from hand to hand. What did Dr. Zeki know about how Orhan felt?

"OK? Please say you'll come."

"I'll come. I'll come tomorrow."

"Why not today?"

"I'll come tomorrow."

"When? Please come early. Come for lunch."

"Tomorrow I'll be working half day."

"All right, I'll come early."

"Thank you, my dear, thank you. I'll see you tomorrow then. Take care of yourself. Please take care of yourself."

The next morning found Meral sitting once again in her mother's chair. She was wearing a halter neck outfit with tiger spots all over it. She was holding a coffee cup in her hand and neither the dress she wore, nor the mug she held seemed real to her. She placed the mug on the table next to the chair and tried taking steps around the room in her high-heeled shoes. She walked aimlessly between the chair and the window several times, and then started to take strolls around the piano.

She had eaten breakfast some time ago, she had given herself enough time to dress, but she did not feel like leaving the house.

She passed to the adjoining room and sat at her mother's table.

She sat there looking at the orderliness she had imposed on top of it. Suddenly she felt that the table no longer belonged to the room. It no longer belonged to the house. It was no longer her mother's table. It was hers. Meral, the great organizer, had made it her own. The table was so well polished that she could see her face in it. But what could she see in that face? A pair of large brown eyes which could see nothing! A pair of nicely formed lips which could never say the right thing!

When her eyes fell on the parcel in front of the framed prayer, her anger towards herself subsided. As she lifted herself from the chair, she felt a weight in her arms. She had collected her grandmother's tablecloth from the table. Crackling sounds came from its wrappings as she left the house. Crackling sounds continued as she settled in the taxi and forged ahead on her beaten track to the villa once again.

When she arrived, she unlocked the door with her key by balancing the tablecloth in the crook of her arm.

The turning of the key had alerted Orhan. He appeared in the hallway as soon as she entered. His eagerness to receive her was unmarred until he noticed the parcel she carried. Her careful way of handling it confused and frightened him as if she had brought a friend with her. So instead of going up to her and greeting her, he waited for her to come closer.

"How are you feeling?" Meral asked, reaching the middle of the hall and laying the parcel down on a table. "Zeki tells me that you are feeling better."

The sound of her voice seemed to help him recover.

"I am feeling much better, thank you. In fact I am feeling extremely well." He approached and kissed her hand and then looked at her face to see if his roundabout compliment had reached its target.

"It's my grandmother's work," Meral said, coaxing his look back to the parcel by pointing at it.

After both of them had looked at it solemnly for a time, Meral started loosening the covering paper. Then she unfolded its contents and spread it out.

The tablecloth was made of white Irish linen, finely crocheted and perfectly finished. The extraordinary designs of the crocheted parts were so finely merged with the linen that you could hardly distinguish where the crocheting ended and the material started.

Meral smoothed its folds with long, hard strokes, but her touch became gentler as she continued. This tablecloth was as much a discovery to her as it was to Orhan. She looked at it intently. "Do you like it?" she asked with genuine interest. "It was given to me as a gift. I would like to give it to you as a gift."

"But why?" asked Orhan.

"Because," she said. "Because," she repeated, "I feel that its crocheted patches are woven into my life. I want to trace my life through this piece of work. And I need your help. If you agree to help me, then you must accept this gift."

"Help? From me? But of course, my dear," Orhan said with an instant glow in his eyes.

Realizing that her romanticism had fanned a hidden fire, she hastened to extinguish the flames reaching the green of his eyes. She did it by laughing at herself and at the scene she had created. "If we want to carry this fantasy a bit further," she said, "tracing a life on this tablecloth will not be so hard. Its designs are so balanced. The layout is so logical, so predictable. This tablecloth is very similar to me."

Orhan lowered his dimmed eyes onto the tablecloth.

"Balanced? Only on the surface. Logical? Predictable? Don't underestimate this work."

She begged for understanding. "I recently learned that my grandmother was Armenian," she said.

She studied his face for a reaction.

"My grandfather married her during the Marash Massacre. To save her life. Her name was Satinique."

"So this is Satinique's work," Orhan said. His voice was non-committal, and his eyes were still on the tablecloth.

"Yes. And so was my mother. She was her work. I am her work too."

He looked up. "What about the father's part?" he asked.

"They were not there. Grandfather died when my mother was six. Grandmother was thrown out of the Yali by her stepdaughter. Her stepdaughter was as old as her. Grandmother raised my mother by herself."

"What about your father?"

"He died when I was four. I don't remember him. My mother died only two years ago. She did not imprint a single notion on my life. At present my accusing finger points at my grandmother. I hold her responsible for my mother's negligence of me. I know that my opinions are very fluid these days. I know that I may switch my blame to a new, an undiscovered person, at any moment.

"But whoever I may decide to accuse, I will remain firm in my belief that I am my grandmother's work. An Armenian grandmother's work. A grandmother I do not remember. A grandmother I know very little about. But years and years after her death, this woman is able to shake my identity, my religion, the very ground I stand on. She is doing all this merely by being an Armenian."

Meral realized that her statements left no room for an answer. Orhan would not defy the facts laid in front of him, nor would he dare to offer consolation. This was a dead end. She did not know where to go from here.

"Come," said Orhan softly, and wrapped his arm around her waist. He led her into the kitchen.

On top of the counters in the kitchen were cut vegetables in separate dishes, minced meat in the mixer and some tomatoes in an open plastic bag. He directed her towards the tomatoes.

"You see these tomatoes?" he said, without removing his arm from her waist.

When he was sure that he had attracted her attention, he added something: "I bought them," was what she heard him say. She looked at him and tried to understand the simple meaning of the words.

"What did you say?" she asked, blinking her eyes intensely, as if she was listening with her eyes, and her hearing was suddenly impaired.

"I bought them," Orhan repeated, grinning. "I bought them from the corner shop."

He looked at her expecting a response. But Meral could not give it to him. The blinking eyes which had become misty now were taking their time in accepting the reality of the tomatoes sitting calmly in the bag. She wanted to say many things but her vocal chords had stopped cooperating.

"Zeki bought all the vegetables but forgot the tomatoes. I needed some tomatoes for the salad. I couldn't prepare the salad without the tomatoes."

There was no mistake. He had bought the tomatoes. And his act of unexpected courage had caught her at a vulnerable moment. And this was not fair at all. She had come to him with a load of her long dead grandmother's work, he had met her with a plastic bag full of firm fresh tomatoes.

She turned to him and buried her face on his chest. She cried on his warm flannel shirt. He encircled her with both his arms, tightening his embrace for some time with trembling arms.

At the moment, Meral was a person who had survived unbelievable dangers. She had fallen from cliffs and suffered no impairment. She had been chased by wild animals, but remained unharmed on top of high trees. She had fought with giant waves but was washed to friendly shores. She was invincible. She was jubilant. She was thinking of no one but herself. The serene thoughts which revolved around her at that moment were dervishes in white robes who were bestowing their blessings on her.

"Do you want some food?" Orhan asked, when he released her.

She nodded without looking at him. When he led her to the kitchen she stood there sideways, partly hidden by the curtain. She saw Orhan move swiftly back and forth between the stove and the dishes of vegetables and meat.

She tried to hold on to her elation, but the sizzle of the frying pan and the smell of the fried onions pulled her back into her childhood of loneliness in the dining hall of her primary school. The hall was long and narrow. The tables were veneered with matt formica. They were placed against two opposite walls. Along these walls simmered the flavors of thousands of different foods. The murky heat of that hall steamed in Meral's memory now. Meral saw two of her classmates open their food boxes. She heard them speak.

"I have chicken today. What do you have?"

"I have ladies' fingers."

"Oh, I love ladies' fingers. Put some in my dish. You can have my drumstick."

"OK. But take care. Eat it carefully."

"Why?"

"You may eat your fingers instead of ladies' fingers, that's why."

"Ha, ha, ha!"

"I'm serious, my mother does it so well that. . . ."

"My mother is a good cook too."

"Not as good as mine."

"Who says?"

"I say."

In the meantime Meral peels the wrapping of a meat pie. She quickly crumples the fancy paper which indicates where the pie was made. She stuffs the paper into her uniform's pocket, hiding the name of the Konyali restaurant.

She hopes that nobody has seen the paper.

Nobody had seen the paper. Nobody had looked at her food.

Rebellious tears ran down her cheeks as she stood by the kitchen window. Tears ran down her cheeks after almost thirty years.

Orhan kept on moving from one counter to the other mixing the remaining ingredients and adding mint and parsley leaves to his complicated dish. When everything was in the pot, he prepared a bowl of salad. He carried it to the dining room, inviting her to follow. "This salad is my speciality," he said.

Meral sat at the table and looked at the stains on the tablecloth. She also looked at the meticulously polished silver Orhan was carefully placing in front of her. When he brought in the food, she began to eat in silence.

Orhan continued the conversation he had started before, as if there had been no interruption.

"I went out of this house for the first time in ten years," he said. "I was thirty when I shut myself in. I am almost forty now."

"What is there outside?" asked Meral. Her voice was bitter, and the question was directed at herself. "You haven't missed anything."

Carried by the rhythm of the waves beating on the shore, her question echoed on the walls of the villa. The aging furniture surrounding them held its breath, declining to impart wisdom.

"I am thirty-eight years old. I was twenty-seven when I married Fahri."

"There is no similarity in our situations," said Orhan. "You are a woman of the world. You are intelligent. You are energetic. You are attractive. You have interests. I am sure you have many friends. I have nothing and nobody. Even Zeki is only tied to me by a feeling of guilt. A guilt of his own invention. I am just a heap in the corner. I was not like this before. Sometimes I cannot recognize myself.

"But today I went out to buy tomatoes. I met Miss Emel, the teacher, walking down the street."

"What? What do I hear?" chirped in Dr. Zeki's voice unexpectedly, his pink face appearing through the door. He had arrived home. "Did you say you bought tomatoes?" he asked, approaching the table and taking Meral's hand. He shook it up and down several times trying to tell her many complimentary things through his earnest pumping. But the unlucky man's timing was wrong.

Orhan turned away sharply. The damage done to the fragile moment might be irreparable, but the well-intentioned man should not be punished for his blunders. Meral came to his rescue. She found something to say. She reminded Dr. Zeki of their tentative arrangements for going to the vegetable bazaar. "When are we going to the bazaar? This Sunday?" she asked.

"As you like."

Dr. Zeki's answer came from a distance, as he had already started climbing upstairs.

He was out of sight, but the door was open. So she confirmed the arrangement by calling after him. "This Sunday, then. I'll be here at ten."

When she turned her attention back to Orhan, she saw that all the earlier liveliness had been drained out of him. He was sitting hunched in his chair. He was no longer the man who had bought the tomatoes.

"He will probably never do it again. Why would he? There are others to do it for him," thought Meral. But she did not judge herself too harshly this time. Orhan had to realize that other people also had feelings.

*

Sunday morning Meral and Dr. Zeki went to the Open Bazaar in Sariyer. As soon as they arrived, Dr. Zeki hired one of the basket-boys who stood in the shade of the stretched yards of striped linen awnings. The skinny boy he had chosen followed them cheerfully with the basket hanging down his back as they moved from one vegetable stand to the next, putting everything they bought into his basket. In the midst of all the shoppers at the bazaar, in the presence of the basket-boy, Dr. Zeki suddenly started complaining.

"Orhan is wearing my patience out these days," he said. "I know that he is suffering. I know that his suffering has a double-edge now, but sometimes. . . ."

Hoping that she could stop his untimely complaints, Meral suppressed her curiosity about the "double-edge." "I agree. He has no right to behave in this way," she said simply.

"What hurts me most is his uncaring attitude. He forgets that I too have loved. I too have suffered. Mine too was a hopeless love."

What had come over the man? Meral looked to see the whereabouts of the basket-boy, and she felt relieved to see him talking to another boy at some distance from them.

Dr. Zeki started describing the woman he had loved during his years of study in Germany. And as if this remembrance took away all his energy, he stopped walking. Meral had to stop too.

"The first time I met her was at the opera house," he said. "She was wearing a shimmering dress of light material. It had ruffles here

148

and there and yet it was so light that it was almost invisible. Inside the folds of this dress her body looked weightless. Her eyes, her skin, even her teeth looked transparent. I felt if I tried to touch her, if I tried to shake her hand, I would damage her. She was accompanied by a classmate of mine. He happened to be her husband's younger brother. I was a second-year medical student at the time."

Meral walked towards the stand of a man who was selling tomatoes. When Dr. Zeki followed her, the merchant's strong voice woke him up from his reverie. "Tomatoes, tomatoes. Tomatoes just like apples," shouted the fat red-faced merchant. He looked like a tomato—like an apple—himself. He had filled his long and wide stand with only tomatoes, and had placed his scales in their midst. Seeing Meral look at the display approvingly, Dr. Zeki gave a sign to the merchant, who filled a bag and weighed it while the other customers stood waiting. During the weighing, he stopped shouting. But as soon as he was paid, he resumed his meaningful call: "Tomatoes, tomatoes. Tomatoes, just like apples."

"Our relationship became serious after about a year, when her husband went to Geneva for a conference. Helga and I saw each other daily. When I was with her I felt lighter and graceful. I felt clever and witty."

They took a wrong turn and found themselves in the household goods section. Shiny glass vases, flowery curtains, fat velvet cushions, stainless steel forks and knives, multi-colored plastic flowers were mingled up in successive stands down the narrow passageway. People crowded in front of them, each one wanting a different item. One woman checked the size of a striped bed sheet, holding its two ends and opening her arms as wide as she could. Another woman had taken hold of a large blue vase. "How much? How much?" she asked, raising it above the heads of the surrounding people.

Led by the basket-boy they had to walk the length of that narrow road and turn another corner in order to come back to the vegetable section of the bazaar. On their way they were blocked by an aggressive fat woman who had chosen a tablecloth. She was in the process of paying for it with crumpled bunches of hundred lira bills. The merchant told her that she was wasting his time. He told her that she was keeping the other customers waiting. He talked to her in a low but steadily nagging tone of voice. The woman paid him no attention. She simply continued counting the money into his hand.

"I am sorry that she was a married woman," said Meral.

"It didn't matter that she was married," answered Dr. Zeki. "She had only been married a little over a year and they had no children to hold them together. The problem was. . . ." He stopped talking as they circled around the fat woman. "The problem was that she was not willing to leave her husband for me. She told me over and over again that she loved me, but she refused to leave her husband and marry me. I never understood what bound her to her husband so strongly."

The vegetable stands appeared around the corner once again. The first stand was filled with onions. A woman with a black scarf, holding her little son's hand tightly, approached the merchant. She spoke hesitantly. "Do you have dry onions?" she asked. "What are these things in front of your eyes, lady?" asked the merchant in a loud scornful tone. "Wet onions? Fresh onions?" The woman whispered under her breath while she walked away.

Dr. Zeki and Meral bought some onions from the rude merchant and they came out of the bazaar when the basket was almost full. "I never understood what bound her to her husband so strongly," Dr. Zeki repeated. "He seemed such an unfeeling man." This thought of his had been a pebble flung into a big lake during the foggy days of his life. The circles it created at that time had grown larger and larger as the years passed by and now the same "unfeeling man" was making him look at all human relationships with wondering eyes.

On the way back, Dr. Zeki was lost in thought and Meral was in search of a suitable subject and an appropriate tone of voice. But he shook off his mood when they arrived at the villa. He opened the iron gate and led the basket-boy in. He helped him unload the shopping at the front door and paid him.

As soon as the bags were carried to the kitchen, Dr. Zeki went to the sitting room and rolled up the cover of the bureau. He produced two volumes of the Quran from the right-hand side pigeon-hole. What they were going to do now had been previously planned like their shopping. "Let's start before Orhan comes down," he said in a conspiratorial tone of voice, handing one of the volumes to her. They were going to do the *Hatim*.* They were going to do that, with the hope that this demonstration of their devotion to God would help Orhan.

Meral covered her hair with a white scarf, and settled on the couch next to Dr. Zeki. Like two studious pupils they started reading in steady whispers. Their Qurans were written in a different alphabet. Meral's was in Arabic; Dr. Zeki's was in Turkish. But the sincerity with which the readers applied themselves to their self-imposed assignment was similar.

After hours of concentration Orhan's movements at the top of the stairs started penetrating their consciousness. They kept on reading while observing what he was doing.

He was absent-mindedly searching for a book on the shelves covering the wall along the landing. He pulled one out, but seeing Dr. Zeki and Meral sitting down below, he hurriedly hid a paper between its pages. He put the book back where it had been.

His preoccupation and his later flustered actions led Meral into a hopeful deduction: he had started writing again. The paper he hid contained the poem he was working on.

After coming to this instant conclusion, she turned her distracted eyes back to the Quran and continued reading.

Suddenly Orhan was standing over them.

"What is going on?" he asked.

Dr. Zeki quickly silenced him by putting a finger to his lips.

After a short while, Meral pointed to a place in Dr. Zeki's book. Dr. Zeki stopped reading. He closed his book and stood up.

"What is going on?" repeated Orhan. "What are you doing?"

"We are doing the *Hatim*," said Dr. Zeki in a low voice. He walked away from the couch and Orhan followed him. "I have finished my part. I read fifty verses. Meral *hanimefendi* will complete the rest. She reads faster. She's reading from the original.

"This woman is a genius," whispered Dr. Zeki. "She knows so many things."

The sound of admiration in Dr. Zeki's voice brought out an instant reaction from Orhan. "Yes, so many things," he admitted. "But

---

* **Hatim:** *Arabic word for "completion"; refers to reading the Quran from beginning to end in one sitting*

also nothing," he added, killing the admission he made with his afterthought.

Although he too had talked in a whisper all along, the tone he inserted into the words seemed to ruffle the smooth silence of the room, causing Dr. Zeki to raise his sparse eyebrows in amazement.

Meral continued with her reading, ignoring the conversation between the two men. When she finished, she closed the book with respectful care. She kissed it three times and touched it to her forehead after each kiss.

When she looked up, she met Orhan's fixed stare at her face. There was a fluttering smile on the corners of his lips. Her performance of the traditional gesture expressing obedience to the teachings of the Holy Quran seemed to have amused him somehow.

She averted her eyes from his steady look and laid the book down on the coffee table.

Orhan's awareness of the purpose of the *Hatim* was obvious now. He could not but realize that the completion of the Book at one sitting, and with such great concentration, was for him—to cure him of his fear of life and of his sustained resentment towards the living.

Although he looked pleased, although he seemed to have no objection to what was going on, Meral feared Orhan's opposition. At any moment he might ask her a blunt question. "What makes you think that I want to be saved?" he might say. But her fear was not of a spoken question. It was of a silent one.

She was afraid that he might say nothing, but keep on looking at her. The insistence of that look might seek a deeper answer. It might go down into the source of her true interest in saving him. It might be a question she would not know how to answer. Orhan kept on looking at her, holding the silent question in a secret smile.

He said nothing.

15

One morning Meral saw a strand of white hair on her head lying peacefully on the side of the parting line, and somehow connected her discovery with the noticeable improvement in Orhan's behavior. He had tamed his moods. He had become less irritable in general, and kinder to his faithful friend Zeki. He had stopped hurting Meral with his bitter comments. These changes in his attitude led Meral to believe that her occasionally interrupted but eventually resumed visits were about to reap what they had sown.

It was on the very afternoon of her arrival at this conclusion that the dark hallway of the villa saw her and Orhan exchange their first kiss.

He had come and met her there before she had the chance to slip the key back into her bag. He had come forward and put his arms around her without saying a word. First he had held her like this, steadily tightening his embrace. Then he had bent and kissed her on the mouth with the timidness of a teenager.

Just as the pleasing awareness of what had happened crept on Meral, just as an alien feeling stretched and yawned inside her, he released her. He took a backwards step, threw a frightened look on the dusty mirror above the sideboard, and kissed her hand almost apologetically.

Meral's shaky steps had steadied themselves by the time they brought her to the sitting room. As the person who had difficulty in recognizing herself settled on the armchair, and while that person pretended to be as cool as she had been when she had first arrived at the villa, the dreamlike scene insisted on repeating itself in the dark hall which was not too far from where she sat.

It took Orhan a longer time to come to terms with what his act had brought out into the open. He walked up and down passing his fingers through his hair. When he eventually stopped walking, it appeared as if he was going to speak. But he didn't. He did not sit down either. He went to the window instead. Standing there with his back turned to Meral, he looked like a schoolboy who had imposed a self-punishment on himself without waiting to be accused.

But his cooperative move was not as passive as it appeared to be. From where he stood, he watched the garden path, fiddling with the edge of the dusty lace curtain he had pushed aside.

He waited for the arrival of Dr. Zeki. He waited for the arrival of his savior.

Although Meral had no way of seeing his face, she knew that his gaze was fixed on the strategic curve of the graveled path which would present Dr. Zeki to his view. She knew that he would stay by the window until he caught sight of Dr. Zeki. She knew he would not leave the window until Dr. Zeki arrived.

It was not a long wait. After only a few minutes, he turned around triumphantly. "Zeki is coming," he announced.

*

On her arrival the next afternoon Meral learned something shocking. A disrupting force had passed through the villa wearing the silent shoes of a thief.

When a thief enters a house he usually steals money, jewelry. The thief who entered the villa stole more precious things. He stole flourishing feelings. He stole established relationships!

Meral was met with banging sounds coming from the kitchen, and on entering, she saw boards of wood on the floor, and a hammer in Dr. Zeki's hand.

"What are you doing?" she asked, baffled by the strange activity.

"I'm trying to fix these boards on the windows."

"What for?"

"Are you ready to hear the reason?" he said, mystifying her further. "I'm trying to stop the thieves from coming in again."

"Thieves? What thieves?"

"The thieves who came early this morning. To be exact at 3.30 a.m. That's when I came to the kitchen for a glass of water. But I can't be sure if there was more than one. I heard somebody or somebodies scrambling out of the window. When I entered there was no one."

"What about Orhan?" said Meral in panic, instead of asking what he did after that.

"Thank God, he was not aware of anything. And I did not tell him about it until he was well and ready. I told him after he had his breakfast. But. . . ."

"But what?" Her heart was beating fast. "Did he show a strong reaction. Was he very upset?"

"No, actually he took the news more calmly then I expected him to. But. . . ."

"But what?" repeated Meral more impatiently. Why was the man making it so hard for her? Why wasn't he giving his news in one batch?

"But what followed the theft upset him more. While I was showing him the broken window, there was a knock at the door."

"Who was it?"

"Exactly. Who was that? Who could that be? It could not be you. You had the key."

"Who was it?"

"It was Emel *hanim*. The teacher with the funny walk."

"What did she want?"

"She had been robbed. She wanted to know if we were robbed too."

"What business of hers. . . .?"

"Exactly. But some people are like that. Most people are like that."

"What did Orhan do?"

"The first thing he did was to slip out of the kitchen before I answered the door. He went up to his room as usual."

"What did you tell her?"

"That was the tricky part for me. I did some quick thinking, and decided to deny everything. I figured out that if I told the truth, she would be sure to inform the police. So I denied everything. I pretended to be surprised. I even tried to sympathize with her."

"Did she believe you?"

"I hope so. She was looking around the room suspiciously though. She was obviously trying to see if anything had been disturbed in there. But then nothing was disturbed there as the thieves did not go further than the downstairs bathroom."

Finally Meral started asking questions about the theft itself. "What did they take?"

"Nothing much really. My coming down did not give them the chance. They took my wallet. I had left it on the kitchen table. There wasn't much money in it anyway. And my identity card was at the clinic. It was needed for the post office. The messenger said he needed it for a registered letter. They took Orhan's watch from the bathroom shelf. It had been there for ages. He had stopped using it. What else? Oh, they also took a lighter. Orhan's father's lighter. Orhan kept it because once when his father was angry with him, he had flung it at him. Orhan always said that this lighter kept his father's memory fresh. He says that it has a sentimental value for him. He is being ironic about it, of course. He should say rather that it helps him justify his uncharitable thoughts towards his father."

"Is he still up in his room?"

"Yes, he is. I took his lunch up to him. He is probably having a nap. The rest will help him. I hope the teacher's intrusion will not cause a relapse. Thanks to you, he handles situations better than I thought possible."

Meral wanted to run upstairs. She wanted to hold Orhan in her arms. She wanted to promise him that she would do bodily harm to the woman if she showed up again. She wanted to suggest a new *Hatim* to Dr. Zeki. But she did not do any of these things.

*

Meral visited the villa for five successive days following the theft. Orhan had come down from his room the very next day, and on the following day he had even attempted a joke about what had happened. He said that he was grateful to the thief for stealing the lighter. He said that he must have been a kind man. All he wanted to do was to protect him from being tempted into smoking.

There probably was some truth in what he said. He might have felt grateful towards the thief for removing the reminder of unhappy days from his sight. By removing this souvenir, he might have cleared away the guilt feelings which are the constant companions of every kind of misunderstanding. But whatever his reasons were for being thankful to the thief, both Meral and Dr. Zeki were overjoyed to see that it had taken Orhan a surprisingly short time to overcome the effects of the intrusion—the intrusion of the thief and the intrusion of Emel *hanim*.

*

After spending long, pleasant afternoons with Orhan, after convincing herself that everything had returned to normal at the villa, Meral had to interrupt her visits. She had to stay at home for a day to supervise the recently hired cleaning woman.

After the general cleaning was done and the servant left, Meral took over. She started dusting. She plunged into the work as if removing the specks of dust from the scattered objects in the house were a matter of life or death.

As a girl, her mother had always discouraged her from any kind of housework. "Leave the jobs to those who know how to do them best," she had said, whenever Meral had attempted to do something in the house. Although her words were spoken in a low, hesitant voice, it made Meral feel as if making one or two beds and rinsing a few dishes required a high degree of expertise. "Ironing is hard on the legs. You have to stand on your feet so long," her mother had said whenever she saw Meral ironing a skirt or a blouse. Meral's legs were her assets. She could walk at high speed and she could swim for miles. They would have had no difficulty in supporting her slim body while she ironed one or two blouses.

By the time she was married, she had no desire left to contribute any effort towards housework. She had hired two maids and between them they had done all that was needed, including the cooking. The only joy Meral excused them from was dusting. She herself dusted every single decorative piece thoroughly, every other day.

At this present dusting session, her attention was fixed on an ebony African fertility figure. While she rubbed her cloth over it to remove every hidden speck of dust from its curves, she thought of her mother's story about the Zachariah feast. By now she had read most of her mother's stories. The only ones she had not read yet were the very short stories with uneven spaces between their lines. They looked like poems. They might have been poems.

She interrupted her dusting. She placed the figurine back on the shelf and she walked to the table still carrying the dusting cloth in her hand. She opened the box containing the short pieces and pulled out one of the single sheets.

An Unwritten Story

I will unwrite a story. I will smooth down a crumpled paper with kind fingers as I console it for its past sufferings, and I will unwrite a story on it. I will empty my brain, I will take the weight off my chest, and I will look at the undone work with pleasure. My feelings will flow into the empty paper and I'll breathe with ease while unwriting the story. The story's non-existing characters will have no undesirable characteristics. Unwanted thoughts will pester no one. Every incident will have one and only one reason.

I will unwrite a very good story. It will be a story of simplicity and truth. This story will carry no blemish of words and no suspicion of question-marks. It will be a well-defined story. It will have a beginning, a middle and an end. The beginning will prepare the middle. The middle will carry the story to the end without effort. Not having read the story, everyone will be wiser, without being older. Having unwritten the story, I will be unburdened of my regrets.

When I think about unwriting this story, I feel a glow in my heart and my fingers move in creative actions. They undo past mistakes and unroll the thread of the story into a huge ball of promise.

I will unwrite a story one of these days, and no one will attempt to admire me for it. My breast will cradle no self-doubt. I will be beyond criticism.

Absorbing all the colors of the rainbow, the story will be invisible. Ringing with laughter and shaking with tears, the story will be the thunder of silence. This story of mine will be permanently pregnant with humanity's sweat. This unwritten story of mine will be as good as anybody else's unwritten story, if not better.

Meral knew this story. She had not read it on paper, but she knew this story. The cruel silence of its words had gnawed at her childhood; it had stunted her growth. These "unwritten" words had led Meral to scratch random lines on the lives of everybody who came in contact with her.

"Orhan should read this piece," she said to herself.

As she picked up the next sheet with anticipation, the telephone rang. She assumed that the caller would be her lawyer, and prepared herself to hear the outlandish accents of his creaky voice. But the voice she heard was not his.

"Hello," the voice said, and stopped for a long time.

"Yes," said Meral. "Who is speaking?" she asked.

She did not hear a reply.

"Who is speaking?" she repeated. She was getting impatient.

"Is this a joke?" she said, ready to hang up.

"No, no," said a faraway voice. "It is not a joke."

"Who is it?" she asked again with a voice sharpened by impatience.

"This is . . . Orhan," said the voice. "It is not . . . a joke. Zeki . . . is sick." He brought out the words one by one as if he distrusted the telephone's ability to carry the true meaning of his message.

"What?" said Meral. "What is wrong with him?" She was worried.

"Just the flu, I suppose. He says . . . it is flu."

"When did the fever start?"

"Soon after lunch."

"Is it very high?"

"It's 102. He requests from you. . . ."

"Yes, yes, I'll bring the antibiotics."

"His request concerns me. He wants you to buy two vials of insulin . . . for me. I have run out of them . . . and now Zeki cannot go out."

"I see," said Meral. What she saw was one man lying helpless, and the other struggling with his helplessness. She could almost see the fear that Orhan had to overcome before he telephoned her. He must have written her number on a piece of paper first. He must have checked the telephone directory for the regular first numbers for the Asian shore and compared it with the number he had. He would then have put the paper somewhere near the telephone and referred to it before dialing each number. Suppose he mis-dialed? Suppose the sharp voice of a stranger answered him from the other shore?

She ended his ordeal by cutting the telephone conversation short. "I'll buy the medicines and come right away," she said. "I have my key. I'll let myself in. All right?" she added, before she hung up.

16

D r. Zeki was lying on the couch in front of the winding staircase. A blue satin quilt had been placed over him. It covered
every part of him except for his smooth pink face. His small eyes
were closed. His mouth was slightly open. He seemed to be enjoying
the blissful sleep of a baby.

Orhan appeared, coming from the kitchen with a glass of hot lemonade in his hand. He was holding the glass in one hand and the
plate underneath with the other hand. Seeing Meral already in the
room, his hands shook and produced a jingling sound. He tightened
his grip on the glass and the saucer and placed them successfully on
the table near the couch.

"He is sleeping," he whispered.

"So I see," said Meral, whispering in return. "How high is his
fever? I brought some antibiotics."

"Last time I took it, it was 99."

"That is not so bad," said Meral, bringing a paper bag out of her
handbag. "This is your insulin. And these are the antibiotics," she

said, removing the boxes one by one.

"Thank you," said Orhan. "We have antibiotics. I already started giving him the course. But we did not have insulin."

He looked very tired. He had not shaved and had dark rings under his eyes.

"Thank you," he said again, looking at Meral. "Would you mind very much if I left you alone for a while?" he said, replacing the boxes of medicine in the paper bag.

Meral turned her attention to Dr. Zeki still sleeping on the couch.

"I will not be alone," she said.

As Orhan turned to go, Dr. Zeki's tiny eyes cracked into slits. "Welcome, welcome," he said, and he went back to sleep again.

Orhan was taking his time in returning to the room and Dr. Zeki was sleeping more soundly now. Finally Orhan appeared. He had shaved and changed into a khaki-colored flannel shirt which flattered the elusive greenish speckles of his eyes. The black rings under his eyes were less noticeable.

Her awareness of the sense of relief that her presence created injected a multitude of contrasting feelings into Meral's heart and turned it into a battlefield. A bitter battle for recognition went on between confusion and certainty, between suspicion and confidence, between sadness and contentment. She smiled at the approaching man. She spoke not paying attention to what she said. "How do you feel now?" she whispered.

"Much better. Thank you," he said.

"Did you give yourself the injection?" asked Dr. Zeki, opening his eyes again.

"I did. I did," said Orhan irritably. "How do you feel?" he added after a moment, bending towards Dr. Zeki and laying his hand softly on his forehead.

Orhan's concern received an enthusiastic response. "I feel fine since this lady walked into the house," Dr. Zeki said. He removed his hand from under the covers as he spoke, and pointed his short fingers at Meral to emphasize what he said.

Meral led Orhan to the kitchen and instructed him on how to make a nice noodle soup. About fifteen minutes later, while she sat by Dr. Zeki, Orhan returned with three bowls of steaming vegetable soup.

Orhan helped Dr. Zeki drink his soup by supporting his head with one hand, and feeding him with the other. A part of the blue satin cover was acquiring many spots from the spilled food, but Orhan did not seem to notice this, so long as Dr. Zeki slurped his soup.

"How do you like it?" he asked, talking to Meral over his shoulder.

"Delicious, better than my noodle soup," she answered, drinking from the deep bowl. "I forgot that you are a sportsman, a poet and a cook."

"Cook? Yes. Sportsman? Poet? Not any more," he said.

"It will come. It will all come back to you."

Dr. Zeki had drunk all he wanted. Orhan carefully placed his head back on the pillow.

"Drink your soup before it gets cold," Meral said to Orhan.

Orhan was studying the spoon in his hand. When she spoke he looked up at her. Then he turned his eyes back to the spoon. Finally he dipped it into the soup bowl.

Meral sensed that his preoccupation was due to his indecisiveness. She guessed that he would have asked her to spend the night at the villa, if he could have brought himself to do it. She wanted to be ready for the question. She wanted to prepare herself for the answer. She looked at Dr. Zeki to see if he supported Orhan's wish. But his eyes had remained closed since Orhan placed his head back on the pillow.

It was at this moment that a loud knock fell on the muted words and unspoken wishes.

"Who on earth could that be?" asked Meral, taken by surprise.

The surprise froze into a deep resentment, as she could not answer her question. And the question which circled around the resentment helplessly was not free of fear—a fear which might not be dissimilar to Orhan's.

"It must be that wretched woman again," whispered Orhan between his teeth. His hands clutched the arms of the chair and his neck tightened as he spoke. His face lost its color, and it forwarded all its features to the lenses of an invisible magnifying glass. His forehead looked more prominent, his nose looked longer, his mouth looked as if it was ready to bare its teeth. There was an erratic activity in his eyes. This alert state of his, this preparedness for danger was that of a cornered animal.

When the sound of the second knock pierced the silence of the room once again, the green specks in Orhan's eyes multiplied and became dangerous-looking spears. They seemed ready to send their poison into Meral's blood without informing her of the source of her guilt.

Orhan pushed himself up. Why had he stood up? Why did he look at Meral that way? What was he going to do? Was he going to answer the door? Was he going to send the caller away? The tight-lipped, unpredictable moment could burst into any kind of revelation. Any daring, nasty, unfair act could be expected of him. But all he did was plead. "Please don't let anyone in," he said, softening his sharpened features. He turned his back and walked to his habitat, up the stairs.

Meral went to the window. When she pushed the dusty net slightly aside, her look caught a uniformed policeman conferring lengthily with his wristwatch. With his hand settled on the knocker, and his eyes keeping their anxious look on his upheld wrist, the young man looked like an inexperienced doctor trying to take the pulse of a patient for the first time.

So Emel *hanim* had not been convinced by Dr. Zeki's denials. The answers following his "quick thinking" had had no effect on her. Having guessed that the thieves who had entered her house would not have spared this villa, she had lost no time in informing the police on behalf of the villa's dwellers. Or had the policeman acted on his own initiative? It did not matter what had brought the policeman to the villa door. It was of no importance to know what had inflamed the situation. What was important now was to find a solution and to put out the fire. Somebody had to act. One could not simply ignore a police officer.

She walked to the door as quietly as she could and led the policeman to the room from where she had come.

"He is sick," she whispered, pointing at Dr. Zeki who continued with his deep, open-mouthed sleep.

When the policeman nodded quickly, indicating that he understood the situation, Meral relaxed. The information she had volunteered regarding the obvious state of the man on the couch was accepted as a sufficient reason for having the investigation conducted in a low tone of voice. The policeman would not envisage another, a more subtle reason for the suggested precaution.

"I'm sorry to disturb you at this late hour," he started politely. "But your neighbor lady called the station several times this past week. She told us that the thieves who stole her valuables had entered here as well."

"She is mistaken," said Meral, trying to sound as convincing as she could. "No thieves came in here."

"Is that a fact?" said the policeman, fixing Meral with a professional look which bent towards disbelief.

"What reason do you have to doubt me, officer?" said Meral in an indignant voice. "Why would I hide it from you if there had been a theft? Do you suspect that I'm a collaborator?"

"No, my lady, no. Please don't be upset. I'm simply surprised. I'm surprised because the lady teacher was not the only one who was robbed. The thieves broke into the villa on the other side of yours as well. I simply wondered why they had spared yours?"

Meral decided not to correct the police officer's assumption of her being one of the villa's residents, but simply offered a theory: "Perhaps it's the neglected condition of the garden," she said, realizing immediately that neglected places would be particularly favored by thieves.

But the policeman said nothing to contradict her. Instead he began a question directed towards the reason for the state of the garden. "Why is it so. . . .?" he began, but left his sentence incomplete.

His next question was an expected one. "Have you heard anything? Did you see any suspicious-looking people around?" he asked.

"As you will appreciate from the position of the house, the only view of the street is from the upstairs windows. I hardly have time to go up there these days. I'm busy looking after. . . ."

She could not elaborate on her consciously misleading answer which supported the policeman's assumption that she resided in the villa. She could not do it because she did not know how to affiliate herself with the sick man. She could not bring herself to say "my husband," and to say "my brother" did not occur to her, as she did not have a brother.

"I understand," said the policeman, standing up. "I'm sorry for asking you all these questions, but I'm sure you realize that I have to do my duty."

The officer's closing lines cheered Meral up. She stood up promptly to see him to the door. "Please don't apologize. It's been rewarding to learn that we are looked after so well by the authorities. Thank you for coming, officer," she said.

She returned to the room with a sigh of relief. She was thankful that Orhan had remained away during the officer's stay. But as time went by, and he still did not appear, she started wondering what she should do. Should she go and knock at his bedroom door? Or should she simply stay where she was?

Dr. Zeki solved her dilemma. He woke up and said, "Where is Orhan?"

"He's up in his room," answered Meral.

"How rude of him," he said. "Please go and call him. Tell him that I want to see him."

"Do you need something? Can I do anything for you?"

"I want to see Orhan," he repeated firmly.

Meral climbed up and knocked at Orhan's door. A lazy answer oozed out after a few moments. "Yes?"

"The caller went away; Zeki wants you," she said, attaching the two pieces of information to each other.

Her condensed way of giving the news would not allow Orhan to understand who the caller had been and whether he had been admitted into the house or not. The elimination of the detail would protect him from further anguish.

Orhan did not lose much time in coming down, and found Meral sitting in the same chair in which he had left her earlier.

"Zeki insisted on seeing you," said Meral in a defensive tone of voice, as just before Orhan arrived, the sick man had returned to his sleep.

Now that Dr. Zeki was asleep and there was no one else to back her up, she felt quite helpless and that caused her words to sound like those of a wilfully untruthful child. As Orhan remained silent, her need to be believed became so strong that she almost considered shaking the sick man into wakefulness.

166

Finally Orhan spoke. "What did he want?" he said, talking slowly. He inspected the room by turning his eyes around it. He was making sure that no drastic changes had happened in the familiar surroundings since the knocking at the door had taken place.

"I don't know. He wouldn't tell me," said Meral.

"It can't be that important, if he fell back to sleep."

He stayed on his feet and did not even look at Dr. Zeki, after the first glance he gave him. He did not look at Meral either. He seemed to be trying to find an easy way of escaping from the presence of the two people, and retiring to his room.

But Dr. Zeki opened his eyes, and mumbled, "Why did you leave Meral *hanimefendi* alone? How could you leave her alone?" he said. As soon as he spoke his mumbled words, he closed his eyes again.

It was obvious now that Dr. Zeki had called him back to the room to give him one of his rare scoldings.

Orhan fixed his gaze on him for a while without saying a word, then he started talking in a low but an unusually excited voice. "Suppose his fever goes up. Suppose a doctor will be needed. Zeki has never been sick. I don't know what to do. I don't know what on earth to do!"

He followed what he said by some unexpressive movements. He raised an arm and turned it a little to the right and a little to the left, then lowered it. He raised the other one. He lowered it too, without trying a new gesture with it.

"Do you want me to stay?" asked Meral. She had to make the first move.

Orhan's spirits were revived at once. But his indecisiveness had tired him so much that he looked as if he had been the one with fever and had now returned to normal. "I'll prepare the guest bedroom upstairs," he said, running up the stairs in no time.

He went in such haste that Meral was not sure if he heard her objection. "I don't need a room. I'll curl up on this armchair. I prefer to stay close to Zeki," she said.

17

"Where is Orhan?" asked Zeki the next morning. His small eyes blinked as if he were trying to remember the hands which lifted his head up and helped him drink his hot lemonade, the hands which gave him the tablets.

"He is resting in his room," said Meral, touching his forehead. "Your fever is down."

"Have you been taking turns?"

"Orhan was down here many times. He is the one who made the lemonade."

"Where did you sleep?"

"Right here," Meral said, pointing at the armchair near the couch which had a folded blanket on its back. "Orhan brought me a blanket."

"Poor kind lady! Poor great-hearted lady! How can I ever repay you?"

"What are you saying, Zeki? Aren't we friends?"

Orhan came down looking fresh in an open-necked white shirt with

168

wavy stripes of green running down its front. He smiled and disappeared to the kitchen, reappearing after ten minutes with a folded napkin on his forearm.

"Good morning, Madame, good morning, Sir," he said, turning his face from one to the other. "What would you like to have for breakfast this morning?" he continued, enjoying his waiter's role. "May I recommend a couple of poached eggs, some black olives and a few slices of our special white cheese? Would you fancy a sip of orange juice before having your coffees? Or would you rather have tea?"

Dr. Zeki laughed heartily at his friend's clowning. Meral smiled with pleasure.

"Would you please bring me just a cup of coffee, *garçon bey*," she said, keeping the game going.

"Only a cup of coffee, Madame?"

"Yes. Just a cup of coffee. And after that Madame will take her leave. She'll go home."

"But why?" cried the two men in chorus.

"Because your fever is down," she said, looking at Dr. Zeki. "Because your waiter is willing and able to do anything for you," she said, looking at Orhan. "And because I'm a little tired. I need some rest." She looked at both men as she spoke, turning her head from one to the other so as to obtain both their permissions.

"Can't you rest here?" asked Dr. Zeki.

"I'd rather go home, if you permit me," Meral said, searching their faces once again.

*

Meral had paid so many visits to the villa during and following Dr. Zeki's illness that it felt as though a long time had passed since the shopping trip to the Open Bazaar of Sariyer. But when one afternoon they arranged to repeat it, she was amazed to realize that they had missed only one Sunday.

That Sunday of their second shopping trip turned out to be one of those unusually hot September days. They came back to the villa loaded with food and flushed from their walk.

Dr. Zeki called Orhan to the kitchen. "Orhan, come and see what we got," he said. "Come and see the strange vegetable we have brought."

Orhan was not in the mood to obey. He stayed standing in the middle of the salon and looked at Meral following Dr. Zeki to the kitchen with a lively walk.

While Orhan seemed to be getting ready to ask what Dr. Zeki was talking about, Meral looked back and gave him a smile.

Her smile seemed to prompt action. Orhan entered the kitchen with steps tamed into performing aimless strolls. He looked at Dr. Zeki with a bored expression on his face. "What have you got?" he said.

"Tell him what we got," said Dr. Zeki to Meral playfully.

"We got 'wet onions.' 'Wet onions' are what we got, dear sir," she said cheerfully.

"We met the same onion seller of the other week and we bought some 'wet onions' from him," Dr. Zeki chuckled.

Orhan knew nothing about the onion seller of the other week.

"What are these wet onions?" he asked.

"Fresh onions. Didn't you know that?" said Meral, raising her eyebrows in mock amazement.

Orhan left the kitchen as slowly as he had come in.

"Next Monday is Orhan's birthday," Dr. Zeki said in a sober voice.

Although Orhan's silent exit had disturbed her, Meral tried to prevent their happy mood from slipping away by clinging to their previous tone of conversation.

"Good," she said. "We'll buy him something next Sunday from the bazaar."

Dr. Zeki listened to her mischievous suggestion with a tolerant smile. He was the patient father; Meral was the delinquent child.

"Silly of me," she went on quickly, "what could we buy for him from the bazaar. A pair of rubber boots? A jar of black olives?"

"We could go to Beyoglu on Saturday," said Dr. Zeki. "We could buy him a briefcase."

"Briefcase? What for? I'd rather buy him an illuminated Quran. We could find that at the Covered Market.

"Our *Hatim* did not help him," she continued, feeling her happy mood deserting her. "Perhaps if he reads his own *Hatim*. . . ."

Dr. Zeki contradicted her. "Our *Hatim* did help him," he said.

170

"You helped him more than you know," he added seriously. "I'll be through by twelve on Saturday."

"All right," said Meral, "I'll meet you in Faith Square, near the arch of the university's entrance. That will be a good meeting place for going to the Covered Market. I'll find myself a bench and feed the pigeons. I can just picture myself there. A lady with nothing to do."

"We can have lunch at the Covered Market's tourist restaurant," said Dr. Zeki.

"We can sit at the barrel-tables among the foreign crowd and have a cold *ayran** later on," said Meral.

While they made their plans they waited for Orhan's approaching footsteps. But he did not return.

*

Meral's taxi could not make it all the way to the Arch. So she had to cut her way through the crowds of people who rushed at the *dolmus*†️ cars and at the numerous buses which arrived and took off unexpectedly. When she emerged from this feverish life which had enfolded her completely, and looked in the direction of the university, she saw Dr. Zeki. He stood under the Arch like a stocky lighthouse and turned his round face from side to side.

"Hello," she said, appearing from his blind side.

"Oh," he said turning, "here you are. We should have chosen a weekday to come here. Look at all these people. My goodness, how are we going to shop?"

"There won't be so many people in Sahaflar. Who wants old books these days?"

"You are right," he said, relieved.

They walked towards the iron gate of the Covered Market. Cars whizzed both ways even on that narrow street lined with shops selling chrome pots and pans, huge iron scales and horse saddles. The

---

* **ayran:** *refreshing cold drink made from yogurt*
†️ **dolmus:** *Turkish for "full up"; refers to taxis on set route that pick up as many passengers as will fit, with each paying according to the distance traveled*

171

pick-ups tried to empty the goods they carried on corners and the porters who carried loads of gigantic proportions on their backs staggered over narrow sidewalks.

Meral and Dr. Zeki joined the faltering stream of people until they passed through the open gate. Once they entered, there was peace. There was the musty coolness which smelled of time. The people moved under the domed ceilings with serenity.

They walked straight to Bedesten Street. "Let's look at the antique shops first," said Meral. "Do you think buying him a Quran is a good idea? I'm not sure. I'll keep my options open. Who knows? We might land on an old book of poetry. That would please our poet, don't you think?"

"Anything you say," said Dr. Zeki. He was dazed by the change of scenery. Meral wondered how long it had been since his steps had led him anywhere besides the clinic and the food markets.

They did not stay long at Bedesten. For a little while Meral was fascinated with the filigree silver daggers in a small shop's dusty window, but she soon recovered from the distraction. "If I do not control myself, I may add another useless object to my mother's collection," she said.

They came out of the Bedesten and walked on the main street of the Covered Market. They passed between the dazzling windows of silver and gold shops, they glanced at the fur-lined leather coats and jackets, they rested their eyes on the heaped frilly beddings on the brass beds.

They came to the shady openness of Sahaflar by climbing up and then down again the stone steps of the market mosque.

Meral pointed out a shop at one of the four corners of the square yard. "I know the owner of this shop," she said, walking towards it. But seeing several people inside browsing through the books, she changed her mind. "He is a quarrelsome man anyway. Let's look at his neighbor's shop first," she said, passing it by.

They entered the shop on the right. The owner seemed to be a religious man. He hardly looked at Meral. His attention was fixed on the male customer.

"A Quran. We want a Quran," said Dr. Zeki.

"An old one," completed Meral.

"An old one," repeated the religious man, still keeping his eyes averted from her. He went to the shelves next to his desk, and came back with a volume.

"This is not a Quran," he said to Meral, as she opened the book and looked inside, "but it is a holy book."

"So I see," said Meral, and started reading aloud from the first page. The book was written in Ottoman Turkish.

The shopkeeper looked at her now. He looked at her open-necked sport blouse, he looked at her tight skirt, he looked at her hair, which was pulled behind her ears. Then turning his eyes away, he started searching for her kind in the pigeon-holes of his mind. She was nowhere to be found. This woman was not among his categorized customers. "Perhaps he should reorganize the holes. Perhaps he should allocate a special pigeon-hole for me," thought Meral. But she quickly relieved the man of his confusion. "I studied Ottoman literature," she said. "This book seems to be interesting," she added, turning its pages back and forth.

The man could talk to her now. "There are some sections in it which give formulas for herbal medicines," he volunteered, in praise of the book.

"So it does," said Meral, continuing to flip its pages. "I can almost understand it. I would understand it better if I had my dictionary with me," she said. "How much?"

The shopkeeper looked at Dr. Zeki once again.

Dr. Zeki said, "Let this be my present. You buy him something else."

Meral realized that this was her cue to leave the two men to do their bargaining. She left the shop.

When Dr. Zeki came out with the wrapped-up book under his arm, she was about to enter the larger shop. The browsing people had left it, and the shopkeeper looked directly at them from behind his desk.

"Good afternoon," said Meral in a polite voice. "May we trouble you to find us some old books. Poetry perhaps. An illuminated prayer book?"

"Since you have no idea of what you want," said the man, as if she had counted dozens of different items, "I would say, buy a *sinirname*."*

---

* sinirname: *property deed*

173

He threw a sour look at Meral as he walked to the opposite corner of the shop. The look at once demanded an apology for her disturbance and expected submission to his suggestion. If she did not agree to buy the very first thing he offered her, she was going to be in trouble.

Meral remained unruffled and partially amused. She had been to many shops like this. She had met many shopkeepers like him. He started to unroll the document as he walked back from the far end of the shelf. The exquisite writing on the partly opened roll shone even in the dark distance of the shop.

When he handed it over, Meral unrolled it completely. It was endlessly long. It would hang so well on Orhan's sitting-room wall with its high ceiling.

The document was dated December 1546; and it was graced by the *tugra** of Suleyman the Magnificent. The design of the Sultan's signature was formal but elaborate. Its line swung twice to the right, shot arrows above its bulging middle and rained down gracefully over the document. The inside of the middle part of the signature was filled with stylized flowers. The circling lines were drawn in cobalt blue and outlined with gold. The text was a detailed account of the boundaries of a village which belonged to the Grand Vezir of the time. It read: "Most noble minister, most honored counselor, source of good order in the world, administrator of the affairs of all mankind with penetrating thinking. . . ."

Meral reached for her purse inside her bag. "How much?" she asked, while the man was preparing his speech about the document.

*

The successful shoppers walked to the tourist restaurant. They deserved their meal, they deserved their rest. But Dr. Zeki was not very cheerful.

"Ten years," he said, as they sat at the corner table with its white and red checkered tablecloth. "It is going to be ten years." He looked

---

*tugra: *ornamental monogram or seal of an Ottoman Emperor*

tired. "It was on his thirtieth birthday that Orhan gave up the world. An accident similar to the one you had was used as an excuse. He claimed that his toe hurt him a lot. He 'had to stay at home for a few days,' he said. A few days!"

"Do you mind?" said Meral. "Do you think you could tell me more?"

Dr. Zeki looked like a stranger without the usual highlight of cheer in his face.

"Perhaps another time," Meral said.

But she saw him nodding his head to her question, and ignoring her retreat. He spoke in an even voice as if under hypnosis.

"I certainly could. And I will. I think you are entitled to know. I do not know how much or how little he told you. Whatever he told you, it is not enough. There are aspects of this situation he doesn't know. My sister, Orhan's wife, was a pampered girl. Her every wish was a command for all of us, my mother, my father and I. As children, we never finished a game without her shedding tears at one stage or another and spoiling the game. She could not study—reading hurt her eyes. The eye specialist found nothing wrong with her eyes. She often had a mysterious pain in her stomach. She'd clutch her stomach with both hands, all of a sudden, and start moaning. I wouldn't say she was pretending. Yet when our family doctor Hikmet came over and listened to her complaint, the only medicine he prescribed was iron tablets. He prescribed iron tablets every time. Not being a doctor myself at the time, I didn't think much about it. Perhaps the doctor did not know what to do about the stomach pains so he gave her the iron tablets. On the other hand she might have been anemic. She was always tired. I never saw her get a glass of water for herself. She always called to our old nanny. '*Abla*, get me a glass of water, quick. I am dying of thirst,' she would shout, and poor nanny would run to her rescue with her old, shaky legs.

"I knew more about my sister than anyone else in our family. I should have warned Orhan that he was getting involved with a neurotic. She was not fit to be his wife—she was not fit to be anybody's wife. And Orhan was my dear, dear friend. I should have warned him. What happened to my sister after they married was no fault of his. I saw what was coming long before Orhan fell in love with her, long before they were engaged."

"What would you like to have?" asked a young waiter appearing at their side.

His ostentatious outfit shone momentarily through the gray clouds of the past. He carried an imitation dagger inside the diagonally striped purple material that held his yellow shirt in place over the rich folds of his black baggy trousers.

Instead of handing out the menu, he held it tightly in his hand and smiled. He was trying to take a shortcut to receiving the order of these two local people. After all they must know the dishes this kind of restaurant offered.

Succeeding in his effort, he yelled their order to the chef. "Two salads and two stuffed eggplants!" Then he swung towards the opposite side of the restaurant sprinkling his red-lipped smile all around. He approached the two Englishmen who had been trying to attract his attention for some time.

"What happened was that," continued Dr. Zeki, "a year after Orhan went to college in Germany, he changed his mind about marrying Nevin. He wanted to break off his engagement to her. The reason for his decision was her behavior towards him during his mid-year holiday in Istanbul. After their engagement, Nevin had started to treat him in a very offhand manner. When our friends were around, she acted as if she preferred other young men to Orhan. The treatment he received broke Orhan's heart. He was very much in love with her.

"Everything went haywire when Orhan expressed his intention of breaking off the engagement in a letter to his father. He received a harsh reply. His father ordered him to keep quiet and forget about his silly intention. When this letter reached Orhan's hand, this time he wrote to my father. My father wanted to break the news to my sister, but he did not know how to manage this. He did not dare to ask my mother's help.

"I don't know exactly what happened. I have no idea how Nevin learned about it. I have no idea in what way she was told about it. I was in Germany at the time, and I had my own problems. One thing I learned was, a new specialist had become part of our family. He was a psychiatrist. This psychiatrist was there to help Nevin. But he helped himself, rather than helping Nevin's condition. He helped himself to my motor-boat for water skiing. He helped himself to our courts for games of tennis with his friends. He used his connection with our family for his advancement.

"News of Nevin's state caught up with Orhan's life in Germany in no time. He was bombarded with insulting letters from his father for not having obeyed his orders. His father was particularly angry with him for revealing his intention of breaking off the engagement to our family. He forced him to remedy the situation. He ordered him to deny everything. I remember Orhan writing a poem to Nevin saying something about finding sparkles among the ashes of their love. Even the poem was not up to his usual standards. Even the quality of the poem confessed to there being no sparkles to kindle the old love. But since Orhan was obliged to go on with the marriage, his search for sparkles was a consolation—a consolation for himself and for Nevin. And that was the last poem Orhan wrote.

"There was an element of chivalry in his young love for Nevin. It was her beauty which had captivated him, but it was her helplessness which held him. Nevin was a failure in everything. In school, she was below average. At home, she was despised by our academic mother for her inability to concentrate. Mother pampered her—it is true—like the rest of us did. But she could not hide her low opinion of her daughter. Nevin openly resented our mother's absorption with my progress at school. She resented mother's reaction when she read the headmaster's congratulatory letters about my work at school. My mother had these letters framed as soon as they arrived and hung them in her study. She encouraged father to go in there and admire the visual proofs of my success."

Suddenly Dr. Zeki's eyes were misty. "My mother . . ." he said after a silence. "My mother who used to be so proud of me then, hardly speaks to me nowadays. We meet once a month. I go and visit her in Ortakoy. But this is only an established ritual since my father's death five years ago. During my visits she hardly looks at my face. And it's only because . . . of my 'shameless behavior,' as she puts it. Because of my 'living under the same roof as the heartless man who destroyed my sister's life.'"

He covered the tracks of his involuntary digression with a deep sigh, and returned to his original subject by saying "Anyway," and exchanging the picture of his mother for his father.

"My father was the kind of man who listened to nothing but the dictates of his heart. He was as little concerned with my success as he was with Nevin's failure.

"He loved her dearly. 'My lovely daughter,' he said. 'My lovely daughter with tender eyes.'

"During her childhood, he confided his firm belief to her: 'You are going to be irresistible,' he said. According to father, when Nevin grew up, there were going to be many men who would be willing to walk over fire for her. He was right, there have been many young men to do just that. But at the end only one man got burned: Orhan."

The waiter appeared carrying a plate of salad in each hand. He placed them on the table with a flourish, leaving immediately.

Dr. Zeki studied the long rectangular dishes covered from corner to corner by two orderly rows of sliced cucumbers.

"Orhan came back from Germany during his second year's summer vacation and married Nevin. They lived with his family for three months and then Orhan returned to college. My family did not allow Nevin to go to Germany with him because of her delicate condition. She returned back home."

He stopped and considered what he had said.

The waiter appeared once again carrying the drinks and the large plates containing the stuffed eggplants capped with halved tomatoes. He removed the plates, first placing them carefully on the table while he balanced the glasses of *ayran* on the upheld tray.

"If you ask me," continued Dr. Zeki, not noticing that the waiter was still within earshot. The golden tassels of the attentive young man's cummerbund whipped him as he turned around hastily and then turned back again realizing that he was not the one being addressed. "If you ask me," Dr. Zeki repeated, "theirs was a strange kind of marriage. During the first three years of their marriage, they saw each other only for short periods of time. Towards the end of Orhan's last semester at college, Nevin had a miscarriage. The doctors advised her not to try again.

"When he completed his studies, through his father's influence, Orhan found a job in the Ziraat Bank. He started searching for a house to rent. His father wouldn't hear of it. He gave Orhan the family summer house, the house we live in now. Then the furniture started to arrive. There came some new pieces from stores and there were some antique pieces from his father's house. It was Orhan who told the porters where to place them. Nevin did not take any part in arranging the house. She stayed in her bedroom and read magazines. Sometimes she lay down, sometimes she sat by the window and looked at the sea. She took a lot of tablets prescribed to her by different doctors. And she nursed her old stomach ache faithfully. Her hands felt dry all the time. She had quite a collection of hand-creams from all over the world. She said that her skin would stretch and hurt her. She learned about these creams from the foreign magazines she leafed through constantly. Orhan had to find out the companies' addresses and order them. Once she asked for something it had to be done. There was no way of getting out of it. It had to be done immediately.

"'Orhan do something,' she would call, all of a sudden. 'It's my hands again. They are dry. They are stretching. They'll crack.'

"Orhan would rush to her with one of the cream jars. She would say, 'Not that one. The white jar.' Orhan would bring a white jar. She would send it back again, 'Not that one. The bigger one next to it. Quick. My skin is going to burst.'

"Then she would ask for a tablespoon of the stomach medicine. She had acquired a stomach medicine prepared by a quack. She believed in that medicine more than the other medicines prescribed to her by the doctors. The concoction was kept in a big bottle and its color alternated between pale pink and shocking pink. The medicine in each new bottle was of a different shade that the previous one. The quack could not even keep the color of the medicine consistent.

"She had become less manageable since she had come to live with Orhan on a permanent basis. In spite of the advice of her doctor, she became pregnant again. And while losing the baby she endangered her life. She blamed Orhan for all that happened. She claimed she had got rid of the baby on purpose, because Orhan did not want them to have a baby. But the truth was that her body was not made to carry a baby. She had three hemorrhages during the three months of her pregnancy. The baby had been lost before she did anything.

179

The purpose of going through the motions of inducing an abortion was to hurt Orhan. And she succeeded. She succeeded thoroughly! All these years, I could not convince Orhan that it was not his fault. He wouldn't believe it. And I . . . I couldn't believe my own opinion. Even if I had told Orhan more about my sister, it wouldn't have changed anything. Even if I had spoken to him about my sister's psychological situation before he fell in love with her, before he got engaged to her, if I had warned him not to have anything to do with her, it wouldn't have stopped him from writing her poems and idolizing her. My sister was an extremely beautiful girl."

Meral thought these were the closing lines of his account, but she was mistaken. He continued.

"A few months after her second miscarriage Nevin claimed she was pregnant again. Examinations showed negative results. She was told that she was mistaken. But she insisted that she was pregnant. She pretended to be pregnant. Orhan went along with the game. Anything to keep her quiet. Anything not to see her tears, or to hear her constant complaints and accusations. He even bought her maternity clothes. 'I have a very small baby inside, but the doctor says I gained ten pounds,' she said. The doctor was an imaginary one.

"One day she announced that her pregnancy was coming to its end and she was ready to deliver. 'Call my doctor. Take me to the hospital,' she said, taking spoonfuls of her pink medicine.

"Orhan was not ready to carry the game to that stage. He refused to take her to the hospital. He did not know the name nor the address of the imaginary doctor, so he could not call him either.

"I was there. I saw all that happened. 'You are a heartless man. You hate me. You want me to die,' she shouted at him.

" 'I will deliver your baby,' I said.

" 'You are not a specialist. What do you know about delivering babies?' she replied.

"She threw herself on the floor and her sick mind simulated the whole scene of a delivery. Orhan and I carried her to bed with great difficulty. She was hitting, kicking, biting.

" 'It's coming,' she said. She gave out several piercing shouts, clutching her stomach. 'The baby is coming,' she cried. 'But she is dead.' Tears rolled down her cheeks.

" 'You killed my baby,' she said to Orhan. 'You did nothing for me and for my baby. You did not take me to the hospital. You did not call my doctor. She was a girl. A beautiful girl with tender eyes. She was a loving girl.'

"It was a horrible scene. I looked at Orhan and saw him drown in misery. Nevin had taken leave of the reality of life, and had dragged Orhan along with her.

"After she was taken to the nursing home, he visited her regularly. He took her flowers and candies. But in return he only received insulting remarks from her. She even claimed that he had injected poison into the candies.

"Eventually he stopped visiting her. And soon after that he quit his job. He stopped going out. The last thing he did was to send away the parlor maid, the downstairs maid, the cook and the gardener. I hated to see him do all this to himself. But I couldn't help him by talking. The only thing I could do was to come and live with him. At least I could keep him company. I flatter myself that Orhan is alive today because of me. That is, if you could call him 'alive.' "

He continued in a quieter voice. He was afraid that the elderly couple and their crippled son who sat at the next table had heard his comment about being "alive." The boy's crutches were propped on the wall; the father's face expressed no sign of life.

"Everything changed after you came along, Meral *hanimefendi*," he said. "I can say that you have given him more life in the last three months than I was able to give him in the past ten years."

Meral looked at the two parcels on the chair drawn close to the table. One was a cylindrical tube in blue paper patterned with silver stars, the other was a flat rectangular package in green and gold striped paper. The parcels looked small and insignificant. They looked sad in their gaudy wrappings. Would these birthday gifts mark a new turning point? Or would they remind Orhan of the last ten years. Ten years of wasted life, and perhaps many more to follow.

18

The next day, on the day of his birthday, while the three friends sat at the table laden with cakes and cookies, Orhan fired a sky-rocket. The virile rocket went up to the sky with incredible speed and reached staggering heights in no time. Then it rained down on Meral in a million colors.

"Meral *hanimefendi*," he said in a calm voice, "are you free tomorrow? May I invite you to the Leziz Restaurant for lunch?"

Meral's hand, which was about to pass the cake-knife to Orhan, froze in the air. The coquettish flickerings of the birthday cake's candles became solidified columns of light. The unwrapped prayer book and the unrolled *sinirname* interrupted their continuous mutterings.

After the colors had returned to normal, after Meral's hand had passed the knife to Orhan, after Orhan had sliced the cake, something broke loose in her. Feelings of helplessness and feelings of violence rushed together to her chest.

She wanted to hurt the man for the uncertainties his ever-changing moods caused her to suffer. She wanted to hurt him physically.

CAGES ON OPPOSITE SHORES

She wanted to punish him for playing with her emotions—yes, emotions—and her self-confidence.

The next moment she wanted to cry. She wanted to cry because she felt tired. Extremely tired. Her arms were tired. Her legs were tired. Her eyes, her hair, her quivering lips were tired. She felt she was being pulled down to the ground. She felt she was doubling up in the chair. Why didn't he reach out and hold her up? Why didn't he embrace her? It didn't matter that Dr. Zeki was in the room. Nothing mattered. Why didn't he pull her head to his chest and gently stroke her hair? Why didn't he tell her to cry? To cry, to cry, to scream her joy?

*

It has always been the responsibility of Time to turn the future into the present. Meral wanted the gift of tomorrow. She wanted to have tomorrow. She wanted to have it and to have it to her liking.

Time granted her wish. He made her a gift of tomorrow, and he formed it to her heart's delight. She did not need to change a thing about it.

As Meral approached the villa, she saw Orhan standing just outside the door waiting for her. He seemed ready and eager for the day. He seemed unaware that his hair was being tossed aside by a thoughtless breeze and that the criss-cross lines of his tightened forehead had appeared. Suddenly the man Meral had seen from the distance dissolved inside the navy blue blazer he wore and the silk scarf he had skillfully wrapped around his neck.

Almost immediately after they greeted each other, the taxi arrived. The two of them walked down the garden path listening to the crunchy sound of the gravel under their feet.

Orhan held open the taxi door for Meral. She entered and slid across the seat. He entered and touched the breast pocket of his jacket. The ride to the restaurant took only a few minutes. When the taxi stopped, Orhan took out some money from the pocket he had kept touching on the way, and bent down to read the meter. He bent again as his trembling hands sorted out the fare. After doing all that he came out but remained beside the taxi cab until it pulled away.

He watched it as if this four-wheeled vehicle which had carried them from one spot to the other was the most remarkable thing he had seen in his life.

Meral was already at the restaurant door. When he finally walked towards her, she turned and gave him an encouraging smile.

But the smile she gave him did not take away the anxiety she herself felt. She could not imagine Orhan sitting in a crowded restaurant. She could not imagine him talking to a waiter.

When they went inside her anxiety subsided considerably. Not many of the spacious restaurant's tables were occupied. And the waiter who came to meet them was a quiet man.

He said simply, "Welcome," and led them inside. At the end of the hall, Meral saw a glazed veranda with a few tables in it. The veranda was partly separated from the main hall by a wall with decorative iron netting, and was given privacy by the large leaves of several climbing plants.

"We would like to sit in there, if a free table is available," Meral said to the waiter.

"There is going to be one," said the waiter, seating them temporarily at a table near the separation wall.

While they waited, a middle-aged woman wearing heavy makeup and a tall young man came out and passed them by, hardly noticing Meral and Orhan.

The waiter had disappeared in the meantime. But he came back after a short time with an assistant, and together they cleaned up the table the couple had left. They carried away the used dishes, and laid a fresh tablecloth on it.

When the table was set, the waiter appraised the finished work before letting his assistant leave. Then he came over and invited Meral and Orhan to the table with a wide gesture of his arm. Meral saw the people at the next table preparing themselves to leave as well. A dark man accompanied by an attractive wife and a lively boy of six or seven stood up and said "thank you," to the waiter, pointing at the plate which contained the folder with the check. Seeing the big tip on top of the folder, the waiter bowed deeply to the departing customer and collected the plate promptly. The boy held his father's hand and said, "When will we come here again, when?" The mother inspected Meral's clothes and accessories, assessing her degree of success in combining them, as she followed the two.

The only table which remained occupied was the corner one where two businessmen sat with their briefcases on the chairs pulled next to them. Both were fairly young, both were mustachioed and they were involved in a deep discussion. Although their voices were kept low, the discussion they were having was highly animated. They moved their hands and arms all the time, and even smacked the table occasionally.

Meral's high spirits placed her in competition with these two men. Her talk was almost as animated as theirs. "Isn't ours the best table? Doesn't it give us a marvelous view? Don't you love being so close to the sea? Don't you feel its ever-moving molecules renew your life? Doesn't everything about the sea energize you?" she bubbled, burrowing deeper and deeper into her love of the sea.

She did not mind being obscure. She did not mind sounding pseudo-scientific. She would not have minded if Orhan considered her childish. She was talking for herself, of herself. What she said was free of all concerns.

She had even stopped paying attention to Orhan's way of sitting, which had attracted her attention at the beginning. He had started by being preoccupied with the position of his hands the minute he had sat down. He had placed them on the table several times and then pulled them back quickly, as if the tablecloth burned them. He had slumped on his chair, going deeper and deeper, then had straightened up as if a marrionetteer had tightened the strings attached to his shoulder blades. On one occasion he had straightened up so much that Meral had feared his being pulled up and away from his chair.

It was when she forgot to pay attention to the way he sat, and simply went on and on with her happy talk, that she noticed her strange effect on him. He seemed to be slightly intoxicated by the bubbles in her voice. He looked at her steadily, but blinked his eyes softly each time she turned her look on him. It seemed that a force stronger than his will held his look on hers, it seemed as if the force kept his look there in spite of his better judgement.

"We are going to enjoy our lunch, aren't we?" Meral said diffidently. He had to provide her with some material to help her in protecting the fragile gift the day had presented to her. He had to help her in wrapping it up. She needed a piece of paper, she needed a good quantity of padding.

But when she repeated herself, when she said "aren't we?" again, she suddenly felt shy. She felt that she was acting like the greedy hero of the story who demanded some lining material after he had been given a piece of cloth for a coat.

But Orhan was not disturbed by her insistence. "Yes, my dear, we will," he said tolerantly.

"Oh, I love the decor of this place. It is so simple, so elegant. Don't you love the purity of its white walls? Isn't it wonderful that the windows were left uncovered? I'm so pleased that the curtains were eliminated. I am so happy that the scenery is not hidden behind some stupid curtains. Don't you think it would be a pity? Don't you agree that curtains would have been quite unnecessary?"

"Yes, I agree. They would have been unnecessary," echoed Orhan.

Meral suddenly laughed. "What else could he say?" she thought. "How could he deny me his agreement after hearing all my ravings?"

"Why do you laugh?" Orhan asked.

"I laugh because I am happy. I laugh because I love everything I see around me. I love everything!"

As soon as she noticed that she had mentioned "love" once too often, she decided to cut it down to size. "I love the smell of the place, too," she added. "What are we going to order?"

"I leave the decision to you."

"And I accept the responsibility," she said, looking at the waiter who approached them carrying two huge menus hidden in their wine-colored, gold-lettered covers hung with dangling tassels.

The waiter's attention was fixed unwaveringly on Meral as he must have sensed that she would sum up the order as quickly as she had decided where she wanted to sit.

As he departed, still writing down all the different kinds of dishes Meral ordered, she turned her attention back to Orhan. "I have an enormous appetite today," she said.

"So do I," said Orhan, straightening up from his slightly slumped position, and staying that way.

Meral continued with her comments about the place. Having already spoken of its looks and smells, she started speaking of it sounds.

A popular Arabesque song was being played on the stereo system. But the music hardly reached the veranda as it did not have a share of the speakers unobtrusively fixed to the walls of the restaurant.

"What is your opinion of Arabesque music? Do you agree that it should be banned from the radio stations? Do you think it is depressing? Do you think we would be better off without it?"

Orhan stopped the flood of her questions by an unexpected answer. He said, "You can't stop the music! Nobody can stop the music!"

"Well," said Meral, "well, well, well! I never imagined you would be acquainted with that kind of music! I never imagined you would be aware of the existence of The Village People. Does it mean that you listen to them? What a far cry from Chopin. I'm so surprised!"

This time Orhan sang out his response. "You can't stop the music!"

His singing voice was low, and his speaking voice, which was equally low, disclosed a secret. "I have to surprise you from time to time. This is the only way I can hold your interest."

The arrival of the *hors d'oeuvres* censored the remaining part of the conversation.

The waiter departed silently after removing the dainty dishes from the trolley on which they were carried one by one, and carefully distributing them over the table.

During the sampling of the variety of dishes, Meral talked only once. After tasting the cigarette *boreks,** she prompted Orhan to do the same. "They are so nice and crisp. Won't you try one?" she asked.

But when they finished drinking their soup and the main dish was placed in front of them, the conversation was resumed once again. This time it was Orhan who talked. He talked about Dr. Zeki in a slow and thoughtful manner. "I'm afraid that I am turning Zeki into a captive," he said. "He goes nowhere except to his work and occasionally to his mother."

Dr. Zeki had mentioned to Meral once that he visited his sister regularly at the nursing home. But she prevented herself from upset-

---

* **cigarette boreks:** *cheese rolls shaped like cigarettes*

187

ting Orhan by reminding him of the overlooked sensitive item on the list of Zeki's activities.

"What kind of a woman is his mother?" she asked instead.

"A strong-minded woman. A stubborn woman. She lives by herself."

"Nowadays most old women prefer to live by themselves. It is better in a way. It prevents friction between the two generations."

"She is able to make Zeki's life miserable all the same. She strongly objects to his living in my house. 'You became a nanny to him,' she says. In a way she is right. But Zeki is stubborn too. In the end he does what he wants. And your friendship gives him some relief from me. Your trips to the Open Bazaar and your lunch at the Covered Market made him so happy."

"And you did your best to spoil it. When he tried to make a joke about the onion seller you became angry. Why?"

"Because I felt left out."

"Why should you always be at the center of everything? Tell me, why?"

"I suppose I'm insecure."

"I don't agree with the contemporary usage of 'insecure.' I feel that the word is alienated from its true meaning. It is forced to cover artificial concepts. It is transformed into an 'all sizes' garment to be worn over all kinds of behavior. Do you think that I am secure? Do you think that Zeki is secure? Do you think that . . . Emel *hanim* is secure. Why do you think she smooths the creases on her skirt as she walks? But being insecure doesn't give us the right to behave the way we want."

"I agree. I absolutely agree. I suppose I'm also spoiled. Who spoiled me? I don't know. I didn't have a mother to spoil me. She died when I was a baby. I had no brothers and sisters. My two aunts were as harsh as my father was. I don't know who spoiled me."

Why couldn't Meral accept his feeling of "insecurity" as a reason for his moodiness? Why did she encourage him into searching for other faults in himself? He could not have been spoiled, as he clearly explained. One could not spoil oneself!

Suddenly Meral's resentments towards him for his unfair behavior of the past flared up, reminding her of something she had read. According to that semi-scientific article scorpions were able to poison themselves using their own flexible tails.

Towards the end of the lunch, she became pensive. Pushing the dish of *crème caramel* away from her, she started watching the fatherly strokes of the waves on the round shoulders of the nearby rocks in silence. She coveted their touch on her body. It was with this longing in her heart that she told Orhan about the dream she had had some time ago. She told him the dream about their swim. When she came to the part when he left her and started swimming towards the shore, she asked him sadly, "Why did you do that? Why do you always give me hope and then take it back?"

Orhan was taken aback, and Meral covered her sentimentality with a laugh. "I'm sure you know the story of the two friends," she said. "One tells the other that he has had a terrible dream. The other asks, 'What was it about?' The first answers, 'Why do you ask? Weren't you in it yourself?'"

But Orhan was not laughing. "I was in the dream. I was!" he said, looking sad and happy at the same time. "I accept your accusations. I shouldn't have left you in the middle of the sea. I apologize for my behavior."

"You are taking all this too seriously," said Meral. "It was only a joke. Believe me, it was a joke. You don't need to apologize, we are friends."

"I do apologize. And you are more than a friend to me." He stopped and thought for a while. Then he talked again with unexpected determination. "I'll make it up to you. I'll make your dream come true."

"Dreams don't come true. That's why they are called dreams," she said, with a sorrowful voice.

"Yes, they do, and I am going to prove it to you. How about going swimming one afternoon?"

"Swimming?" said Meral. "Swimming? Swimming? Swimming? Swimming?"

The two businessmen interrupted their lengthy discussions and turned their mustachioed faces to her. The waiter who was coming to collect the dessert plates looked at her for a moment trying to understand the question. And having understood, he decided to satisfy her curiosity.

"Yes, *hanimefendi*, we do have facilities for swimming here," he said. "The changing cabins are right below the restaurant." Having assumed that the woman who repeated her question in a louder and louder voice would wish to learn more, he continued: "And as you see," he said, pointing at the sea, "our restaurant has a floating platform over there. You may use it for sunbathing if you wish."

"Thank you," said Meral to the waiter, but her looked remained fixed on Orhan's face. She looked at the mighty artist whose one brush stroke had changed the sad color of her eyes, to the mighty artist who had painted a glowing business in both her eyes with a single stroke of his brush. "Let's go on Thursday," she said, struggling to contain her excitement within boundaries.

*

When they arrived at the villa, right after lunch, Dr. Zeki welcomed them. "Some tea?" he asked. Then he corrected himself. "It is too early for tea," he mumbled. He seemed preoccupied.

Meral's mind was too busy weaving fantasies about the promised "Thursday" to pay attention to his mood. Meral's feelings were too heightened to be depressed by the clouds which passed in Dr. Zeki's eyes.

He did not come and sit with them.

19

Thursday morning was the day fixed for their swimming, Thursday was the morning when all kinds of pleasant thoughts paraded through Meral's mind, and left her limp with happiness.

She lingered in bed to keep the morning fresh and unlived as long as she could. She knew that even the most longed-for times could suddenly turn against one and crush one's dreams.

Hope rose in her chest as she walked to the bathroom, and fear ran down her body as she showered. Fear and Hope ran up and down several times, warming up for the serious race.

Her heart announced the winner as she put on her dress. Hope was the winner, and all the roads were open for her that day. Even the taxi she rode did not meet the usual traffic jam over the bridge.

*

The scene was similar to that of the last time, but the location had shifted forward. Orhan had come out of the garden gate. He was standing by a taxi and waiting for her. All Meral had to do was to switch taxis.

During this transitory period, she gave a cautiously festive look at her host, who opened the car door for her. She asked him a crucial question: "Did you bring your bathing suit?" she said.

"I did," answered Orhan softly. His voice seemed to hide their plans from the driver's ears.

He was dressed in a lightweight suit. As soon as he sat next to Meral, he touched his breast pocket, as he had done the last time. And when they arrived he took the money from it and handed the driver his fare without hesitation. Having learned how much the ride would cost from the last time, he had prepared the exact amount.

Recognizing them promptly, the head-waiter took them to the glazed veranda and seated them at a table overlooking the restaurant's?

Meral was having difficulty settling down. She kept on changing her position by shifting her weight on the seat every now and then. She put one leg over the other. Then lowered it. She bent her knees and tightened them close to each other. Then she stretched her legs and pressed her feet down on the heels of her sandals.

Orhan was quiet. His eyes were studying the green bohemian glass ashtray on the table.

"Are we really going to swim?" Meral asked.

"We are. We are," he answered without moving. There was a desperate determination in his voice, but his eyes had not left the ashtray.

"Come on," said Meral after a while. "Let's go down and change."

He was still immobile, not saying a word.

She repeated herself. "Come on, Orhan," she said.

"Give me some time," he said, almost whispering.

"Time?" said Meral. "Time?" she repeated as if trying to remember the meaning of a foreign word. "The time is late," she said. "The days are getting shorter. If we wait too long the sun will set."

There was a tearful lump in her voice. The lump was adding overtones to what she said. Suddenly she added something she should not have added. "You are forty; and I am thirty-eight."

She had shot down the sun in the early afternoon of her happiest day. And a sober answer from Orhan paid tribute to the darkness she had created. "I was almost forty when we met."

Although the frozen tears in her eyes barely allowed her to see, Meral thought that she should take her turn in examining the irregular form of the ashtray on the table.

At the beginning Orhan did not seem bothered by her thorough inspection of the object. He watched her lift it up, turn it around and place it on the table. But when she lifted it up again, he took it away from her and pushed it to the far corner of the table.

It was then that he started speaking in a bitter tone. "What do you want of me?" he said. "You want me to shed the last ten years? You want me to lose them like losing weight? Losing ten pounds?"

"Losing ten pounds? I don't think that you are overweight. Even if you were, it is none of my business."

"None of your business?"

"Yes, none of my business."

"Well then, dear lady, I would like to inform you that those past ten years will remain with me all my life. They'll remain with me whether you like it or not. Whether I like it or not."

Meral hated to be lectured. A childish fury, a tearful riot broke loose in her. "I am going to change," she said and started to walk out of the veranda. Then she turned and recited an old, childish poem.

"Cry for the keeper,
Cry for the kept,
Cry for the joys,
Left outside your net."

The shore was lined with deck chairs. At a short distance from the beach was the floating platform. The name of the restaurant adorned the platform's sides in bold letters. But its surface was empty. The velvety seaweed which covered the supporting barrels underneath was hidden from view and then exposed again by the playful waves.

Meral was not going to lose time. She went down to the changing room and came out wearing her bathing suit. She started walking towards the sea. The looks of several people who sat on the deck chairs lingered on her tall figure and determined walk before they returned back to the color photographs in the magazines they held in their hands.

Although September was the best month for swimming, as the water would be warm, even warmer than during the summer months, there was not a single swimmer in the sea.

Meral dived in hoping that Orhan would forgive her and follow her to the sea. She was certain that he would take the last daring plunge into recovery. When he caught up with her, would he laugh and talk like he had at the beginning of her dream?

She was close to the platform when the waves suddenly became rough. First, she started swimming further, in spite of the waves. After passing the platform, she changed her mind, and tried to swim back. But the more she tried to approach the platform, the further it moved away. Meral loved the sea. She refused to be intimidated by the swelling waves. She swam harder.

She advanced towards the platform in spite of the unruly waves pounding it from all sides. But when she was almost there, its weakening planks groaned several times and started to rock erratically. The heavy curtain of the climbing waves had been concealing the platform's condition from her. Her efforts were futile and the platform she tried to reach was not fit for refuge any longer. One of the anchoring chains was broken and it had turned it sideways. The raging waves hit the rolling platform. They hit it and hit it until they broke the other chains loose. The platform turned upside down, exposing its fat barrels covered with seaweed. Transformed into a sea-monster, it rushed at her, and whipped her again and again with its loose chains. Then it passed her by, and attacked the waves which had taken away its security.

One of these waves lifted Meral up and revealed the happenings on land. She saw a line of people standing alongside the shore and looking in her direction. She saw Orhan running between the deck chairs towards the sea.

The next wave which carried her up showed her only Orhan. He was diving into the sea. Meral forgot the monstrous platform, she forgot the ferocious waves. Every time a wave lifted her up, she looked towards Orhan. He was a marvelous swimmer. His strokes overcame the waves. One minute he was down, the next minute he climbed up the waves. But the same waves carried her further and further away from him. They carried her towards the opposite shore. She felt a

194

sharp pain in her chest. Her knees were no longer able to bend. She continued to swim using only her arms. The salty water filled her eyes, her nose, her mouth, her whole being. The sea filled her with a delicious helplessness. It filled her with a pleasant, sleepy helplessness. She wasn't swallowing water, she was swallowing happiness. There was a silent laughter in her whole being. She knew that Orhan was close to her. "He will save you. He will save you," roared the foamy waves into her ear.

*

She was to learn in the hospital that she had been saved by Orhan. She was saved by no one else but Orhan. He had reached her before the coastguard boat. He had raised her limp body out of the waters and into the boat when it arrived.

"But where is he?" she asked the nurse, who told her all about the accident.

"He was here with you," said the nurse. "He stayed till you were out of danger. Then he made a telephone call. After that he left. He must be resting. I told you, he almost was drowned himself trying to save you."

"Did Dr. Zeki come to see me?" she said.

"Is he one of the hospital staff?" the nurse asked. "I don't know him."

Orhan did not come, nor did Dr. Zeki. There wasn't even a telephone call from either of them.

Meral was discharged from the hospital that afternoon. She took a taxi home.

The driver was a talkative man. Seeing that she was leaving the hospital all by herself, he sympathized with her. "It is tough not to have relatives," he said. "Once I had an accident. All my relatives visited me in the hospital every single day. The hospital staff were happy to see me go. They were fed up with my relatives."

*

It was three days later when Dr. Zeki telephoned her. Hearing his voice, Meral tried to hang up. But he was able to talk before she had the chance to do it.

"My sister is dead," he said. "She killed herself."

There was silence at both ends of the telephone line for a time. Neither of the two knew how to continue.

"When?" asked Meral finally.

"On Thursday. At about eleven."

Meral was fighting with the waves at the same hour of the same day.

She understood Orhan's departure from the hospital after his telephone call to his house.

"I am coming," she said.

"No. I'll come," Dr. Zeki answered.

He might have volunteered to come to her out of consideration for her accident.

*

Dr. Zeki could not ask Meral about her accident. Meral could not ask Dr. Zeki about his sister. They sat facing each other and could not speak a word.

Finally Dr. Zeki shook off his silence. Meral sensed his visit had an important purpose, a message—a message which was to affect her life.

"I want to tell you everything that happened," he said. "Exactly as it happened," he added. There was an urgency in his voice. "What I want to tell you are the circumstances of my sister's death," he said.

Meral was listening.

"You see," he said, "recently the doctor told me that Nevin was getting better. I had my doubts about his judgement, but that is what he told me. He insisted that she should come home for a day or two, to see if she could adapt herself to family life. We had tried this some years ago, several times. That time there was a young doctor in the nursing home with some new ideas. He had great hopes for Nevin's recovery. We brought her home for two days at a time. It didn't work out. It didn't work out at all. And her presence made Orhan more retiring then ever. He used to lock himself in his room so as not to hear her abusive comments. I had my suspicions that the situation would be the same if we brought her home this time, but when the doctor says there is hope, you want to believe him. Wouldn't you?

"So I arranged that she would come home on Thursday. Then I learned from Orhan that the two of you had planned to go swimming on that day. Orhan sounded so happy when he told me your plans. He was so much like the Orhan I had known as a youth ... I couldn't spoil his mood. I couldn't break his newly found confidence. I couldn't tell him about my arrangements.

"So, I went to the nursing home that morning, before you left for the beach. My intention was to postpone her coming home to the next day—to Friday morning. Just a delay of twenty-four hours!

"When I went up to her room, I found her dressed and ready. Her overnight bag was near her bed. She met me with a beautiful smile. My sister was looking happy and all ready to come home. This is the picture of her I would have liked to keep in my memory. But it was not meant to be. I wish, oh how strongly I wish, I could erase the scene which followed.

"I told her that I'd spend some time with her at the nursing home that morning, but I'd take her home the next day. She became spiteful. She said things about Orhan and I, I do not care to repeat to you.

"I told her with finality that I would come the next day at the same time and walked out.

"It seems that she had a good amount of accumulated sedatives in her possession. She must have swallowed them right after I left. I was called back to the nursing home at three. They told me what had happened.

"When Orhan called me after your accident, I asked him to come home. I told him everything as gently as I could."

Meral was becoming aware that the trembling urgency of his speech had a point to make. It was becoming obvious by the minute that in this sad moment of his life, Dr. Zeki was forced to forge his outpourings into a sharp and hurtful shape, a spear. The summation of his account could not evade wounding her mortally.

She helped him to go ahead. She stood in the clearing outside the tragic event, and dared him to do what he had come to do. "How did Orhan take it?" she asked.

And Dr. Zeki did it. He sent the spear right to her chest. "He doesn't want to see anyone anymore," he answered.

It happened so quickly. One moment she was full of sympathy for the deceased, the next moment she was dying herself. Her crippled legs . . . would they carry her out of the room? Her blind eyes . . . would they show her the way?

She stood up and walked out of the room. She came back with the key to the villa. She handed it to Dr. Zeki.

Dr. Zeki seemed to have continued talking while she was out. "All this is my fault," he said. "Just a mix-up in dates caused all this tragedy."

She did not wish to listen to his explanations. She did not want to understand more than she already understood.

*

She found the key and the skeleton key-holder on the piano after Dr. Zeki left. She held it up, her eyes asked questions of the lolling head and the dangling feet of the skeleton. What was holding back her tears? From whom were they hiding? Herself? When would they start to flow? When? When? When?

*

Meral met Dr. Zeki at the steps of her house when she opened the door to go to her lawyer.

"Oh, hello," she said in her surprise, as if she had bumped into a neighbor. "I am on my way to my lawyer," she said, as if he wanted to know the reason for her going out. "He wants me to sign some papers."

"I should have called you before coming," said Dr. Zeki. "But I didn't dare. May I accompany you?"

"As you like," said Meral, and they walked down the street to the taxi rank together.

"There are more things I must talk to you about. I don't think that I made myself very clear yesterday," he said, when they settled in the taxi.

"You are mistaken. You have made everything very, very clear," said Meral. She was not ready for petty details.

"You see," he said, "I don't know what to do. I came to ask for your help."

He remained silent during the short ride to the ferryboat landing, but started talking again while he followed Meral to the boat. "I have not seen him since Thursday," he said, when they found seats. "I could not even convince him to attend the funeral. I take food up to his room. I knock at his door. I leave the tray outside his door. Sometimes he eats a little bit. Sometimes he eats nothing. I hope he still gives himself the injections."

He stopped and looked at her. "What have I done to him? Why is he doing this to me? I have sacrificed my own sister for him . . . I have done everything for him." He made vague, helpless movements with his hand, still looking at her.

Meral put an arm around him and left it there. ". . . . And for me," she said.

"What have I done to him?" he said again, going back to the beginning. "What shall I do now?"

The rest of the trip passed in silence. When it was time to leave the boat Meral became aware of the curious looks of the passengers who sat near them. They threw backward glances at them as they walked to the exits of the boat.

They reached the lawyer's office and Meral signed the necessary papers. When it was over Dr. Zeki offered to accompany her back to her house.

Meral invited him in, and he came. He was a man with leisure time now, as his voluntary responsibility of looking after his friend had been withdrawn from him. Meral also had a lot of time to spare since her only remaining concern was seeing to it that the lawyer followed her divorce case properly. But, as Dr. Zeki had already completed what he wanted to say in the boat, there was only one subject open for conversation: her divorce case.

"When two people discover that they do not get along, I don't think there is any point in prolonging the marriage," Meral began. "The only thing I regret is that I didn't do this sooner. I thought about it when Bekir left. I thought about it when my mother died.

But somehow I kept on pushing the thought to the back of my mind. Even when I left my husband and came here, I wasn't seriously thinking about divorce. What helped me decide was learning that my grandmother was Armenian." A mirthless laughter escaped her. "Can you connect my grandmother's being Armenian with my divorce?"

"Your grandmother was Armenian?" said Dr. Zeki, raising his eyebrows. This was what he did when he was surprised.

"Didn't I tell you that? I told Orhan," said Meral. Mentioning Orhan's name made her feel embarrassed. "I didn't mean to hide it. I didn't know about it myself till a few months ago."

"Why should you hide it?" said Dr. Zeki. He did not show any curiosity about the circumstances which had kept Meral in the dark concerning her grandmother's identity. He simply expanded on "Armenians."

"Personally, I like Armenians very much," he said. "They are artistic people. Look at the work of the Armenian silversmiths and goldsmiths we have in the Covered Market. They are also very good photographers."

Meral said, "My husband is a good photographer too. But he is not Armenian. According to him photography is the highest form of art. He thinks that he can capture the deepest thoughts of a person with a click of the shutter on his camera. He thinks that the truth is on the other side of his lenses waiting to be discovered. Of course he is wrong. To me, this is a simplistic way of looking at life."

They had exhausted all they could talk about.

"Would you come to see us again? Please?" said Dr. Zeki before he left. "I need your help. Come for my sake. Not for him," he said. He could not mention Orhan's name to her.

20

Days passed and the people passed in the overflowing streets of Istanbul. The people huddled into their coats. The people hung onto their umbrellas. The cars honked their horns on the seaside avenues and the ferryboats sent warning whistles to each other on their misty way between the shores. These eternal weavers of the sea never lost track of their destination. Cutting the rough waves with accustomed ease, they advanced in blind determination.

During the changed rhythm of the autumn days, Meral's thoughts remained centered around the traffic on the sea. She constantly consulted the timetable of the boats between the European and Asian shores, and took mental notes of their positions at sea. She felt as if she traveled in each and every one of them, although hers was an established routine. She took a boat at 11 from the Asian shore and returned with the same boat at 11.30. While the boat was breaking through the waves, she made her way on its wind-swept decks, she crossed its glassed halls with their steamed-up panes, and went down to the non-smoking section on the lower deck. She ignored the good-hearted people who, assuming that she was looking for a seat, pressed themselves next to each other to make room for her on the long benches. She ignored the curious looks of the people who seemed to recognize her from her previous trips. She carried on with her relentless search disregarding every hindrance on her way. On these daily trips of hers, she was a big, mindless wave. Reminding herself of the futility of her search did not help. Her mind refused to part with hope. And the hope was hammered into a definite shape. A chance meeting! A chance meeting between two people. It had to happen. It was bound to happen.

She started appealing more earnestly to her commonsense towards the end of the second week. It was at the time when she had almost succeeded in convincing herself of the absurdity of her anticipation when she received a telephone call. It was not the telephone call she had been wanting and hoping to receive. The call was from Bekir.

He wanted to come and see her. Meral wondered when and how Bekir had learned that she was separated from his uncle. She wondered who had given him her telephone number. She wondered what had prompted him to wish to see her after so long.

"When would you like to come?" she asked.

"Any day that is convenient for you," said Bekir.

He came the next day at five. They talked to each other as if no time had passed since he had moved out of his uncle's house leaving a gaping question mark behind him.

He had not been able to go to the university, as Meral had guessed. But he had made quite good progress in his work. He was the accountant of several important companies now. He was earning good money.

The purpose of his visit became clear after he finished drinking his tea. He was engaged to a girl—a colleague. They were getting married at the registrar's office next Saturday. The same evening they were going to have a wedding party at the Guvenli Palas Hotel. He wished very much that Meral would attend the reception. An invitation card came out of his pocket as he told her his news.

"I owe you a lot," he said. "I owe you everything I am today," he said.

This speech of two sentences had been prepared before he came to visit her. There was no hesitancy in his voice. Meral believed in his sincerity, although his voice was drained of color.

His coming marriage seemed to sap his confidence somehow. "She is from a very good family," he said.

"You are from a good family too," said Meral.

"I mean her family is well-to-do," he said, adding to his statement.

"I don't think that is important," said Meral. She wondered what he was driving at. "Does your uncle know about this?" she asked.

"No," he said. "I phoned him. That is how I learned that you are separated. He did not ask me why I wanted to know where you were. He just gave me your telephone number. He asked me nothing. So I could not say anything."

"You know how he is!" said Meral.

"Yes," he said. "I wish I had told him, though. I would like him to come to my wedding very much. Perhaps I should call him again."

All he said sounded like a question asked from her; or a permission begged of her.

"You should," she said.

She was pleased with herself. At last she was giving only what she was asked for—nothing more. If she had been faced with such a situation before, she would have called Fahri herself. Asked his support for Bekir in every way. Financial and otherwise.

Now, she only told Bekir what he needed to hear. She just confirmed his own thoughts and opinions.

"You are different, Auntie Meral," he said, all of a sudden. "You are more relaxed."

Meral smiled sadly. "This is only the second time you have called me 'Auntie,'" she said.

She regretted reminding him of the occasion he had called her "Auntie" for the first time. If he had forgotten that it was during their first and last argument, he would want to know when it was, and her answer would open up the past. But he must have remembered. He lowered his eyes.

As if this last bit of conversation was a sign for him to go, he stood up. He took his leave by kissing Meral's hand three times and touching it to his forehead after each kiss. Meral let her hand remain limply in his, as he expressed his gratitude and respect with this action. She did not consider pulling her hand back in a gesture of modesty. Meral could not deny that the gratitude and the respect she received were well-earned. Bekir would never forgive himself if she denied it.

Just before she opened the door for him, he bent down and picked up an envelope from the floor. "Somebody must have brought it by hand," he said, handing it to her.

Meral stood by the window, holding the envelope in her hand, and watched Bekir's stocky figure walk away using the inner edge of the sidewalk. He looked at the flat faces of the new buildings as if asking for their approval as he walked on. He seemed to be asking the approval of these alien surroundings for his future plans. Was this because the newly changed face of this street, where he had never been before, offered itself to him as a random traveling companion? A companion you can ask any question from, a companion to whom you can say anything, as you do not expect to see him again?

Bekir turned suddenly. He looked back at the window and waved at her. Meral saw a boy of thirteen or fourteen in place of the stocky man. She raised her hand eagerly in answer, then moved it slowly to her face to remove the wet lines of tears.

*

She turned back to the room with a resolute movement. The past walked away outside; the past faced her from inside. But Meral was at peace with herself. The room did not appear to be caught unawares as it used to be before. As her stay in this house grew longer, the room seemed to have accepted the change that her presence had brought. It accepted the newly bought table lamp near the couch. It accepted the pressure of the dusting cloth over the surfaces of its tables and chairs. Even the carpets were less conscious of the exuberancy of their designs.

From the table-top in the adjoining room the willowy women of her mother's miniatures seemed to beckon to her. One of them was bent forward and looked intensely at her. Did she have a secret to tell her?

204

CAGES ON OPPOSITE SHORES

Meral came closer to have a better view of all the people who crowded the strip of wall alongside the edge of the table. What did they have to say? She slid her hand blindly up and down the polished table-top as if in search of something mislaid. Her wandering hand met no obstacles on its way. The box of stories was the only object which was left there, and it was pushed to the far end.

She went to the bedroom and carried back the shoe boxes from the wardrobe. She spread the papers and the diaries all over the table. She removed all the labels she had stuck on them. She had no right to label them. All she could do was to read them over and over again till she really understand them.

She touched the covers of the diaries. She opened them and ran her fingers through the fading papers inside the covers. It was thanks to these diaries that her mother was no longer behind successive closed doors. These diaries did more than exhibit her sufferings. They contained her fights. They contained her victories.

Her mother had lived and died; and she had left behind a grown-up, almost middle-aged, childless daughter who refused to look into her swarming depths even at critical times. She had left a daughter who gave a grievous, accusing look to everyone who pushed her into her own depths. The daughter surfaced for air as soon as she could. The daughter got rid of these people—she surfaced for air! Her mother had impoverished her life unwittingly. "I leave everything to my daughter," she had written in her will. Meral had not known then that her greatest inheritance was hidden among the pages of the diaries.

Meral read and read that evening. She read every bit of paper, she read every word under every scratched line. She read the lines about her grandmother who said, "Why don't you share your bread with me?" She remembered the echo it had created in her heart when she had first read it. She remembered how she had silently asked the same question from her mother.

Reading it once again she realized that the person who was reading the question now, was not the same person who had read it a few months ago. The person who read it now weighed every worthwhile detail of her life, by adding and removing tiny pieces of weights to the goldsmith's scale.

The last conversation with Bekir did not tip the scale one way or the other. The needle remained in the middle. That is how it should be. Bekir owed her nothing. Because her own giving was a pay-off in itself. She wanted nothing from him—she had passed the stage of wanting at last. Her life was saved during a storm. She had reached the other shore and had touched the land. It did not matter that she had been pushed back into the sea once again. It did not matter in the least that she had drifted back to her own shore.

"Orhan, I have so many things to tell you. Do you remember your remark about my treatment of Bekir? You said it was unfair. You thought that I had left what I started unfinished. But it had finished. I have the proof now. He came to thank me. Would you say that this is a good ending? I am being sarcastic. I didn't agree with you then. I wouldn't agree with you now. I absolutely disagree with you if you think that the story is completed at last. To me, stories are never complete. Stories never end. Stories only shift sides, shift perspective, shift emphasis. Stories go on as long as we live."

The well-settled evening listened respectfully to her silent words spoken to Orhan. When she stopped, the languid voice of a woman filled the blindness of the room with a classical Turkish song.

The song came from the café. The song came through the window. "Tell me, my darling, tell me. Tell me, tell me, tell me," said the song. Meral remembered an episode connected to this song. Once, before she was married, listening to the same song in a café with friends, she had become impatient and had shouted. "Tell her! Tell her and be finished with it!" she had said. Several people from nearby tables had laughed at her sharp and loud comment. Now, Meral laughed at herself. The loved one was right in insisting. The lover was right in hesitating. "Telling" was not that easy. No, it was not that easy.

She remembered the envelope Bekir had picked up from near the door and turned on the table lamp to read it. The envelope had been pushed under the multitude of thoughts and feelings Bekir's visit had left behind. Now she tore open the envelope with sudden urgency.

It was a poem.

CAGES ON OPPOSITE SHORES

To the keeper,
Aren't you the lucky one.
Your animals are in their cages,
And your key is in your pocket.
But my loved one
                    roams
The jungles inside me.
She knows no borders,
Her pace is free.
I need to tell her
                    to let me be.
I have to hold her.
Give me the key.

Meral ran to the bureau and brought out an envelope of her own. She dropped the key to Orhan's villa with its attached skeleton into the envelope.

She intended to send the key back. The old heedless Meral was about to take over. Then she stopped herself.

She read the poem again.

Other titles in the series

Wild Thorns
by Sahar Khalifeh
trans. by Trevor LeGassick and Elizabeth Fernea
ISBN 0–940793–25–3   paperback $9.95

A Woman of Nazareth
by Hala Deeb Jabbour
ISBN 0–940793–07–5   paperback $9.95

FROM SOUTH AFRICA:
Living, Loving, and Lying Awake at Night
by Sindiwe Magona
ISBN 1–56656–141–8   paperback $11.95

FROM YEMEN:
The Hostage
by Zayd Mutee' Dammaj
trans. by May Jayyusi and Christopher Tingley
ISBN 1–56656–140–X   paperback $10.95

FROM ZIMBABWE:
The Children Who Sleep by the River
by Debbie Taylor
ISBN 0–940793–96–2   paperback $9.95

   Titles in the "Emerging Voices: New International Fiction" series
are available at bookstores everywhere.
   To order by phone call toll-free **1–800–238–LINK**. Please have
your Mastercard, Visa or American Express ready when you call.
   To order by mail, please send your check or money order to the
address listed below. For shipping and handling, add $3.00 for the
1st book and $1.00 for each additional book. New York residents add
8.25% sales tax.

Interlink Publishing Group, Inc.
99 Seventh Avenue
Brooklyn, New York 11215